The Second Chance Bus Stop

The Second Chance Bus Stop

A Novel

Ally Zetterberg

///MIRA

/IIMIRA

ISBN-13: 978-0-7783-8762-6

The Second Chance Bus Stop

Copyright © 2025 by Ally Zetterberg Literary Ltd

Recycling programs for this product may not exist in your area.

All rights reserved. No part of this book may be used or reproduced in any manner whatsoever without written permission.

Without limiting the author's and publisher's exclusive rights, any unauthorized use of this publication to train generative artificial intelligence (AI) technologies is expressly prohibited.

This is a work of fiction. Names, characters, places, and incidents are either the product of the author's imagination or are used fictitiously. Any resemblance to actual persons, living or dead, businesses, companies, events or locales is entirely coincidental.

For questions and comments about the quality of this book, please contact us at CustomerService@Harlequin.com.

TM is a trademark of Harlequin Enterprises ULC.

MIRA
22 Adelaide St. West, 41st Floor
Toronto, Ontario M5H 4E3, Canada
MIRABooks.com

Printed in U.S.A.

To Mamma and Pappa

The Second Chance Bus Stop

Part One

Thinkin' maybe you'll come back here to the place that we'd meet.

—THE SCRIPT

Prologue

I'M SITTING ON the kerb of a cobbled pavement, not far from the bus stop, feeling as old as I am: sixty-four. And I have felt like I was waiting for something my entire life. Even as a child I'd stare out the window, expecting something where there was nothing other than the cars lined against the road and the black bin bag on the ground, uncollected, because Mother had gotten the day muddled again. At first I thought it was a sign that things would fall into place and I could simply put my life on autopilot until they did. Perhaps it was a psychological thing. Lately I've come to accept it's more likely my mind playing tricks on me. Old age? Some kind of progressive disease? Who knows.

There is a breeze today on Hornton Street. I've counted thirty-one chewing gums on the ground, varying shades of dirt-marbled pink, grey and coal-black. People come and go, and I try to look for patterns. I always find patterns in everything, much like some people see the face of Baby Jesus or George Washington in potatoes. There have been four blonde ladies, so a brown-haired one must come soon. Or three men have walked past, so a child should be coming next. I'm trying to figure out after which sequence of passersby the one

I'm waiting for will appear. And what he will say? I have been through it in my mind a hundred, a thousand—more than that—times.

'Hello,' he might say. Or, 'I've missed you.'

Maybe, 'So this is where you are.'

I'd like him to simply say, 'You came.'

Smile wide. Or perhaps with a serious face.

Of course, I know he won't say any of these things. People never say what you expect them to.

While I'm thinking, someone does come up to me. It's a gentleman who works at Whole Foods on Kensington High Street.

'How are you today?' He hands me a five-pound note and walks on before I have time to answer the question or object to the note now nestled in my hand. I'm not broke. I'm broken-hearted.

Only two more hours until home-time now, when I board the bus and head back to the warmth of my house where my son will lecture me until he decides it's no use and gives up. I ate the plate of lasagne he'd left me before I headed out this morning (it was a better breakfast than the lamb stew we had last week), moved my crossword to a new place and left a half-drunk cup of tea on the living room table. I even pulled off and flushed half a metre of toilet paper down the loo. Extreme? Trust my son to notice any little trace I leave behind. Like this, for all he knows, I've had a productive day at home, eaten my lunch and had a bowel movement. As long as I'm back before he comes through the door I'll be fine.

I glance at my watch. It's 15.14, on 8 June, 2023.

I've been waiting twenty-seven years.

Sophia
Svedala

WHEN YOU KISS someone, as many as eighty million bacteria are transferred between mouths. This is for a ten-second kiss. Don't get me started on those long, slobby affairs that happen in, say, backs of cabs or on doorsteps after a fourth date. But wait—it gets *worse*. Couples who kiss more than nine times a day (first of all, who are these people? Do they not have to work? Or like, *eat*?) actually share communities of bacteria. So you don't just share a home, you also share a saliva community. Which is, to cite my teenage self, *GROSS*.

It's all I can think of as the perfectly handsome man in front of me who's just treated me to dinner and half a bottle of wine leans in and tries to slide his tongue between my lips. I press them firmly shut. Because, well, *bacterial transfer*. He kind of moves to the side to see if there's an opening there, and I'm forced to twitch my face to withhold. He gives up, draws back and looks at me.

His name is Ed, and he has brown eyes and hair that kind of shines without any hair product. He likes travelling and cars, works for a digital creator brand and wouldn't mind settling down with the right woman. He seemed great; I was even willing to overlook his very clear *You don't seem Autistic at all* greeting. On paper he looks good for me, a twenty-five-year-old woman who has blue eyes and hair like unruly yellow straw, is taller than most men, owns her own florist shop and wouldn't mind having her first boyfriend right about now. Or yesterday. In fact, I've been trying for God knows how long to have my first boyfriend. But looking good on paper doesn't always translate to real life.

'Are you okay?' he asks, shifting his weight back and forth as if he needs a wee.

'I am okay.' Roof over my head, no ongoing war or conflict threatening my livelihood, and I just ate a bowl of pasta. Sure, I very much wish I had one and a half million kroners to buy my brothers out of my flower shop so that it was mine alone, but I can't claim to not be *okay*. I'd call my current mental state *slightly unhappy*, but then lots of people go through their whole lives that way. My mother's words come to me: When there are those worse off, we don't complain. Sure, there are those worse off—some single ladies may not yet have discovered the Le Wand 3.0 vibrator.

'We had a good date just now. And the one before.' He starts to recap our dating history. Which, although brief, has shown great promise. He has only a few annoying habits, chews with his mouth closed and, as opposed to the man I dated previously who I spotted in the town centre wearing socks and crocs and thus immediately cancelled, wears sneakers.

'Yes.' It's true. I've enjoyed getting to know him. I may have even fantasised about pushing my body against his, feeling my chest stop heaving for a moment, grabbing his hand and placing it somewhere I'm practically aching to be touched and—'But somehow you're not that into me . . . ?'

'That's not it, Ed.'

I realise I have to give a reason. And that when I do, this will be over. Much like my teenage years when I would sneak back into my parents' house even before curfew, tonight I'll go back to my flat still *unkissed*. I don't like labels. Like *Autistic or control freak. Anxious. Eating disorder. OCD.* Those types of things. Somehow I collected these kinds of labels throughout childhood the way others collected Brownie badges. Hence I've made it my mission to appear as normal as I can to avoid accumulating more of them in adulthood.

So here I am. With the chance to get rid of one of my most stubborn labels: *unkissed*. It's meant to be good, isn't it? Otherwise people wouldn't brave the bacteria. *The eighty million of them.* An army. An invasion. Foreign bodies in my body. Well . . . okay, I wouldn't necessarily mind that last one. Can we skip straight to it?

Ed leans in again, and I finally blurt it out, ending any prospects of Ed and Sophia ever creating a bacterial community or any other form of community.

'I'm sorry. I can't do this.'

'It's okay, we can take it slow. Just kissing.' He leans in again, completely unaware of, and not intending to find out, *what* it is I can't do. I put my hand on his chest, and it drums against my palm. I don't like it. It feels too excited—like a dog's tail wagging. Drumdrumdrum.

'I don't *kiss*. I thought I could, but it turns out I can't. I wrote it in one of my messages to you?'

He looks genuinely confused.

'I thought that was some pun or turn-on technique. Hot girl wants to skip foreplay? Any guy is all in and down with that.'

Great. Remind me to add it to *The Autistic's Guide to Life*'s chapter on getting the attention of a man: *How to make your quirk work and really turn them on.*

'Well, no, it's an *actual* no to kissing.' We stare at each other for an awkward minute, as if we're children checking who will blink first. I think about placing a hand on his body but am not sure where I'd put it. I leave my arms hanging by my side. He attempts a joke.

'Sure you're not some kind of a prostitute?'

It's not a funny one, so I don't reply. He shifts uncomfortably on the spot.

'The no kissing. You know, *Pretty Woman*? I thought that's what working girls do to not get attached.'

'Ed, I am trying very hard to get attached. However, I do not wish to attach my lips to yours. That is the point I am desperately trying to make here. All other body parts would be okay to attach.'

'Gotcha. Erm, listen. I'm all for attaching stuff and all, but . . . we may have different goals here.'

I want to argue that no, we do not have different goals (we both want a relationship) but rather different paths and ideas about how to achieve them (no lips versus lots of lips). But then I think of all the inspirational quotes I've ever been fed that say things like *Enjoy the Journey*. I think how others are usually uninterested in my different-looking journey. And it's clear Ed won't be coming along with me on *my* journey.

'I'm going to go now,' I say. 'Thank you for the dinner, the wine and the ice cream.'

I am about to turn around and leave him there when I have second thoughts. Kissing is essential for getting attached. I can't meet someone and get them to like me without that part of the deal. I pep-talk myself. *If this is what you need to do, then go and bloody do it, Sophia*, I hear my uncle's voice saying. I'm fairly sure he wasn't talking about kissing men named Ed, but I think his words apply in this scenario too. I have tried a lot of things in order to advance my life, to become a happier, more fulfilled version of myself. The one thing I've failed to try so far is a relationship. And I'm convinced that it's the answer to this nagging feeling of not quite having it all. It *must* be.

So I decide to try. At least once. I'm twenty-five and getting a little antsy, not for love and marriage and cute babies and getting to romanticise sleep deprivation. But for someone to like, hold and do *those things* with. I will look up how long bacteria live, and I will survive it. There's always mouthwash. I have it at home. Perhaps if I do it once he will be satisfied, and we won't have to do it again. *Okay. Ready.*

I lean towards him, and that's all the encouragement he needs. Excited to have changed my mind, to have converted me, he puts his hand behind my head intertwining my long hair with his fingers, and I can sense all my follicles protesting. Then he ravishes my mouth. Devours it. Heads into battle, bending open my defence and rushing his army of bacteria in via a wave of saliva. He tugs at my bottom lip, and I stiffen. It's wet and horrid, and my brain can't anticipate where his tongue will move next so every touch is a bloody horrendous surprise. A shock to my nervous system and a complete sensory overload. And there are so many *tastes*. A hint of fresh mint. Deep tones of arabica coffee.

It's *awful*.

And in that moment I promise myself to never kiss anyone again.

This is the first and last time.

I'm Sophia, collector of labels, and my most recent one is Single—*Unhappily*—for Bloody Life.

Blade
London

I GET THE call when I'm racking up the weights. Two dudes are watching me to see that I really have wiped them down. But then, I could just be imagining it. Always feel watched even if I'm not, but try to remind myself that sometimes it really is all in my head. Actually, usually it's all in my head. I focus on the feeling of all my muscles being tense, worked to the limit, so that my brain can't even utter any of its normal anxious shit, but that bubble is burst as soon as I put the dumbbells back on the rack. My mind goes back to reality. To bills, to work, to mum. *Mum.* There's a missed call from an unknown number on my phone. I turn the device sideways so my finger can touch the uncracked area of the screen and call back.

'Hello?'

'Is this Edith's next of kin?'

'Yes,' I admit reluctantly, as if confessing a crime. Or rather, waiting to hear what crime she has committed. Shouldn't it be the other way? I'm twenty-nine, and she's sixty-four. Surely I should be the troublemaker?

'That would be me.'

'I am a social worker in Kensington and Chelsea borough.

I am here with your mother. I was called in to assist an hour ago. We have tried to get her home, as it appears she's in fact not homeless but gave us an address in Streatham. Is that correct? She seems to have a bus card and enough cash for a taxi but is insisting on staying put. She isn't in pain or injured. Just very stubborn.'

All my muscles suddenly ache, but I know I can't blame the weights.

'Right. I'll be there in—where did you say you were?'

'The town hall. Between the town hall and the library. Just off Kensington High Street. The street is called Hornton Street.'

My legs wobble, and again, it's not from a strenuous leg day. She's back there. We've had months with no incidents, months when she's agreed to stay home except for special occasions, but here we are. *Fuck*, here we are again.

'Can you make your way here quickly, please? I've tried to reason with her, but she keeps saying she will stay here until the 16.14 bus and be back in time for dinner.'

'Forty-five minutes,' I tell her. I wipe the sweat from my forehead, gaze longingly at the showers as I rush past them and take a deep inhale when the cool summer air surrounds me. The realisation that I have one more problem in my life now hits hard. Can't help feeling that this is a turning point.

Care home, my brain tells me as I run down the road. Two words that could solve this, change our lives forever. Safety, comfort and pudding every day! I can't do this any longer. It was meant to be a solution, me spending time with my mother and supporting her after her diagnosis. I didn't take the decision lightly. It was a long, guilt-infused process, and I knew it wouldn't be easy. But this constant, relentless fear was never part of the plan. Even as her full-time carer, keeping her safe is becoming more difficult each day. I hop on the bus because I have no time to make it back to the house first, plus there is no damn parking where she is (I mean, come on, Mum, if you're impersonating a homeless person, why do it in Kensington of all places? At least if you chose Romford I could find street parking that wasn't ten quid an hour). My phone battery is low, so I spend the time it takes the bus to get there caught up in my thoughts, annoyed thoughts, thoughts that push at the chest angrily. I get off and let the frustration out by running the rest of the way. I run past shops and coffee places. Everyone is so well-dressed they scare me.

The social worker—I've forgotten her name already—is still there when I arrive. In a big cardigan with a tote bag hanging off her shoulder and shoes that look like she treasures them and takes them to be restored rather than buy new ones. She stands a few metres from Mum, hovering like a bodyguard, attempting to see but not be seen.

'Mum,' I say, nodding a silent thank you to the lady, hoping this is it, that she'll leave us and there'll be no reports, home visits or follow-ups.

'There was really no need for you to come here.' Mum's cheeks are rosy, and she looks as if I've just turned up to her primary school playground to embarrass her. She looks around to see if there's anyone watching. But who apart from the social worker would watch us? An older lady and her young adult son. I notice that Mum hasn't changed out of her home clothes. The soft brown velvet pants I bought her and which she initially resisted and dismissed as inappropriate attire are now apparently appropriate for outings to the city centre.

'Let's go, Mum. We'll talk later.' I usher her away, happy that she is okay, but also far too aware of what this means.

She's back at the bus stop.

Sophia
Svedala

IT'S 11.30, AND I'm in my flower shop, the morning after my disastrous kiss, and I've just moved to close my tenth transaction of the day.

'A flower is the reproductive structure found in plants. The biological function of a flower is to facilitate reproduction by providing a mechanism for the union of sperm with eggs.' I say this to the man who's just walked into my shop, picked up a dozen of pre-banded pink roses and shared that he's off to a date this evening. For good measure, I add, 'Good choice. Hopefully they will help facilitate the union of sperm and eggs.'

He looks around me as if trying to make sure no customer is next to us. The doorbell hasn't rung, so I know we're alone. He doesn't look reassured which means I may have misread the interaction. Perhaps he was hoping for someone to walk in. Perhaps he was hoping for a crowd to appear so he isn't alone with just *me*.

'I know there are people more comfortable with other terminology, but I think it's degrading to speak of the reproductive process like that,' I explain helpfully.

'Got ya.'

'There aren't many customers through the doors at this time of the day. If you look at Google, you will see that our peak times are 12.30 and 17.30,' I inform him as he yet again fixates on the door. 'Card?' I add as I tap in the price.

'Contactless.'

'Like my contacts list,' I say, but he doesn't laugh.

He taps his card, holds it mid-air as we both stare the machine down waiting for the rattle of receipt paper to break the heavy silence.

'Wonderful,' I say when the card goes through. 'Would you like me to wrap these for you? We don't sell them with plastic wraps as they're harmful to the environment, but should you wish I can package them for you in compostable paper.'

I ready the shiny paper and the stickers with our company name on them, Blom's Blooms. I am not called Blom. That would be too much of a coincidence. But my uncle's mother did have the maiden name Blomberg, and so the name was born.

Hearing my therapist's voice in my head, I remember to put my heels down on the floor as I move across the room. I have a tendency to walk on my toes, but there really isn't any need to add to my height. Mum always attempted to make me feel better once we both realised I wasn't going to stop growing at sixteen. 'There are some women who are like Arabian horses and others that are like large Shire horses. Big-boned is just how we're built,' she'd say. It was just that later when I went to search for these breeds online, it became clear that the Arabians went for a lot more money than the Shires, so what she told me didn't actually make me feel better.

'I don't need any wrapping, thank you,' the man says apologetically, just as I'm about to start. 'I'm in a bit of a rush.'

Once he's run off, I defeatedly do what I do after every human interaction: go over what I could possibly have done wrong. I can't read strangers, and my two options are to trust that every person means well and adores me or to assume the opposite, that they hate me. I can't think of anything I could have done wrong this time. I shared interesting and situation-specific knowledge, I wished him good luck (a polite pleasantry reserved for even remote acquaintances or strangers), I made a joke that has a track record of making customers smile, and I offered to package his purchase beautifully.

I think how my uncle would have laughed at my joke had he lived to know what *contactless* meant. My uncle left me more than the shop. He was safety and stability, cinnamon rolls and strawberry squash with floating ice cubes. He always took the time to explain things to me, with words that somehow also managed to cover the answer to the next question, the one I hadn't even asked yet. One week in summer and one week at Christmas break I was allowed to take the train by myself all the way from Jönköping and stay with him here, in the house attached to the shop. My brothers never came; they were too busy with hockey training, Lego assembly and friends. 'Tell me which flower you are, Sophia,' my uncle would say. And I'd think carefully, swing my legs back and forth on the chair and remember all the large, colourful pictures in his Latin dictionary of plants.

'I think I may be a *Tridax procumbens*. A grass flower. It's not so fancy and just smells like grass. It's small and unnoticeable, but still a flower with its own melancholy.' I stumbled on that last word, knowing how to spell it but not quite how to say it. I hadn't had an opportunity to try it out yet. I liked the dance it did on the back of my tongue.

He nodded contentedly.

'Grass flowers are one of nature's most understated arts. They're exquisitely designed, Sophia.'

IT'S CALM IN the shop at midday, so I pop over to the next-door café, which happens to make the best coffee in the world. It also has a food hygiene rating of five, as can be seen on a sticker on the front door. I ask for a hot chocolate, like always. And a pasta salad.

'This may be an unpopular opinion, but there's no nice pasta salad.' Lina prepares it in a deep bowl, tossing it with dressing.

Lina is clearly a sunflower, a *helianthus*. She never shrinks back and always smiles at strangers even if they don't smile in return. She is the closest thing I have to a colleague, seeing as she works in the building right next to mine. This is also as close to friendship as I get. It's not that I don't want friends but more that, once I have them, I don't know what to do with them. I don't necessarily enjoy going to loud places, and I have no energy left in me once I close the shop and leave for the day. I've collected quite a few friends over the years but find the relationships wilt if they don't get watered, much like flowers.

'Didn't you make this? And aren't you selling it?' I protest.

'I cater to demand. Which includes catering to the demand of a specific returning customer.'

Yes, I have demand for a pasta salad. Its humid temperature, familiarity and non-overbearing flavour makes it the perfect food.

'At least it's not breakfast food. It contains some veggies,' she says.

'I only eat breakfast foods when I'm overwhelmed!' Which, to be fair, I am a lot of the time. Cereal and porridge always taste the same, can be prepared in minutes and eaten with a spoon. It's my favourite thing about adulthood, being able to eat cereal for dinner. That and living a thousand kilometres away from my family.

I like my daily chat with Lina and am grateful when it revolves around pasta salad, rather than, you know, why I'm lonely and why I don't have evening plans and when was the last time I bought new clothes? None of which I have satisfying answers to.

'You added olives,' I say, nodding appreciatively to the pasta salad.

'Yes. Speaking of, where have you added yourself lately?'

It looks like we are swiftly moving on from the safe domain of pasta salads.

'In fact, I've just deleted myself from the Ed dates.' Lina knows that I don't like kissing—we agreed to disagree on that subject—but she never tries to persuade me or, like that one guy, force me to watch videos of people's wedding kisses, to change me. Like some form of conversion therapy.

'Human bacteria *is* transferable. Because we're the same species. Even a dog wouldn't be as bad,' I share.

'You're saying you'd rather kiss a dog than a man?'

'Their bacteria isn't compatible, and so no bacterial community can build up. It's definitely preferable in terms of hygiene.' Info-dumping is my love language.

'Don't say that out loud when anyone other than me is around, okay?' She laughs and puts my salad on the table closest to the counter, pulling out one of the chairs and sitting down opposite me.

'Got it.'

'You can't stop dating because of bad dates. Same as you can't stop eating brownies after one bad batch.'

'It's not just one bad date,' I object. 'It's the exhausting, bewildering and alien process of making myself appealing to men. I read the Latin floral encyclopaedia for fun, drink milk to unwind and consider my favourite outfit to be my Christmas elf onesie from 2019.'

Lina whimpers out a *no*.

'Yes,' I reply empathetically. 'On top of that I can't even make up for it with a hot make-out session because, as discussed, I don't like kissing.'

'Okay. Houston, we may have a problem.'

'Finally.' I get up and grab a warm cookie from the tray behind the counter, writing the price of it down on my standing tab that I pay monthly. Lina would give me anything I want for free, but entrepreneurial women deserve to get paid for their work even if they're your best friend.

'But I do think you're wrong to believe a boyfriend will magically transform your life. It hasn't happened to me yet. I think it's a myth sold to us when our sole purpose was to marry and take care of a home so that we'd be more willing to do it. But if you insist on dating, you're gonna have to warn them in advance. Not just in a sexy sentence at the end of a text but properly. It's just like any other 'thing.' *Will only date vegetarians, will only date man above six foot, will only date men who don't kiss.* Got it?'

Okay. Be open with who I am. Easy, right? *Easy, right?!*

'So maybe I don't really need a man?' I ask, giving it one more shot before accepting defeat.

'Need? No, and again, no one else is going to suddenly give your life meaning. But want? That's a different question altogether.'

'That's my point. What exactly would I want one for? I have my own business, a place to live, a pasta salad hookup—and I can, you know, take care of myself just fine,' I try to add subtly.

'I know you're a big fan of adult toys, but let me tell you, a vibrator is not the same thing as being with someone.'

'I've been told that having a vibrator's battery die on you during the act is like having sex with a man. It's a very realistic representation of the experience. And one I don't particularly enjoy.'

'Not arguing with that. But just think about it, if you find a man that won't try to kiss you? Could be a whole different ball game. I hate to say *not all men*, but in this instance it really is a matter of not all men.' She looks around to see if any customers are incoming, and as they're not she leans across the table. 'Okay, to cheer you up, I have a good story. The Volvo employee I was dating? Just up and left me.'

I feel awful now for not asking about Lina, for being consumed by my own problems. This doesn't happen because I don't *care*. It's the opposite, really. I feel everything and anything. I sympathise too much, because the level of sympathy needed for each person is like a well-guarded secret, known by everyone else other than me, so I don't know how much to sympathise in any given situation. How am I to know that I shouldn't cry as much over my co-worker's grandmother as I did for my own? I mean, I *feel* her pain because I too have been there. Luckily, Lina doesn't mind. She just tells me.

'So listen to this. I've been left for many reasons, but never over a jar of chocolate spread.'

'Chocolate spread? As in Nutella?'

'Apparently me finishing it and never replacing it is selfish behaviour and showed him that I'm not a woman he would like to share his life with.'

'Ouch.'

'I mean, what sort of a joke is that? Finished a jar of Nutella and he's gone? Am I not worth more than a jar of chocolate spread?'

'Nutella has a recommended retail price of 34.99 kroners,'

I say, picking at the cookie and putting soft crumbling pieces into my mouth.

'Well, thanks, bestie. Now I know my worth: 34.99 SEK. Freaking amazing.'

I get up to give her a hug because hugs and wine apparently help in situations like this, and it's too early in the day for the latter.

'Thanks. That was great, but it's okay to stop now,' she says and pulls away from the embrace. 'He had the emotional maturity of a hamster. Finding emotional connection is a bloody nightmare.'

I'm about to reply but pause and realise there's something I keep seeing in movies and now see right in front of my eyes. Something I missed when I walked in earlier. Something which worries me.

'Are you okay?' I point to her new hairstyle, finally putting two and two together.

'Yes!' she says and laughs. 'Sometimes people cut a fringe when everything is fine.' She laughs at me again and shakes her head so her dark hair swooshes. 'Jesus, I prefer Nutella to him anyway.'

'Incoming,' I say. Because in that moment Americano walks in. All we know about him is that he's tall, blond with brown hazel eyes and incredibly unapproachable. Lina hops off her chair and is behind the counter in seconds.

'Is he on time?' I whisper in a hiss to Lina before he's close enough to pick it up.

'Of course he is.' Every day at 13.30 Americano walks in and orders, surprise, a white Americano.

'Hi there.' His American accent would be quite charming if he weren't so short in his tone.

'The usual?' Lina asks, already preparing the coffee. I decide to leave them to it. Somehow the air gets thicker when he's in the room, and Lina gets more preoccupied: She starts to fiddle almost like I do, touching her lips, smoothing out her apron.

'Catch you later,' I say. Then I add, 'See ya,' to Americano because I heard it in an American office show once.

MY APARTMENT IS quiet when I get in that evening. I walk around turning all the lights on. The lights are off most of the day so I do this with a clean conscience. Living area, tiny kitchen, lights above the stovetop, bedroom and shower room—can't leave any room out. I feel sorry for things other people don't feel sorry for. Every time Mum forced me to throw away my old toys or clothes I felt pain like a physical stab. 'Oh, grow up, Sophia. They're only things, and you have lots of them,' Mum would say. I'd reply that I couldn't grow up any faster than I already was. 'A child grows on average seven centimetres a year, and I can't speed it up. It's scientifically impossible.'

I think back to what Lina said earlier about clearly stating my boundaries, that I do not kiss, for example, and that's something I won't budge on. Won't change for a man. And then I think about a book I'm reading, *Unmasking Autism*, it's called, and it's all about being your authentic self. Perhaps it's time. Mattias, my youngest brother, gave it to me for Christmas saying it had called to him in the bookshop.

I was five the first time Mum brought me to therapy. The therapist was named Karin, and she had glasses with greasy marks on them, and I had to resist the urge to say anything because any urge I had in that room was meant to be resisted and controlled. I got rewarded with my favourite toy if I held eye contact for more than a second. And I got touched on my hand when I repeated words in a stammer.

As I got older, I read more about this therapy I was given—*applied behaviour analysis*. I learned more about the intention behind it and also that it can often be anxiety-inducing and considered harsh. It made me feel that who I was was not acceptable, and ultimately I only grew scared that I would fail in my effort to mimic others in the way I was apparently supposed to. So all I could do was try and try and try, but I never knew if what I'd just done was a failure or a success. People like to say that failure is what makes you stronger, but what if you can't tell the difference?

When Mum picked me up after my sessions, Karin would say, 'She was a good girl today,' and Mum would look like it had been worth the long drive there and back. But inside me something had shrivelled up and died. When you can't be yourself in front of your family, is there even any point to try and go out in the world and show who you are?

Now I'm starting to understand that there's a whole tribe of Autistics who are healing their traumas and moving on. I'd very much like to be one of them.

I open up my phone and check social media briefly. I follow @Autistic_ProfNed on Twitter and today he tweets, ABA meets the need of neurotypicals—it makes Autism invisible so they don't have to face it. I like the tweet, but I don't comment. Then I think about this no-kissing thing again. I open up my dating profile. *Will not kiss for any money in the world*, I write. Because it's the truth. Then I think maybe I should continue this true Sophia. If I can be honest to the world about this, perhaps I can be honest about other things?

I call Lina. I wish she lived above her shop too so she'd be right next door, but she says that if she gets no break from smelling like flour she'll go insane.

'I've done it. It's added. The no-kissing criteria. It's explicitly stated now.'

'Good. And you didn't add that you're not a prostitute?'

'But I'm not.'

'Doesn't matter. Just don't say it.'

'Okay. But I'm not very hopeful. The problem with people, and men in particular, is so many of them seem to just be alpha males who want to change me. I become a challenge for them,' I say.

'Honey, those are the ones you ignore. Alpha males should really be called beta males. They're the early version of a male before testing and bug fixes. They aren't stable and suitable for the public.'

'So the finished product hasn't reached the market yet?'

'If we're lucky, these alpha males will be gone circa fifty years from now and we can all date freely and happily ever after.'

'Excellent.'

LATER THAT NIGHT, when all the lights have been switched off and I've drawn the curtains so that I'm in the dark, I lie in my bed with eyes closed, and the face of the man buying date flowers that morning plays in my mind. There is always a face playing in my mind. I can't imagine things I haven't seen, and even though I live in a semi-rural location, I haven't seen enough sheep to fill a sequence long enough to last the time it takes me to fall asleep. What I remember and know is faces. I wish it were historical facts, the times tables or even maps, but here I am, able to recall a face I once spoke to at a bus stop.

I move over the imaginary face of today's man in my head now. The outline of the lips with a scar, the gap in his left eyebrow, the stain on his shirt collar, his hands holding the recently purchased flowers, until I finally drift off to sleep.

THE NEXT MORNING I check my dating app. Surprisingly, my honesty seems to have worked. I have three new matches, a high score for me. One who would love to have some fun, one who says he wants other things than kisses wink-wink, and one who says I'm a beautiful girl and how was my day?

I message the middle one because it seems the best match: I, too, want other things than kisses.

Blade
London

ON THE BUS home Mum insists on standing until a seat becomes available all the way in the back. I try, in vain, to get her to take a priority seat that's in front of us.

'I don't have a walking stick, do I? And my pregnant days are long gone. Only used that seat during those nine months with you. But boy, did I use it then, pushed my middle out as soon as I found out and cupped it,' she says.

'It's okay. Sitting in a designated seat isn't a sign of weakness, Mum.' But she keeps her eyes averted from me, and I can see there's no point.

Giving up, I follow her to the very back of the bus. Huddle next to her like I'm a kid again.

But I'm a twenty-nine-year-old man, and this shouldn't be my life. I allow myself a moment to think about where I was three years ago. Making a sweaty morning commute in a shirt that still smelled of ironing-spray mist, going to an office with people who weren't in need of round-the-clock care, other people to email to say, 'Hope you had a nice weekend' and 'Thank you for the below.' I always had plans, was always hours or days away from the next event or meet-up or sponsored half marathon. I spent too much money eating out and stressed when I'd forget to text my girlfriend during the day. I had a life.

I haven't been back to the area where I used to work. Avoid the whole length of that Tube line in case I run into someone I used to know whose life has progressed and didn't just halt one October like mine did. I wonder what the owner of my favourite lunch place thinks, if they asked about me or just assumed I dropped dead one day, never to be seen again. I've kept renewing my Office 365 subscription out of principle, even if the only time I've used Excel since leaving my job was to make a medication timetable for Mum last year. At £7.99 a month, I feel I'm still part of the club.

Now here I am in coffee-stained sweatpants, and the day's only excitement is an outing to pick up another prescription. When my girlfriend finally left me, she kept the friends, the car and the libido. I was left with Mum, her Clio from 2001 and the only climatic experience I can imagine coming from a cheese fridge-raid at midnight.

Mum stretches her legs out in front of her, leans her head back so that the tip of her chin points in the driver's direction and closes her eyes. I want to catch her whilst she's still making sense, whilst she's a hundred per cent here, not when she checks out for the day and all that's left is a shadow. I lean my head towards her, bending my neck in a curve to reach the top of her head, where I rest my cheek. Feeling guilty for letting my mind wander, for thinking of where I might be if I wasn't here. Because of course I'm here. There's nowhere else I'd choose to be.

'Are we going to talk about it?' I ask.

Her eyes flutter open. '*It* being . . . ?'

'*It* being you being mistaken for a homeless person and identified by social services. *It* being you escaping the house to sit at that bus stop on the corner of Hornton Street once again.'

'*Escape* implies I have been kept prisoner. Am I a prisoner, Blade? I thought you maintained that I am not confined to the house or living in the absence of freedom.'

I sigh.

'No one is trying to restrict your freedom. We're worried about you.' Somehow *we* has more authority than *I*, but of course, in reality there is no one else. A cousin who lives in Australia and sends a Christmas card that always arrives after New Year because of the postal service. *We* implies there is someone behind me, nodding at my words and carrying some of the weight of it all. Not just me and Mum, alone.

'I have that button they gave me,' Mum argues.

'Yes, the one you mistook for a direct line to my phone. Concierge service.' Mum had called up the emergency on-call nurse asking to have her heating turned down and could Blade please bring a glass of water? For someone who wants to maintain her freedom, she can be astoundingly dependent.

'What's it matter anyway? By the time they come I'll be dead already. In which case it won't matter. I'll be damned if my last action in life is pressing an emergency button. Asking for help. That is no way to end a life.'

This is a top contender for Mum's headstone inscription. *I'll be damned if I ask for help.* It's right up there with the location of the bus stop if she carries on like this.

'You haven't answered my question. Why did you go there?' I try again.

'Blade.' She says my name so sharply it sounds as if it's a razor, my namesake. 'You cut through my heart like a sword. I couldn't call you Sword, could I?' That is the one-line full story of how I got my name.

She has opened her Thermos, the one I prepared for her before I headed to the gym since she shouldn't be handling the kettle anymore, and takes a sip of her tea as if the sheer mention of my name means she has to fortify herself. She licks her thin lips where a trace of bright red lipstick is still visible on the edges. I wait for the verdict: *too milky, too sugary, did you make this with the compost ground?* But it doesn't come.

'Have you ever felt drawn to something so strongly you simply can't resist? Like you can only be you in that particular instance, and if you don't go there you may well die an early death?'

Well—no. Unless you count the times McDonald's or a late-night kebab has pulled me in with its magical powers at two in the morning. Maybe that's my problem? I have no pull anymore; I'm just drifting through life, following after Mum, in a blur of love and guilt.

'Mum. It simply can't go on like this.'

'It will go on until I find him.'

Here we go again. *Sven.* Tall, blonds and strong, a boyfriend Mum has lusted after since she got her diagnosis three years ago.

'He didn't turn up. He told me to wait for him there, and he never turned up.'

'It's called *ghosting* in today's society.' Like many of us moderns, Mum is convinced something happened to him. That he'd have met her there against all odds and must have been prevented by some terrible force beyond his control.

'He loved me.'

'He left you.' I'm not usually this harsh. I have to remind myself to treat her gently when she gets like this. I remember reading leaflet after leaflet on what to expect with her diagnosis. *She may find obsessions, and they may be rooted in the past as her dementia progresses.* Wasn't it the fact she'd wandered off here that had alerted me that something was wrong in the first place?

'You can't leave someone if you never turn up. In fact, non-arrival is the very opposite of leaving,' she responds.

'Fine—he never turned up.'

'Something happened to him. I was sure of it then, and I'm sure of it now.'

'Mum, you looked for him. For years. You waited and waited. I tried to find him online—do you remember? Isn't it time to move on? To let it *go?*' She looks at me as if I've suddenly given her an idea. Somehow I don't think I'll like this idea, whatever it is. Mainly because I know that however frustrated I feel, the love for my mum is stronger, fuelled by a realisation that I will have to let go one day, and until that day I need to do and be *everything*.

'Fine. I'm ready to make a deal. It involves letting *you* go. To Sweden.'

I nearly bloody spit out my water because the idea is so absurd. I can't even make it to the gym most days because I'm needed to ensure Mum is safe. The time I used to be able to squeeze out of the day, fifty minutes when she watches TV after lunch, is rapidly slipping away from me too. Sweden is a different country, which would require a flight, a suitcase and a valid passport to get to. Something I haven't had the need for in a long time.

'And why exactly am I going to Sweden?'

'Well, that's obvious, isn't it? I can't go myself, can I? You don't like to talk about it, Blade, but my condition is progressing, and there are some things I want clarity on before that happens. I need you to find Sven.'

She leans back in the seat as if the conversation has now ended, eyes half-closed again. I press grubby red button because our stop is next.

'Find him and I'll move into any care home you want. Even

to that hideous one in Berkshire where mindfulness is a core subject.'

I sigh. She sighs. The bus sighs as it stops at a light.

'Don't think I haven't noticed you browsing and leaving information packs around the house.'

We turn the last corner before our stop, and the words slip out of me before I realise what I'm saying.

'Fine. You have yourself a deal, Mum.'

Sophia
Svedala

WHEN I WAS twenty-one my uncle passed away, and as he must have known, the only thing that got me through it was that he left me the shop. His message to me in the will simply said *Taking over this shop changed my life and kept me going when I thought I couldn't. I know it can do the same for you.* My family tried to sell it, but a clause had been added which prevented its sale for a period of five years. This meant I had five years to make it work and during which no one could take it from me. I now have one year left before I need to pay my three brothers their share of value—or sell.

The day after my university graduation I boarded the train I knew so well and headed south, with an envelope containing keys for the shop and the two-bedroom apartment above it and a suitcase with my belongings. My brothers were all hung-over so they never said goodbye, but my dad drove me to the station, and when I looked out of the window I could see him still standing there at the platform looking at the train leaving. Even though he'd said, 'The short-stay parking charges a bloody fortune, so we can't be long, Sophia.'

The relief to get out was immense. I had almost-kissed too many boys in my hometown, and my parents' house seemed a constant chaos ground with my three brothers all living within a mile's distance and dropping in without notice. In my new life no one would question me or my choices.

And I've been doing okay in this new life ever since. The shop makes a profit, I no longer have to hide certain parts of myself to please my parents, and I've made some friends (well, really just the one, but still). I really am okay. It's just that I always wanted a little bit more than just okay. Lots of people wish, dream and yearn for okay. Yet I'd like one part of my life to be extraordinary, to stand out. To give me shivers or take my breath away or make joy bubble up in my throat. There isn't too much joy lately. There is also the dark cloud of the payment to my brothers. One and a half million kroners. That I don't have. And I've not much reason to think that one more year is going to make much of a difference.

I check my phone to see what my family has been up to. Pulling up the group chat, I see that I've missed seventy-three new notifications. All those conversations and they haven't @ me once.

The chat is muted, and I manage to stay under the radar like this. Its name changes on an almost daily basis, and the current one is Mattias Has Worn the Same Socks for 10 Days. There's an amazing amount of immaturity between my brothers. They even have their own special group chat, a sibling chat, that I'm not in despite very much being a sibling.

When I was younger I thought if only I were a boy too I'd fit in with my family, I'd get along with my brothers better. I tried to play hockey but never made it past the stage of clinging to the railings, legs shaky on the skates. Even when they let me play Lego, my job was to find the right pieces and hand them to them, not actually build. An enabler.

Today's seventy-three messages seem to focus on when either of my super successful brothers plans to give my parents grandchildren. My mother is obsessed with the four of us procreating, as if their semi-detached four bedroom in Jönköping is a stately home in need of a bloodline to pass it down to—or else, in the absence of a rightful heir, a mob of illegitimate offspring will storm in and turn it into a donkey sanctuary making my mum and dad homeless.

I ran into Niklas's mum today and he is expecting twins. He was in your year, Mattias! Mum writes.

I am only one year younger than Mattias, I contribute now. My cheeks feel flushed and warm.

You don't even like children. My mum's reply comes fast, as if it's a ready-made template on her phone.

No, I don't, in fact. But that doesn't mean I should be excluded from the bring-forth-an-heir harassment. Why *couldn't* I have a child before my brothers? Is it so obvious that I will end up alone?

I'm a bit like an annexe to this family. Not part of the main house, but this bit that sticks out and looks off because you couldn't get the same colour or the same tiles and the ceiling height is lower. You put all your spare furniture there, the toilet flush lever only works the second time you pull it, and the heating doesn't quite function the same way because it's, well, *the annexe*.

I HAVE MY breakfast on the balcony and wear a floral dress which is floaty and makes me feel well-ventilated and free. I love summer clothes. No scratchy wool or fluffy cashmere. Just cotton, dresses and soft, well-washed hoodies when it gets chilly. I have an hour until I open up the shop, so I decide to tackle my finances, which is a much less painful task than the family chat. As I pull the most recent spreadsheet up on my screen I sigh. Even I can see that my spreadsheets have become faster to compile. People simply aren't buying as many flowers as they used to. And the ones who are buying require deliveries far out in the countryside, meaning my petrol spend and time invested (since I'm the only employee, I have to make deliveries while the shop is closed) is too high. I have no expensive habits apart from silk underwear and organic oats, but even with my modest living for one, the business has to make a bigger profit. It needs to make sense. And working around the clock for almost nothing makes no sense to me. Not when I need more than a million by the end of next year to even keep this going.

I go over my options again. Employing someone is out of the question. It's a small town, and the extra cost won't do me any favours. Then there's expansion. To someone like me, that word is scary as it relates to things like *expanding one's horizon*. If I can't figure out a way to make having another employee work, I'm not sure expanding is even a viable option.

I have had a few enquiries to do events, decorate corporate conferences and take part in markets but so far have ignored any such requests. The most recent one left me a voicemail five days ago, and I only returned the call because it was an old friend of my uncle's. The phone call lasted twenty-five minutes of which I spoke for three and a half, which was just enough time to say, 'No, thank you, I am simply not in a position to take on the project as it stands, but thank you for thinking of me.' The other twenty-one and a half involved my uncle's friend explaining that they were in a bit of a pickle and needed someone to decorate the annual markets across seven locations in Småland county. It was a lucrative and utterly frightening proposition. Thinking about it, perhaps I should have thought the offer over for more than two seconds.

I text Lina.

> **ME:** I could use some company tonight. Do you wish to be that company?
>
> **LINA:** I'll close at 6pm and come over right after.

Blade
London

THE NEXT MORNING I wake up before Mum does. Six thirty, like always. Get myself ready quickly because I don't know what state she'll be in today. I imagine one of those rating displays you get at a public service office or train station with four smiley faces that range in colour from red to green. Yesterday I would have pressed the far left one—red like an inferno, mouth turned downward in a clearly identifiable frown. Today I hope for the green one.

It's a laundry day. I can tell because I'm out of clean sweatpants. I pull open the curtains in the sitting room so I can see the world and it can see me. I look at the people rushing past outside. A little girl drops her hair tie, and the mother attached to her arm only reluctantly stops for it. *Rush.* All those people wishing to give it all up and have no fucking clue what they wish for. People with reusable cups and briefcases walk past, making me wish I could keep the blinds closed so as not to see what all I'm missing out on, but I remember the advice to *Differentiate between day and night always, to aid your loved one being present and in the moment.* The blinds are always open, and whilst my instinct is to duck and hide, Mum likes to wave at neighbours as they walk past.

At the kitchen counter I hesitate. I have photos taped to the cabinet doors so she can know what's behind them. Whatever we can we have in clear view, so Mum can easily pick it up. Keys, pen, paper and timer.

I prepare her toast and put small pills next to it on the plate, watching them roll around like flipper balls when I balance it with one hand and bring it upstairs. Mum is awake.

'Morning,' I say.

'Is it not a good one? Or are you saving your words for someone more interesting than me?' She used to say that to teenage me. *Who are you saving your words for?* When I'd mutter a short reply to prompts about how my day had been, or where I was headed at *this goddamn hour.* For a minute I wonder if she thinks I'm sixteen again and will start rubbing her thumb at a spot of breakfast staining my shirt, then say, 'Off to college you go, now. Buses and opportunities don't wait for you.'

'Not sure if it's a good one yet, that's all. But fine. Good morning, Mum.'

People supposedly look the oldest when they wake up. Groggy and lined from creases in the sheets, and eyes with blue bulges underneath them. But Mum looks her youngest, her most peaceful in this moment. All the lines have relaxed overnight, her eyes are alert and glossy as if she's had a particularly vivid dream.

I place the tray on her lap.

'Tea or coffee?' I ask.

'I know very well what you're doing here,' she replies, and I smile a real smile. Caught.

'You're giving me choices so that I feel involved and in control still. Don't think I didn't notice that you put two pairs of socks out for me to choose from the other day. Although I wouldn't call the Christmas socks from a decade ago a valid choice.'

Again: it's laundry day.

I look at her, my hands outstretched with what she correctly identified as intentional options. I'll drink whatever she doesn't choose.

'Tea,' she answers, and I hand her the cup, waiting to let go until her two hands are firmly wrapped around it.

'We don't have any appointments today, so I thought we'd go for a walk after breakfast.'

I never walked for the sake of walking before. Always walked with a destination in mind, always towards something. Now Mum and I just walk. Slowly. Past things. Then back to where we came from.

'Wonderful,' she says, already halfway through her toast. 'Then, when we get home, we can discuss your trip.'

Oh. *She hasn't forgotten.*

AT NINE O'CLOCK, once Mum is settled for the night with an audiobook and the laundry is dry and folded, I do what I always do when I have a huge fucking problem that seems to have no solution: I ask Zara.

The pub is one street down from ours, offering an average food menu and peanuts that seem to have lost all of their salt. Its unique selling point is that it's the only place my newly purchased baby monitor will reach and therefore my only escape. Mum tends to get restless at night after taking her medication, and I can't trust her to sleep through. I lower the average patron age by a good thirty years when I walk in, and I spot Zara in a far corner in full conversation with the owner Raj and his band of regulars. They leave us with a hello so I assume they've now exhausted the pool of potential ladies to introduce me to. Ever since Jade left me, I have been tortured with set-up after set-up with local girls, magically appearing alone in the pub on nights I'm there.

'Hey, stranger,' I say to Zara. Feels like it's been ages since we met up like this.

'Tell me.' Her pink hair is held in place by a collection of small white clips. There are two drinks and a bag of cheddar crisps on the table.

I press the baby monitor to my ear: Everything appears quiet. It's a long-range model which I bought from Mothercare. When I paid for it, the sales-person told me congratulations, and I wasn't sure what to do with that or how to explain that I didn't have a newborn, just a mum who needed similar care, so I ended up just saying thank you.

I summarise for Zara.

'Apparently in order to stop my mum from playing homeless outside Kensington town hall, I need to go to Sweden. She just sits and sits at that damn bus stop, waiting for an old flame who didn't turn up there almost thirty years ago. She said she'd move into a care home, any care home, if I can just find Sven.'

'Haven't you looked for this guy before?' She opens the crisp bag with a pop.

'Well, yes.' I did a thorough Facebook search, which should have yielded something, considering everyone has Facebook still, but no. 'But I'm tired. Tired of worrying about her. Tired of being on edge constantly. Every time I leave the house I check my phone is on highest volume about fifteen times. Every time there's a call I jump. Where has she been now? What's she getting up to this time? I need to know she's safe and that I can leave the house for more than a half hour at a time without suffering a panic attack.'

I stop for air and a gulp of cold cider then continue to fill the silence.

'Her latest scans show that it's progressing fast. I've got all these nurses asking how I'm coping, and that's all there is. Questions. Because there's no solution. No answers. I can't stop the disease, and I can't be what Mum needs all the time She needs more than what I'm capable of. She needs to be happy, and I can't seem to give her that.'

'Unless you find Sven?'

'Unless I find Sven.'

I stop for a minute to ponder how I ended up here, in a pub with my best friend discussing taking a trip to Sweden. Some people are busy climbing a career ladder or honeymooning in the Maldives or running marathons or hell, even just catching up on the latest show. I got left behind big-time. I wouldn't change it for the world—but also wouldn't have chosen it.

'You want to come along for the ride? Could be massively entertaining to watch me search aimlessly for a man I've never met,' I say. Zara is my only constant. Other friends have been circumstantial, there whilst we had a joint location to be, a class to share or a desk opposite one another. I hadn't realised until they all disappeared that Zara is my one true friend, there since we were sixteen, still here despite all the changes in life.

'I only have two weeks of leave left, and as much as I love you, a tour of Swedish care homes looking for some man your mum's obsessing over is not how I intend to spend them. Sorry. Eagerly awaiting the video chats, though. Do you think there are any hotties? Everyone gushes abut Swedish women, but the men are equally gorgeous. All trendy denim, tall and handsome.'

'Unless you're into older men, I doubt you'll find someone where I'm headed.'

Zara falls silent, and I wait. She has been contemplating the problem for long enough that I start to shake my left leg and am about to open my mouth. She puts up a hand to stop me. Don't disturb the genius.

'But this is a short-term thing?' my best friend finally asks.

'For sure. Couple weeks at the most. Find a man, take a picture, arrange a phone call. Let the nostalgia flow and maybe set up a pen pal scheme. Let's say I give myself two weeks? Money will run out, if nothing else. I'm not even sure how I'll make ends meet to be honest. I'll need to look into a carer whilst I'm away.' Shit. Only just realised that cost will add to my travel expenses. I'd hoped to have two weeks. More like two days. In the cheapest motel there is with shared shower facilities.

'Hmmm.'

'Which means?' The monitor rustles in my hand, and my foot starts tapping the floor. I've been out half an hour, and already the guilt is setting in. What if I reach the point where I can't do this anymore? I'm barely able to step out and go to the gym or the supermarket. Yet, I have to hold on because there's no choice. Can't think about what happens if my trip doesn't go well, if no lead turns up and I return without any news. What if she can't cope?

'Okay, so maybe I can't go with you, but I could work from your mum's. I once babysat Natalie's twins, and that's got to be worse. Besides, your mum—I love her. Happy to sit and watch movies and make her some food and talk about whatever it is she feels like talking about that day. Would be rather fun, I think. But go within the next two weeks if you can. After that I'm swamped.'

'You would work from my house so I can go on a wild goose chase across Sweden?' I can't quite believe what I'm hearing. But then, I always suspected Zara was equally fond of my mother as she is of me. Who wouldn't be fond of someone who, when you turn up on their doorstep after having been expelled from school over green hair, exclaims, 'Green is the colour of intellectual stimulation and thinking. A great colour, if I may say so,' and puts the kettle on rather than calling their parents?

'This is important, right? I have some editing deadlines, but I don't see why not. The early nights and being forced to stay in will be great for me.'

'You're amazing.'

'Yes. Yes, I am.'

'I will write you a list—a manual—for everything you'll need.' I've never let go before, never let someone else in to help. My head spins with everything Zara will need to know. 'But I have to say, it's a lot of hard work.'

'You think because it's only you and her, this is your load to carry alone, and I get it. But you're also only one guy, Blade. This could be a good break for you too, a step away from all the responsibility, and one that you need or else you'll burn yourself out. I've got this. You're not the only person capable of caring for your mum.'

I want to believe her.

Badly.

WHEN I GET back to the house an hour later, I go straight upstairs and lie down next to her. Half my body fits on the bed and the other I keep propped up with the help of my leg. My hand finds hers. I stroke it and let my mind pause for a second on my mum. She's strong. Despite the erratic instructions from her brain, her body is still going, still working everyday, harder even than I am. Me and you, Blade. *Me and You,* she'd say to me. *Yes, Mum, me and you,* I'd echo. And it would be enough for her.

One trip. *This may be the last thing your mother asks from you. You can do this, Blade.*

Sophia
Svedala

'LINA, THIS IS madness. You deserve so much better. The *best*.'

I sit at the breakfast bar with a glass of hot cocoa repeating things a girlfriend should repeat to someone who's been recently dumped, as she sips a wine I bought her. I tend to not like alcohol because it makes my cheeks flush and my head spin and I sometimes say things I don't mean. I always tell the man in the wine shop that I'm having a dinner party and am cooking a fish or a lamb shank and would he recommend something, please, as I don't drink very often. It sounds more sophisticated than saying I need something that my best friend can slurp up whilst discussing her latest break-up. It turns out Mr. Must Have Nutella in the House at All Times has bombarded her with a string of text messages sharing his unsolicited advice on how she could be a better girlfriend, not so he can be with her but, you know, so she may keep a boyfriend in the future. How generous of him. So far his suggestions include not taking guys to her apartment as it's *too* nice and a lot of men may feel intimidated by her clear and apparent success. He also suggested she make more of an effort to cook dinner for her boyfriend. You know, just a suggestion.

'He just wasn't ready for a grown-ass woman who does what she likes in her home. Think of him, he said? I have better things to do than memorise every taste and need he has and to restock the cupboards every other day before he comes over. I'm not his mother.'

I refill her glass, which was empty surprisingly fast.

'I take it that since it's now been twenty minutes of talking about this, you want to change the subject,' I say.

'Yup. No more than twenty minutes to be spent on him.'

'Great. Can I show you my revenue spreadsheet?' I ask.

'Wow, that's a cracker of an invitation on a Friday night, girl.'

'Is that a yes?'

'Of course. Anything you ask is a yes from me.'

I'm not quite sure how I got this lucky. I had friends before. I realised early that to make them, you just do a little bit of what everyone else wants and become this mosaic of a person that everyone can tolerate. I said this to Lina once, and she said maybe we need to tear all those mosaic tiles down and go pick a style that I, Sophia, actually like.

I enter my password and hand her my laptop.

She studies it, taking a sip of wine every time she scrolls down.

'Excel drinking game. Shame for my kidneys you have so many rows.'

'Hang on. You told me you said no to a commission for the Sweden markets,' she says.

I had told Lina about the offer and why I decided to pass on it. The markets are lively, old-fashioned events with fun fair rides, fresh doughnuts and gyros. I was dragged to them enough as a child as they were my family's idea of a fun day out. I found them stressful, loud, oddly smelly, and somehow I always wound up with sunburnt shoulders.

'Too stressful for me.'

'Maybe they're stressful, but you're forgetting what you'd gain. Money, Sophia. Looking at these—' she nods at the screen '—I think you need to call up your uncle's friend and say you've changed your mind.'

'How would I even do the job, though? The farthest market is in Jönköping. That's close to a three-hour drive. How would I transport all the flowers there? I'd need a car, probably a van, and I would need help. I'm not sure I could do it all.'

'Often I find a solution will present itself. But only if you're open to it.' She drains her glass and closes the document. 'Thank goodness there wasn't a second page as that would have meant a second bottle, and I have to open up at seven tomorrow. But seriously, you keep saying you need the shop to make money. Or, rather, more money if you want to buy your brothers out and keep Blom's Blooms.'

'I thought about expanding to sell vegetables. Broccoli is a flower, and I'd love to stock them. They are useful, strong and green, a very peaceful colour. I think they'd do well in the store. 'You and your wife just had a huge fight? Here, have a side of broccoli with your flowers. Bring home dinner and an apology all at once.'

'I somehow don't think people will want to come to a flower shop and walk out with broccoli.'

'Or I could try offering faster delivery? An Uber Eats–type thing but with flowers?'

'You want to tell me you'd bike across Skane delivering flowers in one-hour slots? Since you don't have a delivery van currently, remember, or anyone else on staff to help with that.'

'Okay. Maybe that isn't the winning idea.'

'I tell you the winning idea. You have an offer that will fill a second excel page. Take the job, sort out the logistics later. Don't your parents live near to those last few locations? Maybe they could help, or even if you stayed with them, saved a little on lodging? This could be a huge moneymaker for the store, maybe an actual opportunity for you to keep it.'

My parents. I shudder. Not at the thought of them exactly, but rather at the thought of their house and everything in it. Expensive ornaments and carpets. Surfaces wiped with antibacterial spray and constant 'take your shoes' off reminders. Then there's the questions about life choices and stories about my childhood friends who have been promoted or had babies or, shock and horror, *both*. My parents are tulips—*Tulipas*. They're formal and elegant, even though their outline is simple. They're very uptight.

But Lina has a point. I need to do *something*. My uncle would expect me to do *something*. That's why he left me shop, right? He thought I could do these things.

'Okay, fine. I will email him tomorrow and see if the contract is still on offer.'

'Good. Just keep an open mind, okay? I bet there's a way to make this work.' She closes my laptop. 'And this wine was excellent. Let's tell the wine shop you're cooking the same fish again next week.'

Blade
London

TODAY HAS CHEERED Mum up. Immensely. Her ankles are swollen from running around all day, trying to get me organised for my trip. She's created folders for me, each one with a different category. 'To complement the letters.' Letters we still have to locate. And that I didn't know existed until yesterday. She's even started letting Swedish words slip into her daily vocab again. This was one of the things that spurred a diagnosis three years ago. First, it was French. *Will you be so kind as to pass me the* sel, she'd say like some posh dame. She'd lived in Paris for six months, I knew that. Made sense. Then the Swedish words happened.

'Did you ever go to Sweden?' I asked when she'd loudly proclaimed that her hat was a *mossa* and I'd consulted the internet to determine the language.

'I almost did,' she said.

'When?'

'When I fell in love.' I knew she wasn't in love with my dad: She'll proclaim that and the irrelevance of men to anyone that will listen. That he was useless and disappeared out of our lives as soon as he had the chance. So then, *who*?

'It was Sven. You almost moved to Sweden because of Sven,'

I state now, years later, as I watch her finish off another list, her handwriting wonky and wild. '*I* almost moved to Sweden too.' Images of a blond sibling show up uninvited. A second language. A *father figure*. I was a toddler back then, if Mum has the year correct.

'Everything would have been different if he'd turned up.'

'Maybe you could have tried to move on. To meet someone else?' I suggest.

'Oh please, you turned out just fine. More good women are lost to marriage than to war. If I'd had a father figure for you, you might have ended up an airhead. You might have become a general manager, middling about in some sort of generic life. We may have struggled at times, the two of us, but struggle is good for children. Happy people are so much less interesting.' I feel the fight rising inside me and decide to refocus. The days of arguing with Mum are behind us. Because her confusion means she will sense my anger but not see the reason for it, which makes for a much crueller experience for us both.

I set the table, bright yellow bowls that I ordered off Amazon. Yellow to contrast the food. Unless we are having scrambled eggs or korma, it stands out, and Mum sees that there is food on the plate. Because dementia doesn't just affect memory, it impacts sensory experiences involving touch and sight and smell too.

'I have no idea where the table starts and ends,' Mum says as if to confirm my thoughts just then.

'Trace your fingers along the side of it,' I say. 'Find your way as if it were dark.'

She picks up a piece of potato with her spoon. Forks are only for cutting now. No more knives, something she's accepted after much protest.

'Too hot.'

'Okay.'

She goes in for a second one.

'If the first one was too hot then don't take a second one. Have some salad first,' I say. I feel my frustration set in, an irrational impulse to raise my voice, shake sense into her.

She goes for the potato a third time, and I give up. It's not her fault.

'What do you *think* happened, when Sven failed to show up?'

Mum pushes her thin lips together.

'I don't know. But he would have been there if he could. He was never late. Scandinavian and punctual. He never gave me reason to doubt he'd always be right next to me, whatever happened.'

Mum in love. It's an impossible picture. If she had relationships over the years, she hid them well. Timed them when I went to camp or succumbed to daytime trysts during my school hours.

'*There* being the bus stop?' I ask.

'"Wait for me there," he said. "I'll have everything ready and tell you the plan, so you can start packing. Time to learn Swedish," he said.'

'Right, but where, Mum? Where exactly were you meant to meet him?'

'"At three o'clock," he said. "I'll be there at three. You'll see me waiting at the bus stop."' She finally manages to eat the potato, chewing it before continuing her answer. '"At the corner of Hornton Street, right between the town hall and the library."'

And there it is again, that damned street.

WAKING UP BEFORE Mum is becoming more challenging considering the summer light causes her to stir at six and either spring out of bed or call the buzzer I installed for her, until I come down the hall with a T-shirt thrown on to cover myself. The next morning is a new scenario entirely.

'Please tell me there is a reason you are attempting to get into the attic at seven in the morning.' Somehow, in the time I had a shower, Mum has managed to locate a ladder and is now balancing on the second step.

'We have to go through all our leads, Blade. Remember the letters?' she says as if we are detectives solving a riddle. 'They're up there.'

I gently guide her down under the promise that I will go up.

'There is so much stuff up here,' I shout down a few minutes later. Cardboard box after cardboard box full of books, summer clothes and lampshades. 'Fuck.' My toe crashes into something hard, just as I finally locate and drag out a box of what looks like old school crafts. I kick my other foot into a box just for good measure.

'Are you all right up there?' Mum's faraway anxiety travels up the ladder and into the void I'm in.

'Yes,' I say. 'That's what I always say when things are going incredibly well.'

I manage to make the journey down, covered in dust but with the box of letters safely in my grip.

I carry the box downstairs, placing it on the coffee table.

When I open the box, I'm thrown by how few there are, a couple of single pages on the cardboard bottom, no more.

'Where did you last see him?' I ask, realising I might have asked that before but not gotten an answer.

She thinks. Sometimes the harder she thinks the less words she finds. Same way the more she looks for an item the more she forgets. But she is clear today; it's a good day to talk. She hasn't even used the flash cards we made. Flash cards that say things like *Harriet is a physiotherapist who has two sons; one hopeless and one not so hopeless.* They each have a label like *Family* (I'm the only content there apart from the one Australian cousin), *Friends*, *Care Team*, *Society* and *Norms*.

'Two days before. All we had left to do was to meet up and for him to give me my ticket.' Then she falls quiet, and I realise that's all that the information I will get for now.

'Do you have a picture of him?'

'He didn't like being in pictures. But he took so many of me. Of you, too. Almost all the ones I have of you and me together were taken by him.'

I stop rummaging in the box and look up at her. We have a lot of pictures from when I was a toddler, it's true, and Mum is in all of them with me. I never thought about who might have taken them, or why her smile was so wide. Or why she stopped appearing in photos when I got older. There was no one to take them anymore.

'Let's go through our photos again this week and see if we can find him somewhere,' I suggest.

WE SIT FOR an hour. Like I feared, there isn't much, and all the gaps I'm trying to fill with Mum's memories are still glaringly empty. I read the letters quietly; they're love proclamations. Begging pleas for him to return to her or let his whereabouts be known. *This can't be Mum*, I think. The image of her head over heels in love just doesn't seem right. *This is not how she talks or writes.* Do I not know her at all?

'Where are the rest of them, Mum?' I ask her.

'The rest?'

'Yes, you, know, the other half of them. From Sven . . . Are there any?' I say. Then it clicks. There are no replies. It's all Mum's letters. Without envelopes and folded up into squares.

'Why were they returned?'

I pick up another note and read it in my head. Not addressed to anyone, no greeting, just a single plea: *If you decided that you didn't want me any longer, I understand, just let me know that you are safely back in Svedala. E.* Mum has long discarded the envelopes. Knowing how she tears and rips paper, I'm not surprised, but that means we have no addresses. Until now. What I hold in my hand is a postcard, an address scribbled across the righthand side, a postal stamp covering half of it. It was returned because of an incomplete postal code.

Finally, maybe there's something.

'Svedala, is that the place, Mum? Is that where you were going to move with Sven? Where he lived?'

I see her reaching for the answer. It's here on paper—I just need it confirmed from this version of my mum, not the hopeless, pleading woman in these letters who I don't recognize.

'Yes. Sven from Svedala. Doesn't that just sound like something you'd make up?' she says eventually, and I draw a sigh of relief as I am able to finally plan the first part of my trip.

Finally. With the help of the internet, I have narrowed it down to five Svens with the correct surname and birth year already, but this could tighten the search further. I open up Google Maps and mark the small tiny dot before zooming out to find the nearest airport: Copenhagen.

Right. To Svedala, then.

Edith
London

SONS ARE LIKE weeds. I say this in the nicest of ways, and if you'd seen my front garden you'd not question the affection in my statement. I quite like eccentricity. I certainly like sons. Mine tends to pop up where he's least expected lately, and always in an attempt to secure my attention. *MUM. Did you leave the tap on in the bathroom? The water bill was huge last month.* My son, Blade, does not ask questions like most people. Instead they are followed by a long string of words and reprimands. The fastest way to deal with him is to simply sigh.

When I hear the front door inform me that Blade is gone, I swivel out of bed and swallow the tablets he's left for me on the side table, a chemical sharpness brushing my throat. I don't remember which day it is, but then I don't remember a lot of things anymore. I try not to dwell on that. I simply move on to the next thought. Some days my mind is one fast string of images and thoughts in an endless scroll of one to the next, and other days, when I remember more, I can dwell on specifics, can pause and sit with them. There is less anxiety when your thoughts move slowly, when you're able to stop and hold them for longer.

I walk downstairs the same way I think I always do. The

floor is cold against the soles of my feet, and I realise I have forgotten my slippers. I stop at the hallway mirror and, as always, feel reassured when my own familiar face looks back at me. I still recognise myself. Marvelous. The kitchen is full of sticky notes that say *Do not touch*. Everything bears a warning. *Cutlery drawer—sharp objects! Kettle—hot! careful!* I finally find something I am allowed to touch: my Thermos flask and a plate containing a sandwich, a handful of grapes and two biscuits. I take it to the table and end up staring at it for an eternity because I am not quite sure what I am supposed to eat first. The phrase *five a day* pops up when I look at the grapes, so I conclude that I'll eat five of them, but the order of events is still unclear. In the end I decide to tackle the sandwich first because I think of Goldilocks and how she first tried the big bowl of porridge, and the sandwich is the largest item on the plate. I eat slowly, trying to halt the imagery and thoughts rushing past in my mind, finding one I can settle on, that I recognise. The house is quiet, and I try to think if I get many visitors these days.

I wonder when Blade will be back. I am so used to my son's presence that I'm not sure he counts as company at this point. Rather, he is part of my environment, like the rug that's been there twenty odd years and that I like to brush my feet against when I sit on the sofa. Or the jewellery I don't take off even for showers. I search my mind for a memory that will tell me when Blade will come home and where he might have gone. As usual the memory I need doesn't come, but others do, flooding into my consciousness. I am overcome with joy as image after image of Blade's smiling face floats through my mind like a computer screensaver. The time I taught him to ride a bike, late, at eight years old, far away from the neighbourhood so no friends would risk spotting him. The pride when he finally learnt and the relief at not having to come up with excuses as to why he couldn't join friends in the park.

I'm there, watching him smile and laugh. Then suddenly my mind focuses on something else, more recent, getting close to answering my question about where Blade might be this very moment. Except it's not, and I'm left no wiser. It's the image of the box of letters we went through.

Sweden.

Then it appears to me. I remember that I have something to tell Blade, something he must know, about lost chances and regret. The trouble is it keeps slipping away.

There's a point in life when your future is behind you. It sneaks up on you. You think, *Shall I go to Greece or Italy this summer?* And then the question changes and bears more weight because it reads in your mind like *Should I go to Greece or Italy this summer—whilst I can?* What I mean to say is that your life is in no way over, but you realise that each decision is now judged against whether you can live with yourself if it never happens.

One day I looked at Blade and that damned thought popped up.

I should tell him about Sven *whilst I can.*

Zara
London

ZARA IS PACKING to her current musical obsession, which is, in Blade's words, 'an Irish niche band for cool people'. Packing means throwing things at random into a small hard suitcase then sitting on it whilst zipping it closed, sweat appearing on her forehead.

She still has a spare key for the house, hers since she was a teenager. It was so much closer to school than her own house and she felt more comfortable there. There were no questions about homework or what had happened to her uniform or anything that her mum and dad routinely asked about. To this day she takes out her piercings before she goes to see them to avoid a debate, hating herself and her weak spirit for it.

She's happy to stay with Edith. It's really not a favour. Sure, she's had to cancel a date tonight, but to be fair she would have cancelled it anyway. Zara likes giving people a chance, and so she finds herself swiping for pretty much everyone. She doesn't want them to end up with no match: life is hard enough without being the last one to be picked. So she swipes and swipes like some relentless serial dater and then has to come up with excuses to never meet up or move the conversation to WhatsApp.

She just hopes they'll all hang in there.

EDITH'S HOUSE IS the type of home that doesn't change. The key lock is the same, the sofa has gained a throw in a mocha shade to hide old stains but is still standing, and the kettle takes about ten minutes to boil water because, well, it's ancient.

'He cleans too much,' Zara tells the walls after letting herself in.

'What did you say?' How he can hear her through two walls is a mystery.

'I said a clean house is a sign of time wrongly spent.'

He pulls her into a hug. Uneven, anxious, too hard, then too loose. It goes on for too long.

'Are you *sure* about this?'

'Blade, you've given up a lot. And I get it, your mum is a great mum, she's special. I'll be the first to say it. But not everyone would do what you did. Give up work and a life? You've always been too involved. This is the last thing you *should* do, and I'm happy to help you, but then there has to be balance.'

She's not here so he can find Sven, not really. She's here so that he can get some distance, realise what he's missing out on. That he's not the only source of happiness for his mum, that he never was, nor could he be. He won't find Sven—how could he? But he might find his way again. At least that's what Zara hopes. If one can even find one's way in only three weeks.

'Will you keep looking for pictures or letters? She could have hidden them,' Blade asks her.

The house is neat but filled with thirty years' worth of things. It will be hard to find anything, but Zara doesn't say so.

'Sure.'

Zara walks into the kitchen and runs her hand, her fingers full of gold rings, over the spotless counter.

'I think you might have OCD.'

'I have not.'

Zara nods her chin in the direction of the counter, filled with orange-coloured plastic bottles. 'You know, I'm capable of reading.' In addition to the prescription labels themselves, Blade has carefully mapped out sticky notes repeating the instructions and uses of each medication. The bottles and pills are laid out in a colour scheme resembling a rainbow. Blade is behind her.

'Stop acting like a parent dropping off a toddler at nursery. Stop hovering. A quick goodbye and off you go. We'll be fine.' She says this with actual confidence because, whether Blade knows it or not, she and Edith will be fine.

Zara hopes he will be too.

Blade
Copenhagen

WHEN I LAND a week later I do so with a phone full of pictures of old letters, a backpack and a feeling of doom hanging over me, since I have only found five Svens with the correct surname in total (turns out there are 101,270 men with the first name Sven who live in Sweden) and one of them happens to have passed away recently and is to be buried this very day, in a village called Skurup. I decide that's my first location. Exploring Svedala can wait.

I have no real plan other than turning up, hoping it's a big funeral so I'll go unnoticed and finding out who this Sven was. My online searches told me that he worked as a secondary school teacher, so if anyone questions who I am I will be there in the capacity of former student. I reread my mum's rather short letter now.

Svennie,

I have many questions about where you ended up, but just know I wouldn't change things. I couldn't. Some things in life you don't get to choose, and like my eye colour and aversion for spinach I didn't choose you. I was programmed to love you.

I stop and think: *What nonsense. Traffic lights and the space landings are programmed. Not the heart.*

THE AIRPORT HAS helpful information desks, fresh cool air despite it being June and hot dog kiosks everywhere. I find the car hire desk easily thanks to Scandinavian organisation and love of signs. I pull up my reservation number and pass the man my driver's licence and credit card as he smiles at me.

'Work or pleasure?'

Neither, in my case. Where is the 'Other' box?

'That's not the car I booked.' I stare at the computer screen and what appears to me to be a camper-van. RV. Mobile home. What are they even called? I can't think of a single time when I've ever needed to know before. The man, name-tagged Mohamed, looks as if he's ready to hand me the Worst Customer of the Year badge.

'It's an upgrade from a Fiat 500. Congratulations.'

'Man, I can't drive this, whatever it is.' Never camped and never driven anything that size. I look at the back of my licence hoping to see the category unticked, but apparently I have once upon a time passed a test which allows me to drive this . . . *thing*.

'It's the wrong side of the road. You're doing the nation a disservice by allowing me out on a road in that vehicle,' I insist. You'd think I'd have acquired good negotiating skills since living with Mum, but any argumentative tone leaves me drained, and if anything that experience has left me avoidant.

'I do understand, but unfortunately my system shows me this is all we have. We can, however, refund you and you are free to look at a different company.'

'Last minute? The prices were already outrageous when I

booked. It's almost the beginning of July. Sweden's statuary holiday month.' I've read up on this. Swedes must take two weeks of their annual leave in July, making it a busy and buzzy time to visit.

Mohamed throws his hands out and nods at the screen where the white mobile home is still showing, as if to say *I'm well aware*.

I hear a cough behind me and notice the line of people waiting. Decision, now.

'Fine. I'll take it.'

'Excellent.'

Nothing is excellent about this.

'You can access the manual by scanning this QR code I see that it fits four people comfortably as the specs say the dining table can turn into a small bed. How clever.'

Four people? What would I need three additional people for? At least there's a bed, though, or two. Perhaps I don't need to worry about the hostel money I had meticulously counted from our care home savings.

'Thanks, man,' I say and head off to deal with this unexpected blow.

Once I finally make it out of the maze that is Copenhagen Airport, pay the toll for the bridge and arrive on Swedish land, I end up laughing out loud because the situation is so surreal: Here I am driving along the Swedish motorway in a mobile home on my way to gatecrash a stranger's funeral.

I make the decision as I'm indicating to leave the highway: I'll cancel my hotel and sleep in this monstrous vehicle. It makes sense. I sigh, pat the steering wheel as if it were a loyal pet and say out loud, 'Welcome to your home for the next two weeks, Blade.'

Now to find the church.

Sophia
Svedala

MY UNCLE'S FRIEND sounded relieved when I called him a week ago to say that, yes, I'd take the job. Relief is not what I get from my family when I tell them I may need a place to stay for a couple of nights. Like a tedious task that has to be done, they start to divide me up, splitting the burden. Although they *like* me, they pass me off to the next person like an unwanted gift you don't have any use for. Part of me wishes I didn't have to tell them at all. But if I don't ask and they find out I booked a hotel . . . No one wants me, but if I choose to stay somewhere else they get offended.

You can do two nights at mine, Pontus writes. Pontus is at home a lot and currently has a friend staying with him after a bad break-up. There are football nights and takeaway pizzas and other friends dropping by at all hours, it sounds like. I feel a knot in my stomach. Then Mum writes and it grows bigger, pushing so hard I can swear I look physically bloated. It's only my mum, I tell the lump. *Who is scared of their own mum?*

Can't wait, darling! It's just that Anita and Ralph are coming to stay on that Friday. We booked an opera in Linköping. If you could get your things packed up by 10am so the cleaner can change the linen before they arrive? Oh, and bring something nice as we have dinner guests on some of the nights you're staying. Love, Mum.

I shudder. Dinner guests and a check-out time from my own family home. This means I need to increase the nights spent at my brothers'. Mattias is the best option, and the only reason he hasn't replied yet is that he works nights at the veterinary practice. His house is shared with two pugs and a girlfriend who drinks green tea and does yoga in a corner of the living room and hugs me when I bring her flowers. When the message finally arrives a few hours later, my shoulders relax a little, and I feel like hugging someone. Maybe a tree.

No probs. Let me know when you arrive and I'll leave the key under the doormat if I'm out. M

I start to pack because I will be working today and have set a target departure time of seven tomorrow morning. The evening will be spent squeezing everything I need into my small car. I still can't believe I agreed to this, but then, agreeing to bigger contracts appears to be my only chance of raising the money I need in order to keep calling this my home. I've made sure the cupboards are stocked with my favourite cereals, and then I leave a note next to the front door for myself saying 'Welcome back, Sophia.' Because it's important to appreciate your roommates and co-workers.

UNPOPULAR OPINION: I prefer funerals over weddings. Less drunk uncles, less single-shaming and less expensive. From a florist's point of view, it's also more interesting to cater and pinpoint flowers that reflect the tune and soundtrack to a whole human life, rather than finding something pretty that simply makes a bride's eyes stand out and matches her dress.

I walk into the church hall to help move the flowers outside onto the grave, and the blend of voices flood at me like a light being suddenly switched on in a dark room. It takes me a second to adjust, then I hear them all. The three types of funeral guests. The ones that are there for the deceased, the ones that are there for others and the ones that are there for themselves.

'Hey there!' An older man in an ill-fitting grey suit pushes his elbow into my side narrowly missing my ribs. 'Have you tried the pie? Bloody delicious, that is.'

I conclude that this man is here for himself. For the ambience, the chat and, apparently, for the pie. Growing older must be lonely, and if the only party of some sort you're invited to is a wake, then make the most of it, I suppose. I mean, there will come a day for all of us when birthday, wedding and christening invitations will be replaced by funeral announcements.

'I will get to it once I finish working,' I say. Truth is I can't stand quiches. Pies. Whatever you call them. They seem to go hand in hand with mourning, a practical dish that can be handed over lukewarm and eaten cold.

I make my way to the coffin as discreetly a I can. The crowd of mourners have now gone to the tables with their first serving, the older man included.

I have just finished moving everything that needs moving when I see a man I didn't notice in the church earlier enter the room then hover in the corner next to the door. He's about my own age. He has a yellow beanie perched on the top of his head, aging him down immensely.

He holds a white rose (boring choice, supermarket plastic wrap, could go on), and I can't help but look at him. I blink twice to see if I'm doing one of my zooming-out episodes where my gaze fixates out of my control, but nope. Apparently

I am in control of my eyesight and where I'm looking. Which is *still* at this man. A man who seemingly arrived late and has a flower that needs to get to the coffin before it's buried. Which means this man, or rather his flower, is *my* responsibility.

There is only one way to deal with this. I start to walk towards him.

Blade
Skurup

I DON'T GET farther than the doorstep. *Because someone is staring* at me and my flower from across the room. A woman. Did she immediately sense that I don't belong here? Am I that out of practice being around people? I watch her for a brief minute. Notice now that she wears an apron. Seems like a funeral crasher too, the way she's standing on the outside of the crowd, not talking to anyone. Is *majestic* a compliment? It should be. Because that's what she is. As tall as me and up on the balls of her feet, gliding around the room with flowers in her hands. I feel like a fraud: I don't belong here, and I'm not ready to explain myself to majestic strangers.

No no *no*. Don't screw this up. Think about Sven. The key to Mum's happiness. To my freedom. I feel guilty for thinking it, but it's essentially a perk of her being happy and safe somewhere. I pull my thoughts back and tell them to stay there.

Except now the woman's right next to me. Saying something in Swedish.

'Sorry, could you repeat that in English, please?' I ask.

'Do you want me to take that?'

I follow her gaze to my hand which is gripping the single white rose.

'It's for the coffin.'

She smiles, and her eyes flicker over mine.

'Well, I assumed it's not for me. I meant would you like me to place it for you? Or if you'd rather hold onto it and walk up and say a personal goodbye, that would be fine too. But you'll have to be fast. You kind of missed . . . it all.'

I hesitate.

'Are you going out there or not?' She nudges me towards the door. People are beginning to look at us. Go through my options. Could say he was a friend of my mum, and I'm here on behalf of her. But then I'd be expected to interact, chat, place said flower. Somehow the student alibi doesn't roll off my tongue.

'I don't know him. I'm crashing the funeral.' There. I said it. I desperately search for something else to say to prolong this moment. Because suddenly all I want to do is stay here and talk to her. Who knew I was so desperate for human interaction? I'm in a worse state than I thought.

She gives me a genuinely interested look and not the judgemental one I was expecting. I have to come up with a better search plan, because this was so very obviously a bad idea.

'Is it for the free food? I can get you a quiche from the deli down the road if you're struggling.'

'I'm not here for the food. You don't have to call security or shoo me out,' I say in an attempt to reassure her.

'So why are you here then? If not for free quiche, then is it for the entertaining anecdotes?'

I don't even know where to start, so I search my mind for an alternative story. As soon as I walked in I realised my former student one wouldn't work—I don't speak a word of Swedish. And I have never really been able to lie successfully. When you are raised by a no-nonsense mother who can sense any lie however small, you drop the habit very quickly and never quite manage to pick it up once you become an adult and realise that lying is considered a valuable life skill. So I tell a very brief version of the truth.

'I'm looking for a man, someone that my mum used to know, who would be around the deceased's age.' I'll never see this woman again, so it doesn't really matter what I tell her. And I shouldn't care what she thinks of me. But I do.

'Your dad? Did you not know your dad? Are you trying to find him?'

She looks at me as if she didn't just overstep and as if I'm meant to expand. When I don't, she continues.

'I heard all the speeches. He was loyal and loved, was a brilliant teacher and never left the local area. Married to the same woman for fifty years. Too good to generate any headlines by the sound of it. I don't get the feeling he had an English love-child.'

Never left the local area. So this is not my Sven. This reminds me of the books I had when I was little. This is not my fairy—her hair is too long; this is not my kitten—his tail is too short; this is not my car—its wheels are too black. This is not my Sven—he was married to the same woman for fifty years and never went to England! This means the number of potential Svens has dropped to four.

In that moment someone calls the woman and she turns with a smile, mouthing the word *Coming* towards the voice. I'd like to shake hands, somehow commemorate this meeting. Or smile and say a proper goodbye. But in the end it all happens so fast, she is already walking away when I manage some speech.

'What is your name?' I ask, desperate to have something to hold on to when she walks away.

She's already halfway across the room and gives her answer over her shoulder.

'Sophia. And I suggest you leave now—before anyone else notices you're here!'

ON MY WAY out I see a stack of small rectangular cards printed with a tiny white flower on each on the table next to the guest-book and find my hand reaching for one. Only later when I'm outside and feel sure that she's walked around the corner do I read the card, and something strange, which should go against the law of physics, happens: My heart sinks and does a twirl all at once. Because the name on the card is one I recognise. Blom.

I rush back to the car park, my computer and the letters and begin to dig. When I finally find what I'm looking for, all I can think is that I get to see her again. Because see her I must: I have some questions about her relatives.

The address half-visible on the card sent by Mum in 1997 is the address of her florist shop.

Zara
London

ZARA HAD HIGHLY underestimated the task of caring for a woman with dementia. She likes to consider herself a reliable person, a caring soul. She has never had trouble keeping house plants alive for starters, something she understands is quite the achievement amongst young people.

But this is challenging, there's no point denying it. There's the fact that Edith never seems to stop talking—asking questions, sharing anecdotes, pondering out loud. Often delivered as she walks behind Zara, or sits right next to her. Looking over her shoulder as she types. It is like having a work trainee that you invite into every area of your life. Or perhaps like being in a reality tv series, and Edith is the camera operator hovering, watching her every move.

Then there is the *not* talking. When Zara tries to get answers such as 'Are you hungry?' or 'Did you wash your hands?' she feels like her own mother asking her what she had for lunch at school to which she'd, of course answer, 'I can't remember.' So who is she to judge, really?

But, already she and Edith are settling into a rhythm, just as Zara knew they would. If nothing else, she wants Blade to see it can be done: He can let go, other people can help, Edith will be all right. While she understands his concern, she doesn't want to watch him continue to recede, further and further into the house, into his role of caretaker. She wants him to live life.

Much like she herself wants to live life. However hard she's been finding it lately. She has work, sure, and friends, clearly. But she's been trying and trying to figure out what else she wants, what else there is, and has been . . . coming up short. How is she supposed to know? How is anyone at this age! Maybe something for her to do, or at least to spend more time thinking about, once Blade is home. They can each start pressing onward together. Then she'll have someone invested in the effort right alongside her.

Zara looks to Edith then, who's been quiet for a while now, and thinks she may venture a question.

'Edith, I was wondering something.'

Edith turns to look at her.

'We all wonder a great many things. What makes this one special?'

Zara can't help but smile at the honesty and sheer brazen quality of the response. Zara closes her laptop and gets to her feet, walking up to Edith who's been standing by the window as if she's watching the world go by, despite the fact the curtain is drawn.

'I went up to your room to find your list of medications and had a scroll through the coffee table book *Britain's Parks and Gardens* and found a letter. Blade said you two had been going through your old correspondence with Sven, trying to piece together where Blade might look for him.'

'Yes, he needed a road map for Sweden. Didn't want him getting lost.'

'Right, well, I was wondering, then, why didn't you give him all the letters?'

Edith appeared to be thinking hard, she paused for a long moment before delivering her answer.

'Because sometimes people aren't ready to see the whole picture. So you give them half.'

Zara stares at her. She's definitely got a point, she thinks.

'There may well be more in the house. Even photos. I've become just like my grandmother who would stuff cash under matrasses and books. Hide *valuables*,' she admits. 'I couldn't tell you where all I've put things.'

Zara nods, thinking that she'll have to look, see if she can find anything to help Blade on his journey—anything to help Edith. Maybe she'll be able to help piece the whole picture together, even if she still can't see it.

Blade

Skurup

I'M UNSURE WHERE to go, there are no campsites open around here and I need to be back in this village—that has a gift shop and a pizzeria, which I tried for dinner, and its main attraction, a flower shop with a very mesmerising florist—in the morning. I pull up Google Maps and look at my surroundings. Woodland, some acres of wet marsh land and what I suspect is an old quarry. Another Google search tells me the quarry is now filled with freshwater and the locals' chosen summer spot for swimming. I decide that will do as my home for the night.

I find it after a quick drive and park as close to the old quarry turned lake as possible. As I start to make the bed and prepare the cabin for my first night in Sweden I feel homesick, like a little boy. I long for familiar sounds. Mum's shuffling on the floor in ten-year-old stolen hotel slippers. The fridge's low humming. Mum's soft snores that I can just about hear through the crack I leave in my doorway.

Zara reports that all is well and under control. She has sent me a selfie of them watching *Magpie Murders*.

ZARA: Mum convinced Netflix is broken because there is no more House of Cards. Told her she watched it all and got her onto a new show.

ME: Did you put an Instagram filter on my 64-year-old mum?

ZARA: We tried the one called Paris but she said she'd rather the one called Marrakech because she's never been there and would quite fancy going. So that's what I gave her. All good.

ZARA: Also, she made me buy extra milk, flour, sugar, eggs and tape. Said people might need to borrow some?

ME: Yup, she's convinced a neighbour will pop by and ask to borrow some milk like the old days.

I've tried explaining about next hour delivery, twenty-four-hour supermarkets and Amazon stores. Pointless. She simply doesn't accept that neighbours don't need her to stock emergency baking ingredients any longer. But somehow seeing the extra bottles huddled together in the fridge, like a group of friends, settles her. So I keep buying them.

ME: Tape?

ZARA: She says it's one of the things you never know you need until you really need it . . . ;)

ME: Any luck finding a picture of Sven yet?

ZARA: Nothing. Do you think she got angry when he didn't show up and threw them away? Burned them?

ME: No idea. Anything's possible with Mum . . .

I SIT FOR some time opposite the water until the sun starts to hint at me that today is running out, and the distant voices of a group of teenagers have disappeared on bikes. The water is flat, dark and framed by soft grey cliffs with ledges and pockets to jump off.

I google the woman I met today. Nothing. The only result for her name is a high school theatre production where she stands at the end of the group looking off-camera. No Facebook, no Instagram, no LinkedIn.

Find two semi-professional hockey players with the same surname, and I find her shop. Pull up the pictures and look at it. A small florist business with pots overflowing the pavement outside it in a way that health and safety would crack down on within hours in London. The website tells me it's a family business and has a picture of a couple with a blonde, almost white-haired girl between them. Parents? Grandparents? No, too young. There is a link to order flowers for next-day delivery, but that's it.

I pull out one of the letters. I've read them all but find I turn to them whenever I think of Mum lately. This one is a single square page with a wisteria illustration on it. I read the short lines.

Svennie,
   I keep coming back to our spot. Thinking about what could have been if we'd met there like we planned to.

                                                         E.

Then I jump. Was that an *owl?* The only wildlife I'm used to is rats and city foxes. Yep. *Definitely an owl.* I throw myself on the bed, which leaves a lot to be desired, and press the pillow over my head, blocking out the nature sounds, remembering the ones my mum used to have on CD when I was younger. Relaxing dolphin sounds. Bird song. Somehow 'Over the Top Owl Hooting' never made it into the recording studio. The surrealism of it all hits me. How have I been nestled in my mum's old love story? And why am I starting to feel like it's somehow my story too?

Edith
London

WHEN I CAN'T sleep the way I used to, I lie still and allow myself to flit in and out of dark stillness, without forcing it or feeling angry. I often don't know where my thoughts end and a dream starts. But last night I'm sure I dreamt. People retelling their dreams are up there with the world's most annoying human habits, like biting into Popsicles. So when I walk downstairs I don't share with Zara that I was back in 2000 and that it was a sunny day and my insides felt soft. I go back to that year a lot. It's as if my dreams have regressed more than my brain currently and are showing me a new reality I will one day be living in once I get sicker. I try to think why that year, why then? It wasn't my happiest time, but I did feel safe. Stable. Having gotten rid of Blade's father. Having given up the destructive habit of dating bad men, which I'd thrown myself into following him and Sven. Having just bought the house, having enough work and enough love through little Blade. Perhaps stability really is more important than joy?

I hear Zara before I see her. It is rather delightful having a female presence in the house. A girlfriend of sorts. I love my son but he can tell me he's domestic all he wants, modern man this and modern man that, I still find his socks next to his bed and my tea served in the fine china because the everyday mugs aren't clean and a total disregard for standards. Zara likes candles with strong, earthy smells and says it's our little secret because Blade says 'No candles. Not even a little one.' Or a birthday one. Zara is different to Blade in many ways. She is not into cooking. Or food shopping. She is into meal deals and has a standing supermarket delivery slot on Tuesdays, even though there's a Tesco Express five minutes' walk away. I enjoy checking the long receipt the delivery person hands me. Sometimes substitutions are nice surprises—did you know they don't charge you extra for a more expensive alternative item?—but sometimes you wonder who packed it. We once ordered a Victoria sponge and got a three-pack of sponge scourers, which made for a rather disappointing teatime.

Zara spends most of her mornings hammering away on her laptop, occasionally grunting about a Pomodoro, then walks around the room six times before she sits down again.

'Reckon I can add random words to reach the word count, then colour them white and no one will notice?' she asks me now. I asked what she is writing on her first day here and she said it's manuals for a flatpack furniture company and I haven't asked again because at sixty-four life is short and explanations about flatpack instructions can be very long indeed.

AT ELEVEN O'CLOCK Zara closes her laptop with the force of someone closing the lid on a box containing a poisonous spider and says,

'Right, what do you say we find a change of scene?'

I want to tell her that you never have to find changes they will happen to you anyway. The landscape, the people, the air. It's not changing the scene we should be trying, or yearning for, it's keeping it. But, of course, people who aren't suffering from memory loss don't understand; they're missing these small details that make the human experience.

'I wouldn't mind going to Kensington,' I say instead, innocently.

'I like Kensington. It's certainly better than Knightsbridge,' Zara replies, just as innocently.

She packs her bag, and when we get to the hallway I watch my son's best friend put her shoes on. Those thick soled, athletic things that she insists on wearing even with smart straight-legged trousers. Did I teach Blade how to tie his shoelaces? I can't remember. I think that I must have, as his mother. Zara ties hers differently to me, I observe now. She folds up the strings into two hoops then simply ties them. Like a knot at sea. Or a knot at the end of a sewing thread. I can't recall how Blade ties his, and for some reason I feel desperate for this knowledge. A good mother would remember those details.

WE SIT ON the bus, and Zara writes notes on her phone whilst I watch the rain outside. It's only a friendly drizzle. When we get off, Zara hooks her arm underneath mine, and she is so much taller that I hang off her like a child.

'Don't do anything I wouldn't do,' Zara tells me as she heads into the library and hands me a paper note with the area she'll be sitting in written down on it. Zara seems to have grown up to be a young lady who would do *a lot* of things, and so I'm quite pleased with her instructions.

I stand facing east, then I stand facing west. I receive hellos from the regular faces and a tea from one of the estate agents at Hamptons. The blonde short one who always wears those black ballet-type shoes even in sub-zero temperatures. She always rushes past me, handing me a tea without really stopping.

Each time I come, I sit on the bench and wait. I have my tea,

I say hi to passing strangers, and I wait. There's an awning that helps when it rains, and when I take fifteen-minute breaks—at different times each day, so as to be waiting at all times eventually—I head into the large brown library building to warm up. Just inside it, where you place your returned books, there's a little girl running in circles, for no particular reason other than the running in itself. Which baffles me, like those people in the park doing laps just for the sake of collecting steps on an app.

'Don't fall,' the girl's mother says. I never said that to Blade. It's a useless statement isn't it? Because we don't fall on purpose. We fall whether we like it or not, and we also don't stop moving because we are scared of falling.

'The average two-year-old falls thirty-eight times per day,' I helpfully tell the mother. 'Although I don't know how many falls she's already had today, I'd be inclined to say that her likelihood of falling now is, indeed, very high.'

The woman shifts uncomfortably, then calls her daughter over. I smile at the girl before she's pulled away.

THE READING CORNER starts to fill up, and I remember, to my delight, that it's Thursday which means Baby Rhyme Time. I lean back in my favourite chair in the farthest corner of the library, just a few shelves separating me from the jolly collection of babies, toddlers, mums and nannies. In my hand are the books I've brought with me, a biography on Churchill and a romance novel I started but have put temporarily to the side (a very chirpy sidekick started to get on my nerve). I flick the pages and look at the images but find the text too small and in a font which irritates me. My foot taps along with the singing of 'The Wheels on the Bus'. We get to my favourite verse.

The daddies on the bus are fast asleep, fast asleep, fast asleep!

I think: *Thank you, Lady Librarian, for speaking truth to those babies. Daddies can indeed be useless. I can think of one who was particularly so.*

I'm sad when the group dissembles and the babies, propped up in buggies with snacks and sippy cups in their hands, exit. I sometimes feel an urge to join in, perhaps put a baby on my lap and bounce it up and down. I try to remember when I got so lonely. It might have been three years ago, but it might also have started long before that, a withdrawal and a loneliness hidden by motherhood and workdays, but none the less there. *It's for the best*, I told myself. But now I see Blade is lonely too, and I wonder if it really was for the best. *Any of it.*

I have forty minutes until I promised Zara I would meet her outside at the book drop box, or so this piece of paper says, so I decide to head downstairs. I find myself in a research section I didn't know existed or I would have come here a long time ago. When I find the archives I start searching the records for the year it all started. The waiting. It was 1996, and I easily find image after image of the library, laminated onto thick paper and free to flick through. There are pictures of author talks and community meetings. Small-crime reports and accounts of demonstrations on nearby streets. This act of stepping back in time absorbs me completely. Then half an hour in I stop and stare.

I look and look and I think: *But this must be wrong. It's not possible.* My mouth is dry and I wonder how the heart can be a muscle. If it really is, then we should be able to control it, contract it, confine it, but I can't, and it hurts so much I'm convinced I'll fall down any minute.

I step to the copy machine quickly, picture against my chest. Before I press it onto the machine for a copy I check the caption again: *Pedestrians outside the new wing of the town hall,*

Hornton Street, Kensington. 4 June 1996. It is simply a picture, so similar to the other ones, but it's all wrong, and I feel like I'm looking in the mirror after a haircut and this person doesn't look like me but I *know* it's me. What I know about that day in 1996 I cannot match with what I'm seeing now. *The date is wrong. You told me the fourth of June which was a Friday, and the weather forecast said sunny with cloudy spells. I know every detail of that day.* I know that I had the right date, and I know I had the right time. So why didn't I see him? My eyes fixate on the face, captured from the side.

There is no doubt: The blond man in the crowd, standing slightly ahead of the others, on the day he didn't turn up to meet me, looking as if he's waiting for someone, on the corner of the street—that's Sven.

Eliza
London

ELIZA USED THE old lady on Hornton Street as the main argument to her girlfriend when delivering the news that it was, finally and without hope, over. The lady with grey-streaked hair and a tote bag, who always stands there, or paces the area, only leaving when the rain pours down. Even then Eliza still spots her through the doors to the red-bricked library looking out with focused eyes, as if waiting for the rain to stop. Or something else. Now she's surprisingly what comes to mind as she pours herself a glass of juice and starts to find the ingredients to assemble a sandwich. Her girlfriend of eight months is on the sofa watching a show. She didn't acknowledge Eliza's return to their shared flat, or the fact that Eliza might, at eight thirty in the evening, not have eaten yet.

'She's there.' Eliza says to Sam's hoodie-clad back. 'Consistent. I turn the corner at two ten and I know she'll be there. I walk into this flat and I never know if you'll be here because you never text, never call, never do anything, really.'

The back turns now, her girlfriend's face animated.

'*She?* Are you seeing someone? Oh my *God*, you are so not the cheating type.'

Eliza wonders what Sam, her girlfriend/ex-girlfriend knows

about cheating types and whether she might actually be one herself.

'No. She's retirement age. I don't even know her, but she's *there*. Don't you see? She's there, and I don't even *know* her.'

There are no tears because this isn't sad, really. It's a necessary evil. Eliza always thinks that when women have made their mind up there's no going back. She herself, can be pushed and shoved and moulded and influenced, but once she finally, amidst all life's shoving, finds her train of thought and holds it, ignoring all the outside noise, managing to make a decision, then there's no going back.

'I'm going to bed, Sam, then I'll leave early tomorrow morning for work but I think you should start looking for a place. I'm too tired to discuss it now.'

She doesn't feel relieved, just icky. The relief comes not when the decision is made but when it's implemented, she's always found.

IT TAKES FIVE days of back-and-forth, tears (Sam's), yelling (Sam's), bribery (Eliza's in the shape of a deposit for a new place), drunken make-outs (both of them equally guilty), but then one Sunday afternoon Sam is out, finally. Off partying in old warehouses turned galleries and rave venues with some crowd from East London, all of whom do much cooler things than sell property whilst wearing smart casual clothes. The only sign of life a few late-night texts saying I miss you, babe, followed hours later, when Eliza's silence has worn down her sweetness and the alcohol has made its way to her blood stream, by Can't believe you kicked me out, you're such a fucking bitch!!!

Eliza doesn't miss Sam. And definitely not her judgemental nature. Eliza wasn't cool enough for Sam or her friends. *Can you just tell them you do interior or some sort of art with houses?*

Photography? You do take pictures of the flats sometimes, don't you? she'd ask. Another thing she won't miss.

Eliza is many things. Good with numbers and tricky clients, she's punctual and helpful, and she makes a great pea and parmesan risotto, but she's never been fun. And she's never seen it as a problem. Apart from in East London warehouse parties, that is.

By Thursday she has deleted Sam's number and downloaded a LGBTQ+ dating app. Maybe there's another not-fun twentysomething out there who likes risotto?

ELIZA SPEAKS TO Edith for the first time a week after Sam moves out.

'Hello,' she says, as always, when she spots her at the bus stop. But this time she doesn't say it as she's walking past in a rush, but after she's stopped in front of the woman. Her whole person is still and there in the moment, as if she's about to stretch out her arm and touch her shoulder.

I can't believe I've walked past this person almost every day, someone that's been a constant in my afternoon routine, without ever saying hi, she thinks. *What sort of a person am I?*

'My latte and you are the two staples of my day,' she tells the woman. Her brown trousers are too big on her hips and her lipstick sits outside of her upper lip, as if she's applied it without a mirror. Eliza is not shy, not really, just unsure what you say to someone you've walked past and smiled to for almost a year yet haven't taken the time to get to know.

The woman struggles to hold her gaze; she seems agitated. Eliza puts her hand on her arm, hoping it's not too cold through the thin fabric of her top.

'This place must mean a lot to you,' she adds. Eliza thinks about places, about the property she sells, and how in the city centre, houses have lost their human value. They're investments and opportunities and prime locations now. They're a landing place until the family moves away for more space, or someone gets a lucrative work contract and relocates to a new world capital. Do places have meaning anymore? She's not sure. She's suddenly desperate to hear what this place, the street where she works every day, means to this woman.

'It meant something to me. And to Sven. It's where we first met.'

'Is he your husband?'

'He would have been, if he had turned up.'

'Oh.' Eliza *hates* people who don't turn up. Who arrange a viewing to which she treks through the neighbourhood to, making sure she arrives early enough to open up the curtains, turn on the lights, make the property look awake. Then she waits and waits until she gets a message saying *Sorry, can't make it*. Or if not that, until she calls and gets a voicemail and is forced to accept she's been stood up.

'I'm Eliza,' she offers.

'Edith.' Edith puts the cup on the ground, maybe it's still too hot to drink, and twirls her hands, as if washing them with soap.

'I have to go to work now but I'll see you around?' She doesn't reach out her hand to her because she has a feeling her touch would stress Edith. 'It's nice to finally meet you,' she says instead.

Blade
Svedala

I'M BACK IN Svedala early the next morning after a restless sleep by the old quarry. First the sound of the owls, then teenagers arriving on bikes at dawn (aren't they all supposed to be nocturnal?). Breakfast was a Red Bull from the camper fridge I really should make an effort to stock.

The floral shopfront sits on the ground floor of an orange-brick house opposite a small mall housing a library and a GP service. It's 9.02, and I'm pretty sure I'm the first person to come through the door today. The doorbell sounds like an iPhone alert, and I think that's a neat touch. I woke up in a sweat this morning thinking maybe there'd be someone else working, or worse, the shop would be closed and I wouldn't get to see her. But I needn't have worried because she appears swiftly from the back room, her phone pressed to her ear, then stops abruptly when she sees me. *Nerves*. I only need to ask this girl a few questions, yet here I am struggling to compose myself.

She fiddles with the hem of her shirt, and her gaze is on the floor in front of her now. I overhear her saying that she's excited to work out the details and that she will email over themes and proposals for the décor. When she puts the phone down, she does a long exhale and turns her focus to me.

'Hello there.'

'Hi. Sophia?' Let's pretend I haven't rehearsed this and googled the Swedish pronunciation of Sophia, which is So-fee-aah.

'You did say I should pop by some time.' There is no hint of a smile on her face to put me at ease.

'Could I steal some of your time?' I ask.

'Sure. I sell flowers, not time. You can have that for free, no need to steal it.'

She looks so pleased with her joke I can't help but smile too.

'Thank you. I just wanted to ask you some questions.' Her eyes are blue. And somehow I can't find anything else to think. Or say.

She helps me out by breaking the awkward silence.

'Oh. Would you like a drink? I guess they're free too. I don't usually sell them, so I don't have a price list.'

I nod. Since when does my mind have a life on its own? I clearly haven't interacted with enough people over the past three years and shouldn't have been let out in public. I should leave. *Right. That's it.* My second interaction with a Swedish person has swiftly ended after—I look at the digital clock on the wall—exactly five minutes. She looks at me like I've lost my mind. Apparently it's my turn to speak.

'I'm alright, thanks. Do you know much about the history of the shop? Of who might have worked here? Do you know a Sven? This is all a bit vague and I apologise but he may have lived in this village.' I blurt all the questions out at once, as if I'm working against a timer.

'I inherited it from my uncle. It's been in the family since his father passed it to him. Funnily enough, his name *was* Sven.'

I stiffen. Could this be it? I walk into a shop on my second day in Sweden and find the man my mum has been waiting for for three decades? Is my job here done? That would certainly be welcome since my anxiety is sky-high, I can hardly conduct a normal conversation, and I've only just started the search.

'I'm sorry to be asking all these questions, it might be nothing, but, did your uncle ever live in London?'

'London?' She laughs. 'He would hardly go to Lund. He hated planes. I can't remember a single time he travelled during my childhood. I don't think he even had a passport.'

Well, there goes that dream. It could of course be as simple as my mum having gotten the Sven wrong. She must have found the same list of Svens and their addresses that I did and tried them all, not knowing where hers had gone. That's why she sent a postcard to this shop.

'Is this to do with your dad search? Listen, Sven is a very common name. I've met several of them.' She doesn't expand but begins to fiddle with the hem of her shirt again. She's unfortunately right. How many Svens would have lived in Svedala over the years? It's like looking for a John in Ipswich. Or a Sebastian or Max in an investment bank. I've crossed the deceased Sven from yesterday off my list and am now crossing the shop Sven off it too. Four left: all in different parts of the country.

'He's not my dad, this Sven. I'm not even sure who he is exactly but I'm doing my best to find him. To help someone who lost contact with him years ago.'

'Oh.' She gestures for me to come behind the counter where she's filled a glass with tap water for me. 'I'm sorry I can't help be of more help. And I actually have to start working now. I have a lot of things to pack up.'

I drink some water, although I'm not thirsty, just reluctant to leave. This was the best lead I had and I'm not quite ready to let it go.

'Do you have kids?' I ask her. There is a drawing on the wall behind her. It shows a man and a little girl and then a woman standing behind them; she's just as big, though. Whoever drew them hadn't learnt perspective yet. They all wear flower-patterned clothes, and to the left is a square house with curtains and a chimney that exhausts in grey.

'No. I made this when I was little. With my uncle. We used to have these characters: Miss Grass Flower and Mr Yarrow and Miss Marigold. We'd draw them in their little house and talk about what they'd be up to.' Her whole face lights up as she's telling me.

'They look like a lovely family.'

'I think they were as happy as stick people can be.'

I smile and she returns it sending my eyes everywhere but hers. Looking down I notice the large cardboard boxes in the back room.

'Another funeral?'

'Won't be telling you in case you decide to crash it.'

'Honestly. Those days are behind me. Well, *a* day behind me.'

'I'm going on tour. Eksjö, Tenhult, Markaryd and Jönköping,' she says listing a string of places and one of them jumps out at me. '*If* I can squeeze everything I need into my car. It's a large job, and I sort of said yes without exactly having a clear plan in place, hoping that I could figure it all out later. But it's proving to be a rather difficult task carting all these flowers all around the country.'

'Jönköping. That's not far from where I'm headed. I'm going to Växjö.'

'It's actually the town farthest away on my contract. The others are a bit sporadically dotted along the way,' she adds.

I pause for a moment, know this is going to sound absurd, but before I can stop myself the idea slips out.

'This is going to sound strange, but I actually have a large mobile home—well, an RV. A camper-van. The rental place at the airport was all out of alternative options, holidays and such, and I needed a way to get around Sweden. To look for this Sven. So I said yes and now I'm driving this large RV around—but it's massive, see, and it would likely have plenty of space—for all your boxes, flowers, whatever else you need to bring. And we're headed to the same location it sounds like . . .' I trail off as my brain catches up with my mouth.

Did I just . . . ? The urge to be wiped off this earth by, say, a falling hanging flowerpot has never been this strong before. I clearly should not be allowed out in public. Fucking *ever*.

Sophia
Svedala

LINA IS HERE, coming in for her usual morning break. And she clearly overheard the conversation that just took place.

'Did you hear that, Sophia? This man here is driving a large mobile home with a lot of space, all over Sweden!'

'Yes, so he said.'

'Space for flowers! And space for a Sophia!'

Oh no. She can't possibly think that—

'You should totally go together! Would you believe—what a coincidence!—you both are heading the same way. I'd say sharing is caring, and also half the price in fuel would help balance that spreadsheet even faster.'

'I really wouldn't mind,' I hear Funeral Crasher say. By now I've decided that he is most likely a red dragon, *Persicaria microcephalia*, which is prized for the beauty of their leaves but can be invasive and will need to be controlled.

'Oh, sorry, I was joking,' Lina says and I see Blade (*Blade? Who is called Blade? Did his parents confuse the Baby Names book with a tool brochure?*) going a shade of purple. He's awkward and anxious. I can spot it from miles away.

'Oh. Right, obviously. Okay. I'm off. Thank you for your time. And good luck with your tour.'

I look to see if Blade has left, but he is eyeing up some cacti very closely in the corner of the shop. *Finally.* He looks back over his shoulder then leaves and lets the door close itself.

Lina hops onto my counter.

'Okay, maybe I wasn't entirely joking. It was a sort of interesting idea,' she says.

'Maddening? Bizarre? Outrageous?' I offer as alternative, more fitting adjectives, covering my eyes with my hands.

'So . . . if a cute stranger with a spacious RV and an offer to share fuel costs is not part of the plan, then what *is* the plan, exactly?'

'I didn't notice any cuteness.' It's true, my brain sees details. Wrinkles, hairs, red lines in eyes. Blade has a mole on his neck, a small spot which may be a skin blemish on his upper arm and hair that stands up in a funny way on the left side. His left eye is slightly bigger than his right, and his back teeth are pointy.

'I forgot. Looks are wasted on you.'

'Besides, the answer is no.'

I know something for sure: I am not joining Funeral Crasher in a mobile home with all my flowers. He isn't my only option, nor is he the best one. It turns out he isn't a customer either as he left without buying anything.

'All I know is he is cute and he is heading the same direction as you and he does already have a storage solution for this growing problem. Some people might call that a sign.'

'Some people should leave subject signs alone and focus their energy elsewhere.' I tap at the screen of my laptop. I will squeeze everything I need into my little car, even if it means holding a flowerpot on my lap.

LATER THAT NIGHT, trying to fall asleep, I find myself going over the blemishes on Blade's face. Except something happens differently this time, and my mind start to count the long lashes he has instead. And traces the outline of his jaw. And the shape of his upper arm. This isn't going to put me to sleep, is it? Why hasn't this happened with other people? Even with Ed, who was a highly attractive and accomplished man and who I went as far as to kiss, I could never move on from the coffee stain on his front tooth where my brain would fixate, and I'd find myself snoring within minutes.

This is . . . *different*.

Edith
London

WE'VE FALLEN INTO quite a little routine, me and Zara. The mornings are spent at home. I rest or putter about whilst she works in the reception room. Then we have lunch, and Zara shows me young ladies and men on various apps who are potential suitors. Then we say *Right* and pack our afternoon biscuits in a little plastic container and leave the house. On the bus, Zara works some more, and I look out at the familiar roads and houses. Today the route is diverted and we drive down a parallel road. I think how I've never seen these houses and yet they've been there all these years, just tucked away off the main road.

By the time we get to Sloane Square, with its flagship boutiques and French brasseries, I've scrolled through my photos three times. I've started taking pictures of my days to remember them. So I don't wear the same clothes three days in a row, that sort of thing. From yesterday I have Hornton Street, a ham sandwich, my green crew neck sweater, the library sign saying 'Public Desks.' Finally, I have the picture I took of the article. The picture that I now remember that I have to send to Blade. But I hesitate. Because seeing him there is wrong. I have no explanation. Blade will say: *Maybe you got the date* wrong? Or could you just have missed each other, Mum? No. I did not get the date wrong. I did not miss him. I will hold on to the photo until I understand it even the slightest. I won't share the picture just yet.

When we arrive, Zara reminds me of where she is going to be. This doesn't stress me, as I know the place so well. She'll be at the public desks and will come and find me at four o'clock, which means I have two hours outside the town hall. It isn't a long enough session really, but I've agreed to the compromise whilst Blade is away. I put my bag down onto the cobbled ground and make myself comfortable, then pick up a chocolate wrapper and an empty bottle of coke and carry it to the bin.

'Hello.'

I'm approached by a young man around, Blade's age, as I sit down to rest against the wall. My knees feel terribly sore. I wonder if I've forgotten to take something (it's often the case when pain appears) or if this is a new normal now. Which is also often the case.

'Hi there, love, how are you? I offer free haircuts to people in need.'

'What a lovely thing to do.'

'Would you be interested in one?'

Now, I find this incredibly rude. *In need!* But hard as I try I can't remember when I last went for a trim. There is something about a red lollipop in my memories but that must have been for Blade, which means it was a very, very long time ago. Surely I must have been to the hairdresser since then? I touch the sides of my face, and my fingers feel the rough strands of hair.

'This is certainly a new business tactic. Hassling women on the street.'

'No, no, I assure you it's free. You can find us here.' He

produces a card with a pair of scissors on it and points at the address. I suppose I wouldn't mind a break from waiting. And one should always look one's best when waiting for their love. I get a flash of memory of hot hair curlers and glossing my lips, then licking them as I waited, not wanting to take my lip-gloss out of the bag and apply more in case he appeared in that exact moment and see my vanity.

'I have an opening just now,' I tell the man.

'Oh, good, I'm so pleased. Just head over, and they'll take care of you. You'll be a new woman once they're done with you!'

'That, my dear, I very much doubt.'

THERE IS A smell which I know. A strong, synthetic one that I recognise but can't put the words on. Memories of scrubbing hard at my hands with it surface. There are two women and a man: Two of them are busy with clients, and the third smiles when I enter. I look around, taking it all in. I can see why they need to do promotional work and hand out free cuts. The chairs are mismatched and the lighting flickers. I can spot no drinks and biscuits, and the shelves behind the counter where you normally have over-priced hair products are empty.

'What can we do for you today?' the woman asks, smiling.

'I have been told I'm in need.'

She laughs and pulls a black cape from the wall hangers.

'Oh, poor love. Let's get you sorted,' she says. 'I'm Gemma, and I'll be doing your haircut today.'

I sit down and look at myself in the mirror. Then close my eyes immediately.

'I can't imagine what it's like at—forgive me for saying it—your age. You know, *the streets.*'

'You just have to wear the correct shoes, I find.'

'Oh, is that so?' she replies whilst spraying my hair with a wet, fruit-smelling mist. I close my eyes, some of it has already landed on my eyelashes, like dew drops.

'Definitely. Not all streets posit dangers, though. They're not all cobbled.'

I WALK BACK to the town hall feeling quite energised and only remember Zara when I, well, see Zara in front of me. On her phone. Anxious. On my street corner. When she sees me, she runs towards me, arms flailing.

'Edith!'

'That would be me.'

'You and I had a deal. No walking off, under any circumstances.' Then she mutters, *goddamn it* to herself. I should remind her of the countless times in the past that I have called up her parents explaining her absence or failure to be back by the curfew. Telling them she was studying with Blade when they were nowhere to be found. Because I trusted her. And she needed a break, a bit of freedom.

'I'm back before our bus leaves.'

'Is that a *bob*?' she notices my hair do for the first time. 'Did you go and get a *haircut*?'

'I believe I was part of some modelling gig. Free makeover in exchange for pictures.' They took three pictures. One from the back with my chin down, one from the side with my chin raised, and one from the front where I smile.

I hand her the business card I was given.

'Haircuts4homeless.' Then she bursts out laughing. 'Edith, did you just let these people give you a makeover? You're probably all over their social media. Oh *gosh*.'

I feel the penny drop, so to speak.

'Please. *Please* don't do this again,' Zara says.

'No, it will be at least six months until I need another haircut.'

'I'm serious. Blade will kill me. Heck, Blade may even *come home.*'

Oh no. Not *that*. Blade has stuff to do.

'Okay. No more haircuts, and I won't accept drinks from strangers anymore either, for good measure.'

'People give you free drinks?' I think that's admiration in Zara's voice. 'Wow, I'll come find you for tips, if the world ever gets rough.'

Then my pocket buzzes, and I get my phone out. +46. I know which country code that is, so I press the little button on the side. Quickly.

'Do you need help to answer that?' Zara is too switched-on. Too tense.

'Just an alarm. Wanted to be back here on time.' I smile. I press the phone firmly into my pocket and make a mental note to ask someone—perhaps the nice estate agent with the ballet loafers—how to activate that Silent function I know exists.

It's not time yet. The call is not for me any longer because I've given the task to my son now. I've been avoiding it for so many years already I can keep it up for a while longer. Sweden has been a closed chapter, that was the only way to stay sane. At the last neurology appointment Blade asked about cognitive functioning training and how to old-lady-proof the house, essentially, though he used slightly more polite words. When he finally stopped talking I leaned forward in my chair.

'Secrets,' I said. 'Small ones, emotional ones, family ones. Things that happened in the past and impacted our direction. How do we hold onto them when dementia progresses?'

The red bus comes into view now, slowing down as it approaches the stop, the horde of waiting people all taking a step towards it at the same time.

'Right, shall we?' I take Zara's hand and lean my head against her shoulder. Sometimes we are able to connect more with those we know less. **No shared** history, no secrets, no complicated feelings. Just a **warm hand** and someone to sit next to on a bus and watch the rain with.

'I will say, your hair looks lovely,' Zara offers.

'It's been ages since I've had a trim. Felt it was time.'

'These things happen to the best of us.'

I nod in agreement, as she is correct.

'Just remember, not a **word**, Edith.'

'Of course.'

I'm still very good at keeping **secrets**.

Sophia
Sweden

WHEN I METICULOUSLY planned this trip, *this* was not part of it. I did everything right. I checked the tyres, the oil, the windscreen liquid and the insurance papers in the glove compartment. All my equipment, scissors, ribbons, décor and the flowers for the first two days are safely stored across the folded down backseat. I did everything right and yet here I am. On the hard shoulder next to my car which appears to have broken down.

This is agony. My worst nightmare rolled into one: being an inconvenience (literally blocking a road) and realising that I will quite possibly have to approach a stranger for help. Because although I have three brothers and a dad who know all there is to know about cars, no one picks up my call. I swear, out loud, not sure what to do. Wave for attention, call insurance? I'm about to start crying when a camper-van with its signal on pulls up behind my Skoda. It's white with black lines, reminds me of a sneaker. I tense. *Focus. Task at hand.* They've probably just pulled over to piss in the ditch anyway and not to bother you, Sophia.

Wrong.

'You okay there?'

'That's an extraordinarily stupid question. Do I—or rather does my car—look okay?' I say with as much neutrality as I can.

I turn around to face the stranger.

'Oh, it's you. The Funeral Crasher.'

'Well, hello to you to . . . Car Crasher.' He looks amused. Less anxious and fidgety than yesterday.

'To be clear, it broke down on me, but fair game.' He's wearing a tight black sweater with sweatpant shorts and I wonder why I'm suddenly aware of men's clothing. He's taller than I remember from the other day, taller than me, which is some sort of achievement considering I'm five ten.

'Sophia.' I had begun walking back to my car to decide who to call but stop in my tracks. What *is* it about the way he says my name?

'Do you need hel—'

I shake my head.

'I mean, I do need help, but from a professional.'

'Obviously. But let's move you off the road at least. Do you have your insurance details? Let me have a look.' He leans across me and his face passes my face. I usually hold my breath when there's a risk of smells—the fridge, the chicken shop and strangers. But this time I find myself inhaling freely. My heart beats at an unfamiliar though not unpleasant rhythm. Perhaps there's verbena in his scent? Or he touched some that is growing on the roadside? I'm a florist after all, and that could totally trigger this response . . . right?

He rummages for a while, doing a much more thorough search than I did.

'Okay, got them.'

Blade places the insurance company's phone number without asking me. If it weren't for my relief at not having to call or think about what to say, I'd ask why he's helping, and secondly, be annoyed at said help. I stand next to the car and listen to cars whoosh past us. Then Blade mouths what looks like 'thirty minutes' at me.

When he gets off the phone, he doesn't leave like I thought he would. Everyone has to be somewhere, and I'm pretty sure that somewhere for Blade isn't next to the E4 dual carriageway with a stranger.

'This may be a bad idea. Especially since you declined help once already,' he says and looks down at his feet.

'Are you planning on crashing another funeral? Then, yes. That is a bad idea.' I watch as his chest inflates then releases all the air out.

'I was going to say that you could catch a ride with me. I'm heading north, as you know. And still have more than enough room in my RV. The offer still stands.'

I look at him, speechless. He continues, and this time he looks at me and as much as I can't stand it when people don't make eye contact, I would prefer he not, simply that because his eyes are just . . . unsettling. I thought I was good at eye contact, after years of practice and rewards in therapy. Turns out I'm not, and that too much of it can make you flustered enough to say things you may not mean. Like,

'Yes.'

'Yes?' he says, his eyes leaving mine just long enough for me to collect myself, my pride and my thoughts. I reverse my mistake.

'I mean—yes, that would be an utterly insane idea, which I'd obviously say a firm no to.' There, order restored. In control.

'Oh.'

'Thank you for offering, and whilst I may seem a little out of sorts right now, I actually quite orderly the rest of the time.'

The opposite, actually. 'Unless you count occasionally eating the dessert before the main course.'

'Seriously? *Why*, though?'

'In case I suddenly drop dead at the dinner table like Pablo Picasso, I'd have hated to miss out on pudding. Especially if it were brownies or anything with salted caramel.'

Blade looks at me with interest before averting his gaze and staring at his shoes again. They're good shoes. Nikes.

'Sure. I'll just wait with you until the towing arrives and then you'll be okay . . . ?' he says.

'I'll be okay.' I only met this man yesterday and if I was okay the twenty-five years prior to that then I should be okay going forward. But . . . something in his hopelessly disappointed appearance makes me feel pity.

'Look. It's very kind of you to offer. I just don't feel comfortable.' This does not have the effect I intended—to soften things. He stiffens immediately and looks almost pained.

'If you don't feel safe around me I understand fully. I should never have suggested it. I respect that. I'm sorry.'

'What? No. I feel safe around you.' As I say it, I realise it's true. And it's rare. Usually there's an undercurrent of subtle threat when I'm alone or even close to men. Men are harder to read than women. I never know if, or rather, *when* they might hurt me, or when they might make a move on me, or when they might want nothing to do with me altogether. But here I've been alone at the side of a road in a ditch that would make an excellent dumping ground for a body, and I haven't felt uneasy at all. Blade has made things weirdly easy for me.

'How far would you say the truck is now?' I really have to be on my way.

'Are you trying to get rid of me?'

'Maybe.' The quicker he leaves the quicker my body can

start to recover from the unexpected social interaction and feel like my own again.

'Maybe there's a live location for it. Let me check.' Blade pulls out his phone and checks. 'Nope, but shouldn't be long.'

'Well, let me take this opportunity to make some arrangements.' I say and unlock my screen.

I text Lina, and the immediate blue ticks tell me she's up and baking already.

> **ME:** Car broke down. Currently with man who pops up everywhere unwanted like a dandelion on a lawn.
>
> **LINA:** As in the man I met yesterday in your shop?
>
> **ME:** That would be the one. Complete with yellow beanie and annoying attitude/general demeanour.
>
> **LINA:** Couldn't have planned this if I tried. Are you at least considering a space in his van now? Or will you not go?
>
> **ME:** Mobile home. Not van. He did offer again and I said no. What I know of him so far: crashes funerals, peculiar interest in old men, pops in unannounced and doesn't spend money in small florist businesses. He doesn't seem like the bullying type but what happened to the Lina who tells me 'Sophia, watch your drink and text me when you get home'?
>
> **LINA:** You're delivering flowers, he's interviewing oldies. This seems like a professional enough venture to me. Also, please remind me of your alternate options? I'll wait while you think.

A minute goes by, then she messages again

> **LINA:** Did you come up with a better option? Anything better than the man with the van?

I feel my shoulders fall in defeat. No, I did not.

LINA: I obviously don't want you to do anything you're not comfortable with, but this guy seems harmless and a bit lost, in the general life sense. I can't imagine he's up to anything sketchy. Just a man with a van driving across the country.

There's an app I can't remember the name of, where you can carpool, but I can hear Lina's objection already, which saves me having to message her. *You won't travel with this stranger that you've at least met but are willing to find another stranger on an app?* I think of the flowers I have in the back of my car, of the deposit I've already been paid and put into my Excel sheet. I *need* this job. If I let Blade drive off, I have about a hundred challenges ahead of me that include changing my plan altogether. Challenges and tasks that could be avoided by giving up my need for personal space for a short period of time. I'm not usually spontaneous but as I stand there opposite this man with a silly beanie flung on top of his head it is as if something malfunctions. I decide I'm going to do it—

'Fine,' I say, surprising even myself a little still.

'Fine?'

'I mean, yes. But it's a yes with conditions. We can ride together, and we will split all the associated costs evenly. I have specific places to be at specific times, in order to complete this job, so we'll need to work out a schedule and stick to it. And I have to be back by the twelfth of July.' He studies me for a long time, then he nods, once.

'So we have a deal?' *Have we both lost out minds?*

We gaze at each other in silence as my lips play with the answer, moving wordlessly as I think.

'Deal.'

Yep, we have both definitely lost our minds.

'You're sure about this?' he asks. Something flickers across his face.

'Sure.' I'm sure I do *not* want to do this. In fact, if I had to compile a list right here right now on my phone's Notes app of things I'd rather do, I'd need to upgrade my cloud storage to fit it.

'Well, I was planning to leave now, as in I was already on my way,' he says.

I think of how I had planned to arrive and meet with Vincent this afternoon. How being unable to make that meeting and prepare for tomorrow's busy day could jeopardise my whole contract. The tow-truck finally pulls up behind us, somehow finding a space next to my car, and I shake my long hair off my shoulders and turn to Blade.

'That's fine with me. We'll wait for the truck to finish loading my car and then—let's go.'

AS WE DRIVE off I keep my eyes firmly at the window. I wish it was legal to travel in the living area of the mobile home, but it turns out even dogs aren't allowed to do that in Sweden so I'm doomed to sit in the front. Next to Blade. I knew this was a mistake the minute we set out. I'm meant to be unmasking with the help of my book and Twitter, and now I'm suddenly finding myself in great proximity to a stranger.

My hands finally make work with the seat belt, releasing it so I'm not strapped in like I'm on a rollercoaster. He studies me, as if he can't figure out why I'm here, inside his car. And in the meantime, I'm wondering exactly the same thing.

'Plug your phone in, if you need to charge. Once it's parked up we won't have power.' I do as I'm told. The seats are large and leather-clad, and luckily there is a gap between them wide enough to enable walking to the back of the home. It means almost a metre's distance between me and Blade.

I message Lina, because I had an idea whilst waiting for the tow-truck.

I'm next to British stranger heading north. Sharing my location so that you can alert authorities if I divert from route. Which I will send you shortly.

WE HAVE BEEN driving for what feels like the longest hour of my life when I decide I can't take it any longer. Even the limited amount of small talk I'm capable of producing must be better than this. If I don't say something soon, I'll have to jump out of the car.

'So you are heading to Jönköping?' My words sound loud falling into the small space that is the front-seat compartment.

A nod in reply.

Okay. *If he doesn't start talking, say anything at all to help me fill this silence, I'm going to have to push him out of the moving car . . .*

'So if it's not your dad you're looking for, who's the person?' I try. He considers this question long enough that I start to believe I really will have to shove him out.

His fingers grip the steering wheel tighter; it was impossible to miss because, well, I have been carefully watching him for the past couple of minutes.

'My mum lost someone. Many years ago. And now I'm trying to find him. She, well, both of us, have been in a bad place lately and I hope this might help.'

'You went to a different country to find someone for your mum?' I think this new information softens me. But then on second thought, it hardens me. Because would I ever do something like that for *my* mum? I doubt she would trust me to look for her misplaced reading glasses, never mind a lost person.

I sit quietly. I watch Blade's hands move up and down the steering wheel, his muscles tensing and my mind wanders off with the same weird sensation I had when he came into my shop. I'm distracted by him. A stranger. His presence and his proximity. I take my pack of anti-bacterial wipes out of my pocket and begin wiping down the door and glove compartment, creating a faint citrus smell around me. I feel more at ease immediately.

'Gum?' he asks me, holding out a pack of Extra.

'No thanks. Spicy mint somehow seeps through my eyeballs and makes me sneeze at the same time. I prefer the fruity ones.'

'They don't make you feel clean though.' He pops one, two, three gums into his mouth and closes his lips around them.

'It's not the mint that kills off bacteria. It's the fluoride and they all have that.' I consider his mouth and all the bacteria dying slowly as he chews, quite a satisfying thought, and whether very hypothetically—*of course*—I could kiss a mouth if there'd just been, let's say, three pieces of gum with fluoride inside it. Perhaps there'd be a window of a few minutes until the bacteria built up again.

Blade is quiet, and I turn my head back to the window, but the glass just reflects his face in it. I sneak a peek at him again. His jaw moving with every chew.

'It just tastes like toothpaste,' he says.

'Exactly. I use children's toothpaste. The strawberry one is nice.'

Apparently that was what we could manage in terms of small talk. Toothpaste. Kill me *now*. But no, I'm in for a long slow death. Close to a thousand kilometres long, to be precise.

'Let's put some ground rules down,' I say. 'Number one, the bed is mine.'

'Okay. I've brought a tent.' Blade continues. 'Number two, we split the driving.'

'Deal,' I say. 'Number three. You help at markets with unloading and reloading.'

'Then, you keep me company in at least one care home. While I'm looking for this person.'

'No deal. Don't like chatting to strangers.'

He shrugs, arguing doesn't seem to be in his nature. 'Happy to help.'

'So based on our route and schedules, you have more free time than me, or at least your schedule is more flexible. So we should set up camp for the night close to where I need to be the next day and then you can drive from there,' I say. Then I stop talking because there's something at the side of the road and—oh no. *Oh. No.*

Blade turns to me.

'Oh God, what is wrong. Sophia? I'll turn around right now. You don't have to come anywhere. Or if you still want to, then I will help with everything. I'll even agree to clean the van bi-weekly. I'll make your bed. Complete with the pillow-fluffing. Please don't cry.'

'Not crying,' I lie badly.

'Okay. We may be experiencing some cultural differences then because in England that thing when wet drops roll down your cheeks and sulking sounds come from your throat? That would constitute crying.'

'Fine. If you must know, it was a cat. At the side of the road.' I start sobbing again, big ugly crying with my sleeve pressed against my mouth, just thinking about it. 'Run over.'

'Oh.'

'I have issues with dead animals.' I sniff.

'Issues?'

'Animals are cute and innocent, and I've never understood how humans relate to humans but not other species. Like bears, they like to sleep and enjoy quiet nature time. I relate to that. Or a giraffe. They pay attention to what's ahead and are extremely gentle. They also have unusually long necks. I can relate to that as well. Sometimes I'll relate to objects too. How could you not buy the display item because it's been scratched? How would you feel if someone rejected you that way?'

I stop because I realise that I've explained enough. Overshared. More than I ever shared with Ed. Blade doesn't look a bit uncomfortable though.

'I'm sorry. I would have stopped,' he tells me, whilst looking in the back mirror.

'And what if the cat was a *mother*? Think of the sweet kittens waiting for mummy to come home.'

'Sure you're not projecting a human family structure on the deceased cat?' He steals a look at my face and decides to stop. He settles on, 'It's very sad.'

'I'm okay. This was nothing.' A scratch on my knee, sun in my eyes, a dead animal. My dad's voice: *This is nothing, Sophia!*

I sit for a moment before adding quietly, 'My dad used to stop the car and make me look at them. The animals. He said it would toughen me up. To see what real life was like. There were three boys and me in the car on our school run. Eventually my brothers let me sit between them in the middle of the backseat so I wouldn't see anything dead at the side of the road. They didn't want to be late to the hockey training just because I had to be phobia-trained with a cadaver, they said.' Mattias never liked seeing the dead animals either—that's why he became a vet. So maybe I wasn't totally a freak, yet I can still remember every word my dad said when showing me roadkill.

Blade looks at me in disbelief and I shrink down, embarrassed. This is not Autistic Twitter, this is real life and real life prefers women like me to keep their mask on and be the high-functioning level-1 end-of-the-spectrum *mildly Autistic* women we're diagnosed as.

'Do you want to stop for a break?'

'No, I'm fine. I'm an adult now and have a heart of stone.' I laugh as I say it, trying to lighten the mood, but it's probably, most definitely, true.

'Still, I can't help thinking that the cat might have been very old. He may have chosen this very spot for sentimental reasons and drew his last breath here entirely peacefully,' Blade says.

'At the side of the dual carriageway? That's his sentimental spot?'

'Maybe it was where he met his cat partner for the first time. Yes, I feel sure of it. That was a peaceful end-of-life death you witnessed.'

I shake my head. *Hopeless.* This man is hopeless. But then I can feel a smile spreading across my face.

The navigation voice speaks and drowns out any thoughts I'd had. Ten days, 2,521 kilometres in total. But our first stop is only a quarter of that distance away.

I can do this.

An Almost-Retired Storage Facility Manager
Malmö

THE RENT-A-SAFE MANAGER is the type of person who dislikes unfinished business. Leftovers, burial places without headstones, to-do lists without ticks. Now that he's approaching retirement and it's within his grasp and only days away, he'd like to leave an empty desk behind, so to speak. He's looking at it now—this unfinished business—having taken it out of the storage compartment. Turning it around, holding it up to the light and wishing it would magically disappear out of his hands, as you so often do with unfinished business. And leftovers. Yes, he'd pushed that dauphinoise to the back of the fridge—arrest him now—because he felt bad throwing it away, but also would very much like a kebab for dinner. Things magically disappear at the back of the fridge. Everyone knows that, so who is he if he doesn't use this to his advantage?

The box arrived on a Tuesday on the manager's eighth day of work. It had been sent over from a lawyer's office, one he didn't know the name of, but then why would he? He only dealt with safes and their secrets. He had to sign for delivery, he remembers that. It came with a name, a cheque to cover five years' worth of rent and a 'Please store this box until collection.' Like bloody Paddington Bear it arrived with a tag around its neck.

So here he is now. Realising this won't magically disappear. *I could dispose of the contents*, he thinks. Yes: cleaned-up, the box could be quite useful. Perhaps for putting newspapers in.

No, no. Empty desk. Law and order, code and conduct. He picks up the phone one last time. Missing a time when people would respond with their surname rather than a general generic greeting. Everything is general now. Anaesthesia, elections. He heard a news anchor refer to a political event as a 'genny lecky' the other day and that's that with the world, isn't it?

He presses the phone to his ear now. He doesn't have to worry about a hello though, not this time and not that time last year or that time seven years ago. Because *in general* no one answers this British number he has on file, belonging to an *Edith* something.

In general, since 2016, he's only gotten her voicemail.

Part Two

And you'll see me waiting for you on the corner of the street.

—THE SCRIPT

Edith
London

THE THING THAT people forget about dementia, and well, so many other things in life really, is that it all has a beginning, a middle and an end. They also forget that it's often impossible to know where you are in the moment. People tend to always assume they are in the beginning, perhaps in the middle quite reluctantly once they hit older age, but no one ever wakes up and acknowledges the end. It tends to just happen. My life is no different to other people's in that sense and it fills me with some degree of hope.

My new estate agent friend is running late and I wonder if she knows what even a few minutes can mean for a person. For a life. What if I had been a few minutes late meeting Sven?

To pass the time, I show people the way to the permit section. The town hall seems to exist purely as a reason for the area's wealthy to park their Teslas along the street.

As I wait, I'm tremendously cheered up by a large corpulent black dog that licks at my hand and my cheek when I crouch down to his level. I can't recall his breed but know they're known for being gentle and kind. They like treats and always finish their meals, a bit like Blade as a teenager really.

'Would you mind holding him for me whilst I pop in and

sort out this council tax?' the dog's owner asks me and I joyously wrap the lead around my wrist, once, then twice, like you would with a helium balloon, so it won't fly away. I resume petting the dog and stroking his soft neck and I think that in a different life I would have had a dog, the life where I wasn't a single mum, working long hours and being so exhausted when I got home that a walk around the block at nine in the evening would have felt like a half marathon.

I hear a voice above me.

'That's a beautiful face right there.'

Even I know I've reached the age where I can be certain a comment like that is directed at the dog and not myself.

'Well, thank you, he says.' Dogs are always seen as an open invitation for conversation with strangers.

'Always loved a Labrador. I have a Newfoundland.'

'Ah yes. *Newfoundland*. Makes me think that we shouldn't feel too bad about not always being creative when naming pets and children. Just think of the man who named the new land he found New-found-land.'

The man laughs.

'Love your spirit. Would you need some dog food? Deworming? Can't be easy looking after him under those conditions.'

I ponder the conditions that he's referencing, which don't appear bad to me at all. It's a sunny, mild day, and the owner should be back in no more than ten minutes.

'I'm looking after him for a friend,' I say, finally.

'Oh, I see. My mistake then. Well nice to meet you and the handsome boy here.' He ruffles the dog's fur and walks off.

I'VE JUST GIVEN the dog back to its owner when the estate agent with the weather inappropriate shoes appears around the corner. It's fairly hot today, and I imagine her toes clumped together with sweat. She jumps over a puddle that's still lingering from a wetter day and narrowly avoids getting her feet soaked. I wonder if she has something against proper shoes. There is much to be said for good footwear, I always thought. She's been stopping to talk to me the last couple of days now. I find myself looking forward to it and notice that, for a brief moment, just after two, I'm looking towards the street corner not for Sven but for her.

'My son used to call puddles "muddy cuddles." I tell her when she's next to me. I'm not sure when I last remembered that little fact, but I'm savouring it now that I seem to remember a lot while sitting here on this bench, next to the rust-coloured brick building with its low metal railing and tall silhouette. *Perhaps soon*, I think. *Perhaps soon I will remember what I need Blade to know and why I'm here.*

'How are you today?' she says, squeezing my shoulder. 'I'm taking a break. Would you like to come and get a hot drink, or would you rather I bring it back for you?'

I think how I can come to this spot and sit for hours but how, at home, I don't even remember the way to the kitchen some days. How do I dare to venture away from here? But going for a coffee with another person is important. Not just another person either. I think she's now my friend.

'I will come with you,' I say decisively.

I've forgotten her name, so I suggest we go to Starbucks. It smells of gingerbread and sweet syrup, and there is pop music playing.

'Eliza,' she says to the barista, and I mouth it in silence. It's a fabulous practice to write the name on the cup as well. When I sit opposite her I twist my head to look at it several times. Apart from having spelt Eliza with an *s* it's a perfectly formed reminder of her name in black marker.

'I saw your son pick you up once. Or at least I think it was your son,' she says as we sip on coffees and I eat a millionaire's shortbread. 'He hasn't been for a while has he? Anyone looking after you? That girl with the pink hair?'

'Zara. She is very good at it. Because she lets me look after her in return.'

'Tell me. If I had a choice to go anywhere in this city, I wouldn't come to this very place every day. Why do you?'

'Not everything we do is by choice. Some things are for survival. It's become the one place I'm myself. Where memories don't float around, they're more organised when I'm here, I can hold onto my thoughts better. And it's the only place I can possibly hope to find him in.'

'Oh.'

'Eliza,' I say and glance at her cup again, worried the name will once again slip my mind. 'Would you happen to know how I can put a phone on Silent mode?'

'Sure. Would you like vibrations on?' she asks.

'Depends on if they're good vibrations. We all need good vibrations in our life.'

She laughs. I put the rest of the biscuit in my mouth and find it is far too sweet.

'Keep them on then, I take it.'

I hand my phone over, and she works her magic in seconds.

'No more loud signals. All fixed.' It looks the same as a minute ago to me, but I trust her. I know that any more phone calls in front of Zara will lead to more questions of me or, worse, she'll ask Blade. I can't quite remember why I can't answer this call, but I somehow know that if I do my world will fall apart.

'Right. I have to get back to the office. At least it's Thursday!' I hadn't noticed what day it was, but I nod knowingly. As if I know what regularly happens on a Thursday in Eliza's life.

'Please, let me.' I take the two empty cups and carry them

off to the counter where I spot metal trays and a three-bin system for recycling.

'Bye, Eliza,' I say when we arrive back to my corner and she retreats back to her office building.

In my bag I touch that the thing I snuck out with me rather than putting it in the bin. I touch it now to know it's there: my friend's empty paper cup, so that I don't forget her name.

I feel refreshed, like when you've come in from a cold walk or stepped out of the shower. Perhaps it's the realisation that even the smallest, most rapidly shrinking world can still grow bigger and that there is always space for a new friend.

The walk to the bus stop takes six minutes rather than the usual nine. I think how I diverted from my daily route to include Starbucks and how that has now made my original route faster. I think that I can't *know* if this is my beginning, middle or end. The thought is quite liberating.

Blade
Eksjö

THREE HOURS AFTER we set off on the trip we arrive in Eksjö, which Sophia tells me with delight means *fairy lake* and is an hour from her childhood home. The market is set to take place on the main square the day after tomorrow, and I have looked up a route to take tomorrow to a retirement village an hour's drive away. While not every location she needs to be is close to where I'm headed, at least it's within the same county. We drive through the town centre, and with an hour until sunset the sky has gone a bruised purple. A small crowd are getting mid-week-level rowdy outside the single bar on the high street and there's a line winding up to a Thai food truck. Everything is clean: Even at dusk, the absence of random rubbish and lack of peeling paint, broken railings and tipped over bins stands out to me. There is none of the chaos that you get in a city with ten million people.

'I googled a campsite a reasonable drive from here. I think that's where we should head for the night,' I say as we leave town behind. We both ate on our last stop, and there is no real reason to dwell here. It's awkward enough sitting next to each other in the car.

'Did you not know that we have right of passage in Sweden? You can camp anywhere if it's just for a couple of nights.'

'Anywhere?'

'Well, anywhere where you're not in the way or in someone's actual garden. In a forest, next to the beach if there's a suitable road.'

'I don't have to pay to set a tent up?' This opens up a whole new world. Rather than finding campsites, we can stay anywhere we want.

'No need to pay, no. We can plan our stops more intentionally, then. No need to factor in campsites. I need to stay three to four nights in our next location but that's the longest we'll ever stay in one spot. So this will work perfectly,' she replies.

'Where should we go, then? Do you know the area?'

'Not really. I know where the hockey rink is. I waited in the car outside it every other weekend when my brothers played. I wouldn't want to sleep there, though. The car would always get really cold, so I'd have to sit on my hands.'

I try to process what she just said. But I need more information.

'Why did you wait in the car?'

'I couldn't *behave* inside.' I look at her, a little confused still. 'In the car it didn't matter if I rocked back and forth, but inside Dad had lots of friends and my brothers had lots of friends who'd all look at me, I guess. *Inside someone might see you, Sophia,* my dad would tell me. As if me being seen would be a catastrophe.'

'Sophia, you were left in a cold car, alone, while your parents watched your brothers' hockey practice? Just because you rocked in your seat?'

'You may have noticed that I always keep the seat warmer

on,' she says, her head bent. I had, actually. The full eight hours the light was on. The bright red light on the side of her chair in July. I'd assumed it was a mistake until she pressed on it again once it got down to one bar. I swallow hard. I decide to always, always make sure that seat is warm for her.

'Listen, it wasn't so bad. I only really panicked if any of the kids from my class came past.' She shrugs.

'Why?'

'Because they would bang on the windows and write swear words on them if there was frost. I had the doors locked from the inside and would just close my eyes. Though, not everything goes away just because you can't see it.'

Well, no. And I sense that this hasn't ever gone away for Sophia. I notice that I've held my breath as I've listened to her.

'How about an area near the woods, away from the centre of town? So that it's a little quieter is all, less crowded. Would that be okay? We can just google it if you don't know any.'

'That would be fine,' she replies, and I think that I don't need this to be fine, for some reason I need it to be better than fine for her.

WE FIND A dirt road with a dead end and a large, gravelled area most likely used by trucks and tractors at the edge of where a forest begins, and I manage to park the van so it's out of any passing vehicle's way. I begin converting the inside, pulling the curtain between the cockpit and the cabin and opening the windows for fresh air. One side is lined with rectangular windows and once the bed is made they are the right height to look out of. I open the storage compartment above the bed and start getting the equipment out. She laughs as I haul it all out of the bag.

'What's wrong with mosquito repellent?'

'Three cans of it?'

'Three for the price of two. Don't come to me when you're being eaten to death at two in the morning.'

'Why would I come to you at two in the morning?' There it is again. She asks such direct questions.

'I wouldn't actually expect you to do that. I exaggerated to make a point.'

'I see. I like how you explain everything immediately. Thank you.'

I'm taken aback slightly. Do others not take the time to answer her questions?

'Anyway, you won't be bothered by them since you'll get the grand suite. The camper-van.' I start unpacking the khaki-coloured tent for two and pushing the pegs into the ground. Mum never took me camping, but even I can erect this simple structure. Or least I thought so. *Where is the instruction leaflet?*

She doesn't respond with 'Are you sure' or any other polite objection but simply nods.

'I picked up some sheets the other day. Feel free to use them.' I'd have bought something nicer if I knew she'd be joining me.

'Oh great, I hadn't even thought about that.'

'Let me show you where it all is,' I say, abandoning the tent and following her back to the van. I have to duck to go inside, and I notice she does too. If ever two people weren't built for camping life, it would be us.

'I'm not used to sleeping on blue sheets,' she says. She looks around. It's a relatively spacy cabin. 'But I guess there's not really any difference when you think about it. I won't see the colour in the dark anyway.'

I show her which button releases the be, and it descends from the wall. There's a two-seater sofa with a table for eating across from the bedroom, and the bed is surrounded by cupboards now that it's down.

She's started taking her items out of her luggage and I notice a drawing she's set on the sideboard, much like the one I asked about in her shop.

'Oh, that is one of my favourites,' she says, following my gaze. 'It's where they have just picked up their new kitten.'

'So the stick family have a pet.'

'Lots of them.'

Mum has some of my drawings on her wall. They're not particularly good ones, and I think she just randomly picked out a couple to display from the vast number I produced, because that's what you're supposed to do. And now they live forever on her walls in her house.

After she's done unpacking, we go outside again.

'I've got some beers and a generally well-stocked snack bag. Swedish petrol stations are ace. I mean, they even sell hot dogs. Would you like something?'

She turns around on the midpoint of the steps leading up to the car and shakes her head.

'No, thank you. I need my space,' she says. 'Good night.'

Good night? Its eight o'clock. If that's not a direct rejection of me and my snack bag I don't know what is. I take my sleeping bag out of the tent and spread it on the ground. The trees are tall and dark green, like Christmas trees. I dip into the snacks, starting with the crisps. Here I am, spending my night alone, much as I've been craving. But this, actually being alone, feels different to what I'd imagined. I can't think any clearer and the anxiety is still there, along with thoughts of Mum and the decisions looming ahead.

Letter time, I think. I've read them all at this point and feel like a case-obsessed detective looking for new clues, as if the Swedish night would somehow shine new meaning onto the words. This is the letter which confirms that Mum found the shop address randomly, that it was simply a long shot and no real connection.

> Svennie,
> I don't even have your—our—address. The one where we were meant to live together. Isn't that crazy? So I'm sending these to the only one I could find. We were meant to move, to escape it all and start our new life and I don't even know where this magical start is supposed to happen.
> I always wondered if you went without me. Or if you changed your plans. Where are you now? I saw something in a movie the other night. Someone called up an airline and checked if their friend had gotten on the flight, as though that was something airlines actually kept track of. Who checks in and who boards. I did call Ryanair, but they just told me that they record calls for training purposes and that I couldn't get a refund.
> Did you take the tickets we booked and go, just without me? Did you put your coat on the seat that was meant to be mine? Or did you keep it free and glance over, imagining what it would be like with me sitting there, Blade on my lap?

I stop here and put it aside. Escape *what* to start a new life? The capital's pollution and inflated rent? The constant din of the traffic, the too small houses, the lack of jobs? Or *something else*? I can't help but let my mind trail after Mum's words. I really do imagine her sitting there in her seat, me on her lap. Perhaps she'd feed me juice from a sippy cup to alleviate the air pressure getting to my ears. The man next to her is blurred and faceless in my fantasy. And I'm starting to genuinely wonder for the first time, *Who was he?*

Sophia
Eksjö

I MANAGED TO sleep. Eventually. Even though the sheets are the wrong colour and they smell of new fabric. Which for me is an achievement.

I'll admit I'm curious about Blade, and what his idea of a good snack is, but a day ahead full of listening to fairground rides zoom and clink and chatting to strangers means I needed sleep and quiet first. So I locked the doors, closed the curtains and all the lights, and got underneath the duvet as soon as I was alone.

I check Lina's location, and she's been all over.

ME: I'm afraid I won't have any chance to have my breakfast in peace. SOS.

LINA: May not help but when I went on first holiday with Kurt I popped down to the reception bathroom to poop in peace.

Sneaking off with my breakfast cereal into the woods *is* an option, I suppose. I weigh it up as I wait for Blade to get ready to drop me off in town.

Seriously, this whole idea, this whole trip is just . . .

Exciting. That's not the word I expected to pop up in my head. *New*, sure, but I wouldn't want it to end now. Or at least not yet.

'Good morning,' Blade says when he sees me. 'Can I . . . make a coffee?' he asks. And I realise I'm standing in the small doorway, blocking it.

'Sure. My home is your home.' I hesitate. 'Or rather, your home is my home. Or Sixt's rental is our home? Technically.'

Blade smiles. It's short-lived but stops me up short. I inhale through my nose, trying to restore my breathing and immediately regret it. Because all I have accomplished is filling my lungs with an unfamiliar, overpowering scent. Blade's scent.

I'm not used to anyone else as part of my morning routine. Or even coffee.

There is not quite space enough for two people so I stand awkwardly at the side, feeling very much in Blade's way. Finally, I decide to squeeze onto the sofa, folding my legs underneath me to make them fit, and look on as he waits for the coffee to brew. Before it's finished, he pulls the can out and empties what little liquid there is into his cup, then quickly puts it back.

'Coffee?' he asks, offering me the mug.

'Wow. That is generous of you. But, no, I won't take it from you. You're practically sniffing the fumes. And I had a glass of milk already.'

He looks at me like I'm some kind of suspicious creature from the nearby forest. As if a human can't run and work properly when fuelled by only a glass of milk.

'Childhood habit. Were you not force-fed milk for the bone growth? A cold glass of milk with dinner was normal. I mix it up now—oat, almond and normal to reduce the guilt of using too many animal products.'

I watch him practically inhale the caffeine as he swallows the contents of the mug in a few fast sips. I take it the tent is not the most comfortable sleeping quarters.

'We need to get some groceries. Unless you, in addition to mosquito-surviving skills, are also trained in foraging the forest for berries and nuts. Meet you at the supermarket after work?' I say.

'Sure. I'm going to some archive in Jönköping. I'll be back by four.'

He runs back out to get dressed and pack up the tent, which can't be left here over the course of the day. I see him crawl into it and watch as his backside and legs are the last to disappear. When the flimsy fabric of the walls begins to shake and shiver, and I see the imprint of an elbow in it as he's presumably wriggling a sweater over his head, I finally turn my back and prepare my bag for the long day ahead.

I'M SUPPOSED TO meet the manager of the market at eight. Blade helps me unload all my equipment at the site and then drives off to do whatever he's planning to do at the archive. I wanted to stop for a drink, like I usually would, but then it's not Lina taking my order and I'm unsure how a barista in a local café would react when I ask for a warm milk or an adult-size babycino. So water will have to do.

At 8.02, still waiting for Vincent, I message Lina. I notice that Lina's location has moved again. I pull the address up on Google Earth and see that it's a block of apartments, three floors high with bikes tied out front. I wonder who lives there.

> **ME:** Survived the first night. Don't think he's a serial killer, unless he's the type that first befriends you with promises of snacks and friendship then strikes when you least expect.

LINA: Great snack taste usually correlates to great person in my opinion. You're doing good.

ME: You've been in the same location three times now? What is happening?

LINA: Too early to say but may have exciting personal news to share . . . ! Clue: coffee.

ME: Oh! How tentatively exciting!

I, on the other hand, have turned my dating app off for the duration of this trip. I can't imagine socialising with anyone on top of the dose of human interaction I get from sharing my space with Blade. So everything is on hold for now, it seems. I focus on the positives: this will give me ample opportunity to finish my Autism book and unmask.

'SORRY I KEPT you waiting.'

Vincent is tall and wide and seems louder out in the world than when I met him in my shop a fortnight ago. Everything seems louder when I leave my shop. Vincent is a dumb cane (*Dieffenbachia*), which, despite the name, is a lovely plant. Like it, he enjoys shady-to-bright indirect light. judging from the aggressive redness on his shoulder and would require little watering to thrive. He'd be sturdy and hard to kill off (literally, I'd imagine, and in conversation, I can testify).

'We're expecting close to a thousand visitors,' he proclaims proudly and I swallow hard. *Crowds.* My favourite. If I work carefully I should be able to place everything so that I don't have to attend during the busiest times. Vincent continues, a hand on his hip, the other pointing animatedly at different things.

'Let me show you around before the exhibitors start to arrive. You have about three hours to get it all set up and then the décor needs to be taken down Sunday by ten, the council advised.'

'Great. I will be on-site to do a daily check and readjust anything that needs it, but I've generally chosen flowers that will last.'

'Nice little buzz here, we are expecting just shy of two thousand visitors.' Oh. The forecast just increased. We should end this conversation before it jumps to ten thousand or I may start hyperventilating.

'You can use the facilities here and someone should be here to open up every morning at seven thirty, even if it's not myself every day.'

'Thank you.'

I draw a breath of relief when he finally trots off and I can disappear, hands and head into the world of my flowers. I go and check that all my stock has arrived with the delivery I arranged before our departure and am pleased to see that it has. I like to source locally so have called up a couple of local shops to get their help filling out what I don't have.

AT FIVE O'CLOCK I'm relieved to leave the busy, loud, fairly smelly marketplace and walk the short distance to the supermarket. I spot Blade's mobile home at the end of the car park, spread across two spaces lengthways. He's standing outside, leaning against the RV, scrolling on his phone. His glances up and catches sight of me as I near, smiling very lightly at my familiar face.

'Hey.'

'Day okay?' I ask.

He nods a brief yes, and we silently fall into step as we approach the supermarket.

Neither of us have a coin for a trolley, so we take a basket each.

I start shopping, grabbing things off the shelves, going for anything with a green sticker and trying to get as many colours in there from the fruit and veg section as I can, because I know it will turn very beige once I arrive at the ready-meal and breakfast aisle.

'That's pretty much all organic.' Blade has so far put one item in his basket—a toast bread with the white and blue label which signals the supermarket's own brand.

'It's meant to be good for you.'

'Pretty sure it's meant to be good for the planet.'

'That too.'

'It's twice the price, though?' He inspects the contents of my basket closer.

'I hadn't noticed.'

I go to the cleaning aisle next. There's a new antibacterial spray fragrance, which I can't help picking up, even though I've already brought two for this trip.

I bring my basket up to the check-out. At the till I turn to Blade.

'What's your monthly disposable income?'

'Excuse me?'

'I've read that expenses are most fairly split according to income. A percentage based on salary seems fairer than fifty-fifty. I myself belong to the high-average bracket.'

'I figured—or the basket wouldn't be full of American-imported cereals and organic oat milk.'

The cashier's gaze jumps between us. Then to the line, albeit short, that's started to form.

'So? I'm quick at maths.'

'How about I get this one and we figure it out later? I'll let you take a look at the receipts in the car, okay? I feel like at this point it's in the public interest.' He nods to the people behind us.

Blade puts his juice on top of his lettuce, and my retinas physically hurt from the violation as I rush to tower my things up appropriately inside my basket, making a base of tins, a next layer of cardboard boxed items and finally soft goods on top followed by berries and crisps bags. By the time I finish he's tapping his foot slightly, but he doesn't shoot the people behind us apologetic looks, roll his eyes or say, 'Christ on a bike' or, 'You're holding up the bloody queue, Sophia.' like my dad would.

WHEN WE EXIT the car park, an open bag of crisps between us, there's a sound of a horn coming from behind.

'What does he want?' I ask.

'Who? What do you mean?'

'That driver. I think he beeped because we were blocking the way.'

I start to roll the window down to explain to the other driver that we were only parked there for a minute and I had to get something out of the bag to pay the parking with and I hope he kindly understands, but Blade drives off and just waves to him.

'But I was going to explain! And what was your wave supposed to mean?'

'I guess I meant it as an apology.'

'But you didn't do anything wrong. As my explanation would have pointed out.'

'Then I guess the wave meant more "all good"?'

'That makes no sense.'

I look out the window, following the other car with my gaze.

'He didn't wave back. Why do you think he didn't wave back?'

'Did you *know* him?'

'Well, no, but if we wave then he should acknowledge that, right?'

'It's a stranger on the road, Sophia. We'll never meet again.'

This is why roads are confusing. As soon as people are in a car I'm meant to interact with them differently.

'The intention, Blade. I'm meant to look for a driver's intention. But they're inside a car and that makes it hard. Is the head turned or positioned to the right? To the left? Driving is not just a system of rules. I thought so when I did my test, but no. The road is a *social activity*.' I say.

'Social?'

'There are all these subtle interactions that you're supposed to pick up on. It's exhausting. This is why self-driving cars will never work.'

'As someone who's been forced to drive and park a six-metre-long vehicle the past forty-eight hours, I regret to hear that. That's why you avoid driving? Because of other people?'

'I don't like when people are angry at me and I don't know why. That happens a lot in traffic because I can't chase them down and ask.'

He smiles. Then the car comes to a stop and I can hear birdsong before I even open the door.

'Okay. Here we are. Back in our spot.'

I GO TO sleep that night going over Vincent's face. Glasses. Age spots. Stubble in three shades of grey. *Damn it, this usually works.* But now there's this other face that keeps popping up.

And is useless for sleeping, because there aren't enough imperfections. It's like I'm unable to see them. I know they're there, but I keep seeing the brown eyes. Then there's the problem of wanting to think of *all* of that person. Not just the face. I move off target. Because there are arms with tattoos. And a chest. Big hands. Thighs where one hand at a time rests when their owner drives. *Sheep*, I interrupt myself. Maybe I should finally do what others do and try with actual sheep. There would be enough fields around here that I can do a field trip and memorise their appearance well enough for it to work. *Great, I have a plan.* I abandon face mapping and close my eyes hard. Waiting in stillness for what feels like an eternity to be tired enough to drift off without any help.

Blade
Växjö

CAMPING IS OVERRATED, I've decided after the second night. At least the type that involves a two-person tent and a man of six-one height. Perhaps my codriver has an altogether different experience in her glamping quarter. New bed linen, oat milk and what I'm guessing is silk pyjamas. I unzip my way out of the cocoon and find that it's a sunny and still day. The light is on in the van so she'll be up. Don't want to disturb her. But also need coffee. *A lot.*

I knock once and the door opens a smudge as if she's checking I'm not a wild bear.

'Just me. Who needs coffee.'

'Two minutes.'

Four minutes later I'm allowed in. Everything is neat, and Sophia's dressed in a long cotton maxi dress with a simple cardigan on top.

'Are you ready for today?' I ask, attempting to make small talk, something she seems reluctant to engage in generally. She shared that the local newspaper is coming to take pictures of the market in full swing and her floral arrangements will feature.

'Impossible. You can only be ready for something if you

know exactly what will happen and when. Days don't work like that. They're unpredictable.'

I think of my own day. Very similar to yesterday, just a different archive in a different location. Obviously we camp where Sophia has to be, which is never the same town that I need to visit, but I am able to make it work with a few hours' driving each day. No luck yesterday and I doubt I'll have any today. In the back of my mind, the idea that Sophia's uncle could be Mum's Sven lingers, but she's sure he never went to London. So I'm on to Sven number three.

Twenty minutes later, with my coffee next to me in an at-home mug, I drop Sophia off at the main square and head on my way. Long after she's hopped out of the passenger seat, I can smell the faint scent of her shampoo drifting up from the back of the cabin.

AS PREDICTED, THE time in the archives was fruitless. A man with a knitted jumper and thin-framed glasses hovered next to me for nearly an hour before I finally gave in and let him help me. After another hour he offered me a coffee, and after the third he brought out the biscuits. But after the fourth hour we had to conclude that we wouldn't find anything, and I left to get back in time to collect Sophia. I don't understand: my mum says Sven went to university in Växjö , but looking through the town's records there is no sign of him. I know some people stay under the radar, graduate and get on with it. They manage to go without making any marks as they progress. I looked at the university graduation photos: nothing. Mum was sure that's where he went to study social sciences. I have now exhausted Sven's university town, and I'm running out of ideas. The man promised to email me should he think of anything, but how often do we get those emails, really?

I have a quick lunch back in Eksjö and call Mum as I eat.

'How is it going?' Mum asks with her usual blend of hopeful scepticism.

'Getting there,' I say.

'Getting where?' she asks.

'You're not meant to ask that.'

'Well, I did. Watch me stir up the English language conventions.' Her camera is off view and I see the green wallpaper. I clench my teeth.

'I went to an archive, following up a lead I got from one of your letters. Checking Sven's graduation history. Whatever there was of it. I still have a list of three Svens to contact, though. Plus the owner of the floral shop.'

'I found some more letters here. Zara and I have been on quite the search mission since you left. I can have Zara send them over to you.' She's clear today. The way the words string together in the right order and she can find each one of them easily. They are words I have heard her use all my life and not new, foreign-sounding ones like *chaise longue* or *Darjeeling* which make her sound slightly off. I decide to try and find clarity in something that's been bothering me.

'Mum, there are no records of him. If you gave me the right details, that is. Birth year, home town and university. Is there anything else? Did you meet him through work?'

Mum has had many jobs. Hotel housekeeping, dinner lady and personal assistant.

'Not all details are important, Blade,' she tells me.

But she doesn't confirm that this one, of how they met, isn't.

'HOW DID IT go?' I ask Sophia when she opens the door and jumps in.

'Surprisingly well. The airborne humidity is perfect and unless the temperature rises overnight I won't have to switch out any of the arrangements. I didn't have to be in any of the photos which was a relief. I hate photos.'

Sophia sits quietly the whole drive back and I don't want to disturb her. She is tapping away at her phone in the passenger seat next to me. Her knees are pulled up against her body, and her feet are rested against the dash. She looks cosy. I guess with her long legs sitting up straight in a seat won't work. She only breaks the silence when I make an abrupt break to allow the car in front of me to parallel park. The red Volvo inches backwards until it halts then abruptly drives back onto the road.

'Wow. Commitment issues,' Sophia remarks.

'Sorry?'

'That Volvo. The way they first wanted the space, but when everything around them aligned—car behind stopping—they still gave up after one try. I bet they'll do the same to another parking space on the next road.'

She peeks out of the window, following the car with her eyes hoping to prove her thesis. A content laugh when she does.

'See.' She nods at the red car which is now again holding up traffic to wedge its way in between two parked vehicles. '*Obvious* commitment issues.'

'I CAN COOK something,' I offer when we are back home twenty minutes later. *Home*, it's a clearing in the forest that I share with a stranger but I don't know what else I'd call it.

'Sure. Stress level is at a *modest 1* so I can handle a nutritious cooked meal.'

The kitchen is so small I have to crouch down and look

behind me each time before I move to ensure I'm not bumping into her.

She finds the table and two chairs that come with the mobile home and sets them up outside. When I appear with two plates of pasta she looks so genuinely pleased something tugs at my chest.

'So did you find the man you're looking for today?' she asks.

'Unfortunately not.'

I'm not quite ready to ask more about her uncle. Based on what little Sophia said about him, it's essentially impossible that it's him. But still, I'd like to prolong the moment I find out this has all been completely useless. That my mum mistakenly sent letters to his shop, that he is not, in fact, the Sven I'm looking for. To find out that I'm that much closer to failure.

'Where is your mum now that you're away?' she asks me.

'A friend is staying with her. She's amazing.'

'I have one friend, but she's a three in one really. Life coach, best friend and sister.'

'Sounds like you don't need anything else. My best friend can be highly critical and too invested, but she always pulls through when you need her. She's the one staying at my house now. With my mum.'

'Do you miss your mum? I find I don't miss people. I can ache and hurt and but when people talk about wanting to hug their mum, I don't feel it like that.'

'I'm not used to talking about this. About Mum. Us.'

'Why?'

It's hard to explain. The mix of pain and guilt and fed-upness that always washes over me when I talk about my mother. These feelings have robbed me of the ability to speak about her, to be proud of her and what we've had all these years. Her illness has robbed me of even cherishing the memories. *Oh don't go and fucking cry, Blade.*

'You can talk about it. I don't always know the right thing to say, but I know how to listen.'

She means it. Somehow I trust her more than someone who's known me half my life. I'm not sure I'm ready for it, though. I shrug. But her eyes are open wide and never leave my face. *Maybe just the short version, then.*

'Do you know anything about dementia? It's a disease, there's no cure for it. It changes the brain, the memory and the personality. Mum has it, and well, I've been her carer for the past three years.'

What I leave out is that it's been three years of no breaks, no travelling, no peace of mind. There has been joy, and love of course, but lately all these other feelings are starting to eat away at it. *Please don't let me lose sight of the joy . . .* I think maybe that's what I'm really looking for, by coming here for her, some way to preserve the joy.

I tell Sophia a little of the brightly coloured plates and how some days I'm only a floating head to my mum, due to changes in the brain and in how things look, feel and sound to her.

'I feel a little like that around my family. Like I'm a floating body part almost, not a proper person like the others,' she says. I smile, my anxiety lowered, then start to stack our plates.

'It's raining.' I'm stating the obvious. It's been raining for a while already. Soft drops fall on us and the table, but I've finished talking anyway, and she doesn't seem to mind.

'I love rain.'

'More than sunshine?'

'Oh yes. I don't like sunshine. It gives me a headache. It's too bright, too loud. Can you hear brightness? I swear I can.'

'So what's your preferred weather forecast?' I ask.

'Overcast, sixteen degrees,' she replies in a heartbeat.

'Here, take my sweater.' I offer her my black hoodie and she pulls it down over her head so only her mouth, nose and blue eyes are visible. She takes it off again as quickly as she put it on.

'Sorry, I can feel the tag. I don't do well with scratchy things.'

'Here, give me.' I take it from her. With my teeth I rip the tag off and hand it back to her.

'That may well be the most thoughtful thing someone has done for me in a long time.'

Only when it starts pouring more heavily do we grab the tableware and fold up the chairs, running towards the van cabin to store them away.

'Thank you for dinner,' she says as I grab a towel from the cupboard and prepare to make a run for the tent.

'Goodnight,' I say. Then, desperate to talk more, if only just for another minute, I add, 'Would you like a gum?' I stretch the pack out towards her.

'No, thanks. I don't like mi—' She smiles. 'Oh. These aren't mint. You bought new ones.' She takes two, weighing them in the middle of her palm.

'No, they're strawberry.'

Edith
London

I VERY MUCH think that chasing pigeons is a sign of future narcissism. I see it all the time, parents smiling when toddlers toddle and older kids throw their hands out laughing and running after the birds. Pigeons are at the bottom of the chain in London.

'Think about how you treat society's most vulnerable,' I say to the group of mothers who have emerged from the doors of the library and now talk about au pairs not abiding by curfew times, or keeping up with their personal hygiene, or cleaning their plate of the organic steak that was bought specially, although they are great with the children and finding a new one is *so* draining.

'Did you need anything?' They smile at me. Because that's what you do with the older citizens. Smile and offer assistance, politely. But never actually engage.

'No. But the pigeons need peace.'

I would have gone on, but I am hoping to spot Eliza and grab her for a quick little chat. I have my flask with tea, and I sit down on the bench by the bus stop, which has just become free as a couple of riders just boarded the bus.

Sven always walked around pigeons, I remember now. Not because he liked them: he didn't, he blinked when they flew too close and he watched carefully so he didn't drop encouragement in the shape of crumbs to them, but he respected them. That's how I knew he was a good egg, even though he didn't exactly look it, a tall and rugged giant that sometimes forgot to smile.

He was waiting for someone else when we first met. I was too, having arrived early for my meeting with the single mothers' group, Blade asleep in the buggy, covered by a soft muslin blanket, shielded from the world. Sometimes, when I pushed him along the streets and he was sleeping, I'd forget he was there and even almost forget I was a mother. I would walk a little taller, as if I had heels on and someone might notice me.

I was early that day and wanted to let him sleep for as long as possible. Sven and I stood next to each other long enough for it to become awkward.

'I'm delivering something on behalf of my boss,' he said finally. He looked straight at me, not first at the sleeping child and *then* me, as if he was assessing me as a mother only. *Unusual*, I thought.

'I see. And what is it?'

'Do you know what? I don't even know. Want to guess?'

'Sure. How about some crickets?'

'Seriously? That's your best guess?'

'You can likely find a lot of weird things in the mail. It was legal to mail children before 1915. Stamps were cheaper than train tickets.'

He laughed then. Which made me take a step closer. His laugh always had that effect on me. As if the soundwaves went straight into my bones, the very frame of who I was.

'You think my boss sent a child from Malmö to London?'

'Why don't you have a look?'

'Can't open another person's mail. I'm a man with principles . . .'

'Edith,' I quickly filled in. Because it seemed like the sort of name a well-built, tanned Swedish man with principles should know.

'Edith.'

The crowd of single mothers' group members began arriving and people smiled and waved at me from all directions.

'Does every last person here know you? They practically flock toward you.' He laughed a second time. 'Hopefully that means your number will be easy to find, should I want to see you again, Edith.'

Sophia
Älvsjö

IT'S THE THIRD and final day in this first location. When I arrive at the market, a new man meets me instead of Vincent. Which goes to prove my point that every day is highly unpredictable. He's around fifty, and I'd put his average step count at two thousand. I wait for him to say something.

'Hi there. Sophia?'

'Indeed. With a "ph" as in "Philadelphia". The city or the cheese spread. Take your pick,' I say.

'Vincent told me to open up for you. Bit of a flu, he's got. I'm the building maintenance manager.'

'Wonderful. Well, I'm ready for you to open up when you are.' I move towards the door. He pushes it open, he's clearly been inside already as the key isn't needed.

'Bit young to run a business by yourself. Look no more than twenty.' He looks me up and down which takes a while considering my height.

'I'm twenty-six next month,' I say. It's more my body language and facial expressions that make me seem younger, because in pictures I certainly feel I look my age.

'Well, I'm exactly double your age then, in August.'

'I like older men,' I say. Then realise my mistake. This is a comment-in-the-lift scenario that's gone against me. I try to save myself from death of embarrassment.

'I mean dads. Grandads. Those sorts of men. Uncles! I was very fond of my late uncle.' The man laughs, and my technique seems to have worked. I'm saved from any unwanted advances.

'All right then, young lady, I'll leave you to it. Don't want you to become too fond of this old man, now do we?' He stretches out his hand, and I shake it.

'Thanks and bye.'

I'VE COME TO enjoy my evenings with company. It only took us four nights to fall into a routine. We eat, then we sit until the forest noises start to grow louder—leaves rustling, trees swaying, owls hooting in the distance—letting us know it's time to sleep. The social hangover is still there, but for the first time I can understand Lina when she says that a night of drinking is worth feeling sluggish the next day. I think talking to Blade makes up for the overwhelm I feel afterwards.

'Where were you born?' I ask. He answers my questions with long sentences now. We have definitely moved past small talk about gum. I might be imagining it, but he seems less anxious, less jumpy, and the dark circles under his eyes that I had thought were permanent have started to pale.

'London. My mother raised me alone.'

I imagine this man's mother and find myself wanting to know more about his upbringing. About him. *Weird*.

'I think we should always set up camp by a lake,' Blade says after a pause, taking a bite of dinner. I've cooked tonight which means we are having ham and cheese toasties.

'There are about a hundred thousand lakes in Sweden.'

'I love how you know those random facts.'

'Who decides what's random?'

'No idea. But I reckon I'd happily visit every single one of those lakes with you.'

I have something hard in my throat, an invisible tennis ball, by the feel of it.

'Cold?'

Shaking my head I turn to him. We're in chairs, but only a few inches separate us and I wonder how we got his close. Didn't he start out on that other log, over there, an hour ago?

'I'm fine.' I'm not, though. I've learnt that when Blade is this near me, I'm something else entirely.

'What's that?' Blade ducks then jumps up from his chair.

'If you mean that black thing that just touched your shoulder ever so slightly I'd say it's probably a bat.'

'A bat? *A bat?*'

'They're not dangerous. Bats are the only flying mammal. They're very cool.' I'm sharing scientific facts, which can only mean one thing: that I'm comfortable.

'He just flew right at me. This one seems pretty aggressive.'

I laugh. 'You're scared. That's sweet.'

'Yes, I'm scared of insects and bats and all sort of nightly creatures that you normally avoid meeting because, you know, you don't sleep in a forest. What else is there in Swedish forests? Don't tell me there are wolves.'

'Not in the south. Bears would be unusual as well.'

'Wild cats? Badgers?'

I stare at him. And stare some more. I stare at this man who just vented his fear of wildlife and is now going through a mental checklist of the forest fauna.

God. Oh *God*. I think I *like* him.

I'M NOT SURE what time it is when I wake and sit upright, pulling the eye mask from my face. It's raining again. I can hear it thudding against the roof. It always soothed me as a child, and I never slept better than to that drumming noise. Maybe I won't need to imagine faces tonight, I thought as I climbed into bed earlier. The drumming is interrupted by persistent knocking, and I quickly throw my night shirt on.

Blade. Soaked by rain.

'How can I help you?' I say. His eyes search my face.

'The tent is letting water in. I hate to impose on your space and a deal is a deal, but we are moving on to the next location tomorrow, and if I drown out there I'll be of no use. You may even have to put your project on hold to dispose of my body, and then technically you'd be on the run from the authorities from then on out, and I don't think that's something you want to do. Which leads me to ask: Can I sleep on the sofa?'

The sofa is about half the length of Blade. I wouldn't sleep there if you paid me. Which is why I stare at him unconvinced.

'Technically that would be fine. Considering the drowning potential. *Obviously*. However, there may be some problems. One, I'd say the sofa is much too small for you.'

'It apparently turns into a bed if we combine the chairs and table. The guy at the rental desk told me when I collected it.'

'I doubt it will be a two-metre one.' I eye him up as if trying to judge if I can fit his dead, drowned body into a given storage unit and if that would be a better option than the sofa.

'I'll make it work.'

'Secondly, I sleep naked.' It's true: The fabric of clothes on my skin as I sleep is almost painful, but it's not the main reason why him in my space is an unsettling thought. The main reason is a school field trip. Rooms with bunk beds, one room for the girls and one for the boys. I had begged not to go, but as Dad put it, *It is compulsory, Sophia*. Bloody hell, *you can't treat school like a drop-in club.* I must have been utterly exhausted, worn-out from the new environment and a full schedule because I fell asleep. Heavily asleep until I wasn't, because there was cold water on me and the boys' were laughing and someone was shining a torch in my face and when I jumped out of bed to get away from the cold, sticky wetness my shirt was soaked and they could all see right through it. My mind flashes back to it automatically, I don't think I've shared a room with anyone since.

'So anyway.' I wonder if I somehow should have padded that statement. I try to fix it. 'Clothes bother me. When I sleep. They're scratchy.'

'Like the tag in my sweater.'

'Yes, exactly like that.'

'So. You. Sleep. Naked.' He looks as if he's just encountered the biggest problem during our trip so far which, considering the ant infestation on our first day, getting lost multiple times and the wet tent, seems bewildering. But then here we are, his eyes rising to the ceiling as if waiting for some help. I wait, hoping he tips his head just that a farther so his ridiculous beanie will finally fall off.

'So—this isn't usually a problem, except now we need to share the sleeping space. I stay strictly under my duvet so there is no real risk. Plus it will be dark.'

'It's light until three in the morning in summer here.'

'You're a great problem-solver, aren't you?' I say.

'I've noticed that your sense of humour relies heavily on me being ridiculed.'

'Blade, I'm trying to solve this for us. Unless you want to sleep and possibly drown in the tent, then sleep here. On the sofa. And I'll stay in the bed.' My initial panic has gone, without me even noticing it. I suddenly know that he can be in a sofa metres away from me and I won't have flashbacks to bunk-beds, bullies and never feeling safe.

'Thank you. I'll go and get my sleeping bag and you . . . can hopefully be in bed by the time I'm back.'

I hear him leave, come back, then turn the key and go straight to his sofa. I turn the light off, and it takes me a long time to sleep.

Blade
Älvsjö

I'M LYING FOUR feet away from a very funny, very smart, very attractive and, as it turns out, very naked woman. I force myself not to think about her. I turn towards the wall and pull my legs into recovery position, my knees touching the outline of the table. I go through where I stand with Sven to get my mind to peace.

'IS THAT A fire alarm?' I jump up then throw myself back down on the sofa pressing the pillow over my ears. My left side is tingling and I'm surprised I haven't fallen out and onto the floor during the night. Must have been too tense to move even in my sleep.

The noise dies out, and I drift off again. Until *again*.

'Good morning,' Sophia's voice says over the noise.

'Jesus, how many times do you snooze? And are you trying to call all the wild animals over? I bet there's a wolf out there somewhere who'd be keen on that sound.'

'I like to call it my opportunity clock. Less of a negative connotation.'

I chuckle, surprising myself. I didn't think a chuckle of any sort was physically possible before seven.

'Could I encourage you to jump at the first opportunity when it arises in the future, rather than miss four of them?'

'I snooze six times. We have two left. I like to think not all opportunities are for me. Everything happens for a reason and all that.'

'But you're awake to watch the first opportunity pass you by?'

'Habit. Here we go. Number five already.'

I pray for a rainless day today so I can move back out to the tent, far from the alarm.

'Okay, that was number six. Now I can get up.' She has somehow managed to get dressed underneath the duvet, don't ask me how, but when she appears it's in a pair of denim shorts and a long-sleeved white shirt. She pushes the button on her phone and shows me the screen.

'Look. Off.'

'I can see why you live alone.'

I watch her walk to the kitchen tap and take her retainer out, drink a full glass of water and put her hair into a ponytail, and I think that maybe everything will turn out okay. I will try to make the most of my time here with a woman who talks in floral metaphors and misses five *opportunities* every morning. But seizes the sixth one.

I go to pack up the soaking-wet tent.

Sophia
Älvsjö

THE NEXT MORNING, knowing I'm waking up in a new place and that I have to find a new town square, I've set my opportunity clock half an hour earlier and swiftly put my T-shirt and shorts on underneath the duvet before I hop out. I can see Blade struggle as he stirs and get up ten minutes after me. He's still on the sofa. In the cabin. As much as I like gloomy skies and rain which have followed us to this new forest, I find myself wishing for sunshine so that the tent set-up will be reinstated.

'Deal is a deal,' I explain when he's still in the sofa bed as I emerge from the bathroom. 'I need a lift.'

'Heard you the first time.'

I pull up a message I just received from my brother Mattias and show the screen to Blade.

'Look, cute pet rabbit. Recovering well from neutering. If that doesn't cheer you up this morning, I don't know what will.'

'That is very cute.' He pauses and turns to the kitchen with a hopeful look on his face. 'Wait, is there coffee? Or am I hallucinating?'

'There is indeed coffee. I don't drink it so I couldn't taste-test it, but I hope it doesn't poison you.' I added two levelled spoons like I've seen him do. It smells like it usually does and looks like it usually does. But then lots of things that look and smell good turn out to be anything but. Like white oleander, *Nerium,* which is sweet with pink and white petals yet has deadly toxins racing through every part of the flower.

'The mug is clean.' I push it towards the coffee machine.

Blade looks at me long and steady, his eyes stuck on mine. I think his eyes haven't quite woken up yet, so I blink to help them on their way.

'I'd like to find some sheep,' I say.

'Sheep?' Blade looks at me as if I've just landed from a far-away planet and asked him for the impossible.

'Yes, I'd like to sleep better, but my imagination isn't as good as others. I can't just create pictures in my head. I have to actively put them there, base them on real life.'

'I guess that can be . . . arranged?' he says, bemused.

'Great. After work. Sheep field trip. Bring something to eat. For the sheep.'

THIS LOCATION IS smaller, on the outskirts of what is more like a village than a town. I step across the not-yet-trampled grass and look for places where I can work some magic. Vincent will be here this afternoon, and it all has to be ready by midday.

By the time I've finished, cleaned up and shown Vincent around, I'm starving and desperate for a bathroom break. There's already a short queue formed at the public restrooms; the beer tent opened at eleven thirty, and already bladders are bursting. I study the back of the person in front of me as I wait. Flannel shirt over jeans, my height or slightly shorter, brown hair cut close to the skin. As if he can feel my gaze he turns around, then gestures to the queue asking without words if I want to go before him, but I'm caught off guard. *I know him.* Unease fills me and I walk in front of him, my head turned down. *He doesn't remember.* My palms start sweating. What do you say to someone who made your life hell year after year? I want to hide, make sure he doesn't recognise me at all costs. He was at my brother's birthday party four years ago. I hadn't known they were still close. He brought me a drink and told me I needed to loosen up. Then he looked me over and said *It's true what they say, the ugliest girls become the hottest women. The cute ones reach their peak too soon. Don't mind tall girls because everyone's the same height lying down, you know? We never quite made up did we, Sophia? I'd love to end things on a good note this time.*

I'm grateful for the escape the toilet cubicle provides, and if it weren't for the fact that Portaloos have on average 3.2 million bacteria per unit, I'd stay here until I knew the coast was clear. As it stands, I choose to exit with caution, disappearing quickly behind the row of Portaloos.

> ME: Why do people say that they saw a ghost from the past? When it's actually a living, breathing, full colour version of your past stepping right into your present.
>
> LINA: Who?
>
> ME: Someone who told me I'd do everyone a favour if I killed myself when I was ten.
>
> LINA: Jesus!
>
> ME: No, not Jesus.
>
> LINA: Yeah, I know.
>
> ME: What do I do?
>
> LINA: Is he still there?
>
> ME: Currently in a Portaloo four metres away.
>
> LINA: Fight or flight.

I stand to the side and wait for him to appear from the plastic box, pulling down his shirt and spitting to the side of the road. I wonder what it would feel like to be him. To be so unbothered by his childhood that he doesn't even recognise a girl he made afraid to walk down the street. Who as an adult is choosing to hide behind a public toilet because she is terrified to confront him.

I walk to the parking to wait for Blade. Then it hits me: why I would recognise the bully anywhere, why I've been obsessed with memorising faces at night-time. Because the first face that ever haunted me was his.

And I've tried to replace it ever since.

Edith
London

IT'S ONE OF those soft, blurry evenings where I can't remember much of the day, but I keep thinking of eggs and how they can go to waste and rot if you forget about them. How you have to hold onto a good egg when you see one. There's no one downstairs when I make my way there. I hear Zara's voice in the garden, but I don't want to bother her. I don't need her to worry. Again. I'm hungry and not sure when I last ate. I look at the dishes by the sink, but it's empty and offers no clues. Zara uses the dishwasher, whereas Blade does the washing up by hand. There is a salad bowl in the fridge with my name on it, but when I open the cupboard to find the vinaigrette I instead find the pasta and rice shelf. I haven't cooked for a long time, and something stirs inside me. *An egg.* I can do this. Somehow I know that eggs have a cooking time of four minutes, and that's about as much as I am brave enough to attempt.

I find a pot, decide against boiling the water in the kettle in case of injury and instead fill it from the tap. It's heavy in my hands, and I hesitate at the hob, not knowing which burner to use. My hands seem to have some sort of muscle memory, and I stretch to the right. Then I set the alarm. The iPad is upstairs, and I know that if I leave the kitchen now I'll forget. So the egg clock will need to do. I also set my phone. *Six minutes.* Then I leave the room and sit in the lounge. Zara sees me from the glass door and gives me a wave. When my phone beeps I don't remember why, but when I hear the egg clock I do. I know there is another step, but I can't figure it out, so I find a large spoon with little holes and scoop the egg into a bowl. I find the salt and pepper. As I sit at the kitchen table and eat this I think: *I cooked this! I did it!* A sense of achievement I haven't felt in a long time fills me. I eat every last piece of the white and yellow egg until my stomach signals fullness.

'Edith.' Zara comes in the kitchen. 'Did you . . . I didn't prepare dinner yet?. Did you cook this?'

I nod proudly. I am—what is the right word?—*happy.*

'Well done. But remember—any time you need me, I'm here.'

'Oh, I do know.'

I take my friend's hand then and squeeze it hard, hard, hard.

I AM JUST about to retire to my bedroom when there's a knock at the door. Zara is there first, but I follow after her, the sound of the knock so unfamiliar and out of place that I have to take a look to ensure it's not an auditory hallucination. The woman on our doorstep has long black hair and balances a baby on her hip. They both smile at me as if on cue. The mum apologetically.

'Sorry to bother you, I know it's late and all, but I was wondering . . . would you have any flour?' She clarifies: 'Bake sale. For the summer fair. Except I haven't baked anything because the leaflet got lost, and there's a class app, but you need a bloody password and I can't remember mine. What

I mean to say is that I need to bake something by tomorrow morning.' I notice the older child behind her now. Short black hair and a superhero figurine in his hands.

'I've been told there are one-hour deliveries these days,' I say. 'That there is no need for neighbours and favours.'

'Oh, right. Sorry to have bothered you . . .'

'No, no, wait here. I'll be back.' I hesitate in the kitchen, not sure where I keep my flour, but Zara grabs it as if she's lived here all her life and pushes it firmly into my arms. Two packs.

At the door I hand it to the woman and receive a shower of thank yous. They fall on me like golden confetti.

'You don't happen to need any tape?' I ask her.

'Not today,' she says. 'But I know where to find you if I do.' And she is genuine.

The following afternoon there is a silver foiled box of cakes waiting for me on my doorstep with a note saying *From your neighbour, Pushba.*

Blade
Norrlösa

I'M ONTO SVEN number three, having discounted the Sven whose funeral I attended and Sophia's uncle. The first thing I see when I arrive at the Norrlösa retirement home is the row of neatly parked mobility scooters. I'm shown into a communal living room where I nod to two ladies on a sofa. The smell of coffee and wool is comforting. I try to imagine my mum in a similar room, her address book in hand, organising and planning for things that may or may not happen. There would be a book circle, surely. And some sort of residents' association to get involved with. I haven't dared look into places yet, but maybe Zara is right, maybe just the fact that I came here will be enough for her, and we can start to think about our options when I'm back.

The man I'm here to meet isn't Sven, I already know that, but I'm hoping he can give me some clues. This is a man who was listed at the same address as the Sven I've singled out as the most likely match. Born the right year, lived in the town Mum remembers Sven being from. I couldn't find any photos of him online, but I'm hoping his friend might have one.

'Good afternoon,' Thomas greets me, reaching out a hand.

'Would you prefer to sit here or in my apartment?' he asks,

and I choose the latter. The apartment is a small, neat studio, and I pick the only armchair there is leaving him the sofa.

'So you're related to Sven?'

'It's a complicated story. I'm trying to find him on behalf of my mother who's lost contact. She would very much like to know what happened to him. Her name is Edith.' A flicker of recognition passes through his face.

'And she was English?'

'Did you know her?'

'I knew he met someone. This would have been years ago. But our contact was sporadic at that point.'

'How come?'

'We didn't exactly fall out with one another, but I kept my distance. There were rumours going around, and I'm not one to listen to them. I'd say I know a good person when I see one, but in the end I had a baby and a wife and wanted no involvement with those types of crowds.'

'Those types of crowds?'

'The types that are up to no good, you know, who run kebab shops and laundrettes as a front for the real business, if you know what I mean?'

No, I don't know what he means. I'm pretty sure the launderette at the end of Mum's road really does wash the sheets I give them once a month. I shake my head slowly. I'm struggling to make out what this new information means and how it fits with my mum and the love of her life.

'Do you have a picture of him?'

Thomas shakes his head. 'I only brought the essentials here. The rest is in stored in my daughter's garage. Although, he wasn't one for the camera, Sven. Handsome enough, but just not interested in the attention. I'll ask Julia, that's my daughter, to have a look for you, but don't get your hopes up.'

I thank him and move on to the question that's bothering me.

'Do you know where he went after London? Have you seen him at all recently?'

'I have no idea. He did give me a ring once and said he was moving back home, could we perhaps have a coffee when he was back in Malmö, that sort of thing. Then I never heard from him again. I'd always assumed he moved over there. To London. I tried a Facebook search some time ago, but the name didn't come up.'

'So the last time you heard from him was . . . ?' I search for the year in my memory, but somehow I know the answer already. And something shifts inside me because suddenly another person, his best friend at the time, tells me that Sven went missing, never to be heard from again, summer 1996. For the first time I realise that my mum could be right. Sven was supposed to meet her, they had it all arranged, and then he really went missing. Thomas's answer sends shivers down my spine.

'I think it was, what, 1996, springtime?'

Sven went to London and never came home again. Or went quiet when he did.

I feel the unease of the question genuinely nagging at me: *If this is the right Sven, then where did he go?*

SOPHIA SITS OUTSIDE the RV, with a mug in her hand and a fidget spinner on her lap.

'You finished early.'

'We should try fishing,' she replies. She sometimes does this. Doesn't say hello or hi and goes straight into whatever was on her mind.

'Fishing? As in worm on a string, standing for hours by a waterfront?'

'You've never fished?'

'It feels like something a dad should do with you. Like learning to ride a bike.'

'You don't know how to ride a bike?'

'I know how to ride a bike, Soph.'

'I used to love fishing because you get to hang out, sit side by side with someone and look out over the water. No talking. Parallel play at its best. Sometimes my brother would take me.'

'Not any longer?'

'We're adults now.'

'You don't have to stop hanging out because you grow up. I wouldn't if I had siblings.'

'My siblings are not very hangoutable.'

'Mattias seems all right when you talk about him.'

'He is the exception to the rule.' She fiddles with a small stick. Seems there's always something in her hands. 'But even he still needs to be paid half a million for his share of the shop.'

Wait, what?

'But you're family! He didn't seem like he needed money. What are your other brothers doing?'

'One is a teacher, and one works for the fire station, handling the incoming calls. They are both fine. But it's the principle of the thing, isn't it? There are four of us, so my uncle couldn't just give the shop to only me. He loved us all, really, didn't want to play favourites. So it belongs to all of us and they've no real interest in keeping it, would rather have the money. My uncle's will put a time cap on it—five years, and we could then either sell it or in order to keep it I'd have to buy the three of them out. I've only one year left and even if I stopped going for the organic oats I still won't be able to come up with that kind of money.'

'Maybe not, but surely they can see what it means to you? How can they ask you to give it up?'

She shrugs and drops the small stick back onto the ground.

'I think they just assumed I would run it into the ground. Have a go of it then sell once it hit the fan and cash out. Go back to school. They never expected me to still be going five years in.'

'You took it over when you were twenty-one? That's incredible.'

'It was the best option. I mean it. I loved the shop, and my uncle, a lot. He was easy for me to talk to, and he understood, he slowed down for me. And I understood flowers. Besides, school was never a good fit for me. I liked the school part, not so much the other kids. I'd have to hold my bladder all day because the minute I'd make my way to a bathroom, people would crowd in and climb on the door and look and laugh at me. Hard to want to keep going with school when that's the reality of it.'

'Where were the teachers?' Who can blame her for wanting to leave school, when you're that bullied?

'My uncle used to say *When there's a will, there's a way*. He was referring to growing orchids in shady conditions but the boys in school were successfully applying it to torment me.'

I clear my throat, which feels strangely clogged.

'Tell me more about your uncle.' I've finally managed to ask the question, but find I haven't done it for the reason I thought I would. I don't see how he could be my mum's Sven, but he seemed to have been a good man, a good uncle to Sophia. And all I want it some sort of proof that she was okay.

Blade
Jönköping

TWO DAYS HAVE passed since we arrived in Jönköping, and we've both grown fond of this spot. It features a narrow leaf-covered path down to the smallest lake I've ever seen. Once you wade past the algae the water is clear and cool. I've just gotten back from a run and I go over my schedule as I stretch too briefly. Today I'm meeting Sven number four, who lives a two-hour drive away. For those keeping score at home: number one was happily married for fifty years, number two never left the country and number three went missing in 1996. Only two more Svens to go, and I'm feeling less than hopeful.

I'm just about to open the cabin and start the coffee machine when Sophia comes around the corner, water dripping from her black fitted swimsuit. Which stops me in my tracks. I stand with the door open, a foot on the step.

'You're letting mosquitos in,' she says, using her two hands to squeeze water out of her hair. I follow the drops as they travel vertically across her skin. I almost turn around because I feel I shouldn't be looking then remember that I'm an adult, and she's wearing a swimsuit. Appropriate clothing for a lake swim.

'Hey,' I manage.

'You should get in. 'You never regret a green vegetable, a pension fund or a freshwater swim' is what my dad always says.'

'I'd like to disagree, as someone who's once attempted a triathlon in February and who is allergic to avocado.'

'Just get in. I'll go grab you a towel.'

'Good idea.' I can't stop following her body's contours, and I think she's right, I do desperately need a bucket, or a whole lake, of cold water over my head right about now. But above all, I have lost all power to say anything other than yes to this girl. I take my shirt off and throw it on the big rock where we hang our clothes to dry, that faces the afternoon sun. With her present, I feel suddenly and oddly self-conscious.

'Are you coming with me?' I ask, and she is looking at me intently, like she wants to say something.

'I just went for one, didn't I? I'll make the coffee.'

Right.

'Catch,' she says as she throws me a towel which I miss and have to bend down and pick up off the ground.

'Enjoy.'

I trod off towards the lake, eyes firmly on the path ahead, looking out for fast adders or a forest snail in front of my feet, fighting the urge to look back the whole way.

Edith
London

I WAKE UP with a funny feeling in my stomach, and at first I'm not sure why. Lying in bed, I go over the possibilities, ranging from food poisoning to nerves, when it hits me. Today is my birthday. I don't particularly care for birthdays anymore. I'm older now and the day usually brings nothing other than a roast lunch in a pub and a book voucher from Waterstones. Both very nice things but not deserving of the butterflies in the stomach. It's a feeling I won't be able to shake, I fear. A feeling cultivated by my parents over the years, one of excitement and anticipation that this was, indeed, *special*.

That is why I never treated Blade in this way. I downplayed it to feel like every other day. *I guess it's your birthday today*, I would say when he was as young as four. *It so happens that this is the day you were born on.* Then we would go to the park and have waffles with chocolate sauce and pick something from the toy shop. A day for specialness, not necessarily a special day.

When he got older I started throwing his birthday party on a different date. I didn't want my son to spend his entire life waking up every February 2 with butterflies in his stomach, just to be greeted with a simple roast lunch. Priming opens up the potential for hurt. Set expectations can lead to disappointment. Waiting for someone inherently means they might not come.

I LOOK AROUND for my phone, knowing that it should be next to my bed, but somehow I'm not able to see it today. I have trouble looking for things. I can't visualise the item I'm missing so I can't see what it is I'm trying to find. In that moment the phone I'm looking for could be any model or colour on the entire global phone market. It's disappeared. But I can see Sven. I would recognise him anywhere. I think that today is a very important day to spend at Hornton Street, so I decide to get ready as soon as I can. Once I finally find my phone I reply to Blade.

Call me when you want. Have a great day, Mum, he has written.
We'll see, I respond.

WHEN I MAKE it downstairs I have those flitting thoughts travelling through me, the ones I don't dwell on because I know instinctively that they'll confuse me and require too much energy to figure out what they mean. Zara is in the kitchen with a cup of coffee in her hand.

'How do I look?' Zara is wearing all black.

'I only see your head. It's like it's floating around freely.' It's the truth. Some days, people are reduced to floating busts and today is like that. The brain is so complex I don't even try to understand the science of it. Blade's Google search says it's normal and so I accept it. Zara laughs.

'That sounds quite liberating, existing only as a head. As long as my face looks all right?' She's beautiful, of course; all young people are they just don't realise it. *I look fat, I hate my hair colour, my lips are too thin*, they say. Then they age, look back at the photos and see how stunning they were when it's too late to enjoy it.

'Your face looks lovely,' I offer quickly but sincerely. 'Now, today is my birthday and I'd very much like to go out if you need to do some work?'

'I know—happy birthday! I can absolutely do some work. At least in the library I don't need to buy a beverage every hour to justify my space there. Much better for my finances. Let's go.'

On the bus, on the way to the library, I'm trying to think. About who I am, now that I'm sixty-five. We define ourselves by the things we like when we're younger mostly. *Oh, I love dancing.* Then when we get older we define ourselves by the things we don't like. *I can't stand reality TV.* Then there's me who exists in some in-between land. Perhaps this definition of me will be different altogether?

At midday we arrive at the town hall, and I find myself a seat at the bus stop, for once knowing that Sven won't come around the corner.

Nothing special ever happens on a birthday.

AT THE END of the afternoon Eliza meets me at the corner of Campden Hill Road with a small paper box.

'For you,' she says.

Inside is a small cupcake with white icing, high and pointy like a pale Christmas tree.

'I got one for me as well,' she says and sits down next to me. I nod gratefully, not having to explain that I'm unsure where to start. I imitate Eliza as she gently lets thumb and index finger dive into the box and whisk the cake up without touching the icing. I resist the urge to lick the white cream and instead bite into it from one side. The sugary taste is intense and overpowering.

'Hey there.' Zara turns the corner and spots us.

'Zara, meet my friend Eliza.' I'm proud to manage the name without a cup.

The girls look at each other, their eyes diverting a little bit too soon. *Oh!* I know that look. It's the look of someone who'd very much like to keep looking but doesn't want to make a fool of herself.

'Nice to finally meet you. I'd have gotten you a cupcake if I'd known you were coming. Edith says you are always very busy.'

'Well, yes. Busy saving the world of flat-pack-buying consumers from assembly-related mental illness and nervous breakdowns. That's me.'

Eliza laughs. 'I'm busy saving millionaires from having to squeeze the nursery into the walk-in closet because there's no second bedroom.'

They both smile. I think how if Eliza came up tonight on the phone Zara and I keep browsing perhaps she'd say, 'What do you think, Edith?' and I'd take a close look and say, 'Yes, do you know what? She looks quite all right.' And perhaps Zara would have swiped, and they'd have matched.

'Right, have to get back to it, then,' Eliza says, her cupcake half-eaten in the box. Perhaps Zara's pink hair is too distracting for her.

'I'll come collect Edith earlier tomorrow as well. To go to the bus,' Zara says. 'I'm sure the flat-pack consumers would understand it if I were to sit down for twenty minutes to have a cupcake.'

Eliza laughs again. 'The millionaires of Kensington would

not understand if I sat down twenty minutes with a cupcake but I'll bloody well do it anyway.'

Eliza trots off, not looking over her shoulder, not once. I pat Zara on the shoulder.

'Look what you can find while waiting for the bus.'

Blade
Lidhult

YESTERDAY I FINISHED another fruitless meeting at a care home in Mjölby. This Sven—number four—had never been to London but told me all about his time in East Germany as an oboe player following the fall of the Wall. I left with the link to his self-published memoir, which had it had some better publicity would have saved me this visit. Five days left and all I have is question marks and one remaining Sven to track down. I asked Sophia again whether her uncle could have maybe done some—any—travelling, and she, again, said no. Mum still hasn't found a photo, but then, what would I do with it if I had it? Put it on Facebook with an appeal for help? I don't want to disappoint her, to see what disappointment does to a fragile brain, but it's starting to look inevitable.

I have found a café with enough space inside so no one should mind if I sit there for half a day. I try the oddest-looking Swedish cake I can find: a green marzipan-covered log with dark chocolate dipped ends called a hoover. I spent the morning catching up on everything back home. Bills and a phone consultation with Mum's neurologist. The doctor told me again to make a list of options in the event her decline starts to speed up, so that I have it on hand as a safety net, a coping strategy for us, even if we are a long way away from needing it. Can't help thinking he's doing the tea/coffee choice thing I do with Mum. Attempting to give me a sense of control where there isn't any.

At midday I get a message from Sophia asking what time I'll be back that evening because she's had a good day and feels able to eat a proper meal rather than cereal. My spirits lift instantly. It can't be denied any longer. I'm seriously, and ridiculously, attracted to the girl I'm currently travelling through Sweden in a mobile home with.

We left the van parked this morning so I'm taking an almost-empty bus back. I call Zara because when you're in the woods (literally) you can't see the trees.

'I need you to come up with a plan B because plan A is not working.'

'No luck with the Svens?'

'None whatsoever. So far they were all either missing, happily married, or never left Sweden. Nothing matches up with what my mum's said.' I wonder if Zara can hear the desperation in my voice.

'Well, there's one more on your list, right? So not all hope is lost.'

'Maybe not, but hope is dwindling at a somewhat rapid pace.'

'I'm sorry, Blade.'

'I know, me too.' I pause for a minute, not sure where to go from here. 'How's Mum though? Everything going okay?'

'Oh yeah, all's well here—we get along swimmingly, much to no one's surprise. But she could do with a bit of good news from you. Anything positive to share?'

'I mean aside from striking out on the Sven front, Sweden is beautiful, all the driving has been fine, and admittedly it's been a bit of a lifesaver having this RV to drive around. Not just for me but Sophia too, she—'

'Oh, the fellow traveller! Yes, how's it going with her?'

'What do you mean? We're just driving around Sweden together. She's off working every day.'

'Oh, come on, Blade. You've been all over the scenic countryside with someone who by all accounts sounds kind, smart, funny and not bad-looking. What do you mean you're "just driving around"?'

'Well, I mean, yes, she's all those things.' And more. 'But this is work for her, remember? Not like she's here entirely by choice.'

'Uh-huh, sure.' Her sarcasm is practically dripping through the phone.

'Seriously. And I need to stay focused on Sven. Not some cute passenger.'

'So she is cute—I knew it!'

I try and eye-roll loud enough that she can hear. 'There's no point, Zara. I'll be back in London in a few days anyway, back to Mum, and she'll be back in her flower shop. Besides, I can't get involved with anyone.'

'Why?'

'You know why.'

'No, actually.' Zara takes on her usual stubborn tone of voice. 'I know that the last time you dated—'

'I was almost engaged.'

'Yes. I recall it with regret. Maybe things didn't go well . . .'

I shake my head at this understatement of epic proportions.

'And I know you feel you are a son above all else, and we all commend you for it, the way you prioritise and sacrifice. But that doesn't mean you can't ever date again. There's still plenty of life left.'

But that's the thing. People don't get it—I'd choose Mum

over everything, every time. I tried to mix, to have a life alongside caring for her, but it just doesn't work. *Have you ever been left behind?* I want to ask Zara. *Have you made space in your very complicated life just to lose it all? Do you know how it feels? Because it doesn't sound like you do.* And I don't want to feel that again.

'You're just scared to be in that position again. To have to choose your mum over a girl. So you figured out how to maintain your emotional boundaries. But there's a world in which that's not a choice you'll have to make.'

I know that she's right. But I am scared. Because what if I'm only human, what if I do have to make that choice again and I pick wrong? What happens if I don't put Mum first because I love someone else more?

Zara's voice brings me back.

'She's fine now, but she has been having more hallucinations. She's had me crawling on all fours checking under furniture for a dead rat.'

'Not again.'

'I tried Febreze, but the odours they promise to tackle in the ads apparently don't include imaginary dead rodents.'

'Make her leave the room and come back in—that sometimes helps.'

'Have done. Then the rat just moves rooms. It's like she has to live it until it's over, no way to break it. The only thing that helps her relax is if I actively look for the rat.'

'What if I'm just living another of her hallucinations right now? I've played along, but when will this episode involving Sweden and Sven end? What if it's all in her mind? She doesn't even have a picture, no return letters, no phone number.'

'I'm not telling you this to cast doubt on this mission or to worry you, Blade. I'm telling you because you need to prepare yourself, no matter what happens in Sweden. Even if you find Sven, she's going to continue to get worse and at some point it'll be too much, for both of you. Look into options for her care.' I think back to my call with the neurologist and realise that Zara is the second person who's told me this today.

I get off the bus and start walking along the road. I take my time getting back, kicking at rocks and sticks along the way like a child. The sense of failure hangs over me. I gave up everything to care for her, and I can't even manage it any longer.

Edith
London

I'VE GONE SHOPPING with Zara. It all started when a lady about my own age began chatting to me outside the town hall last week.

'Are you properly equipped for the winter?' she asked me. She has been bringing me cappuccinos with chocolate powder on top for some time now and we have apparently progressed to conversational friendship. I promised Zara not to take coffees from strangers and I haven't: this woman I have known for months.

Now I look at her and think her question over carefully. I had thought we were still in summer and the mention of winter confuses me.

'Not yet.' Winter clothes are kept in large boxes in the attic, that much I know.

'I'll see what I can find. I work in an Oxfam shop, and if you come in we should be able to figure something out.'

'I usually buy my coats from John Lewis,' I reply.

'Oh?' she says, and I do agree that John Lewis does sound quite posh but at the same time I'm standing in the borough of Kensington and Chelsea, and they do have their own range which isn't that much more than M&S at all.

'Well then, if you're all set for clothing, can I at least keep bringing you coffees?'

'Yes, please. Being a John Lewis customer doesn't mean you don't like coffee,' I say.

THIS THING ABOUT winter nags me and nags me and I can't shake it. I remember waiting for Sven in winter and how I wore a navy blue coat but was still freezing.

'Zara, I need a coat,' I tell her that evening when she's picked me up from the Hornton Street bus bench like a waiting nursery child. I noticed how she looked around hoping to spot Eliza, but to no avail.

'There's a heatwave next week.' She smiles and pours orange tomato soup from the plastic container into my yellow bowl.

'Still, I'd very much like to be ready for winter.'

She gives me a look as if to say, 'Right, if you say so. No further questions.' This is one of Zara's best character traits—her no-questions approach.

'I'll take you. I need some bits and bobs myself. Also, I might have a date tomorrow tonight. With that estate agent.'

WE DRIVE TO a shopping centre, and if it weren't for the bright lights hurting my head I'd quite enjoy it.

There is an escalator that takes us from the ground floor to the first floor. We get on, and I find I can't see the individual steps; they melt into each other like ice cream flavours. I stop and pause. The marble floor below us looks like a swimming pool full of waves, no edges or boundaries. A deep black hole leading who knows where. I feel nauseous and grip onto the handrail. Tone and contrast, everything that holds life together is blurry to me. How am I supposed to know what's real? Blade put a purple pillowcase over the mounted flat-screen in my bedroom so it wouldn't look like a black hole in the wall, but sometimes I take it off and just stare into the hole which feels like space and think what if they're all wrong and I'm right and it really *is* a hole I'm seeing? How do we really know what is real and who is right?

We decide on Next because it feels like a good place to go when you're unsure of what to do next.

When we get off the moving stairs and make it inside the shop, Zara immediately starts grabbing and touching things.

'There's only one colour.' I eye the black padded jacket she's holding up for me. Lots of straight lines and dull material. 'Paying for one colour seems a waste when I can have many for the same price.'

'Right—colours. A better value for the money. No problem.' Zara does a quick stroll around the shop floor whilst I stand there, the bright lights overhead burning my skin. I wrap my scarf around my shoulders trying to block out the sensation.

'Look at this!' Zara yells. 'I've counted five colours, and although I would say the addition of purple would really lift it to the next level, I reckon it's good value for money and that we should get it. What do you think?'

I look at the garment which has an Aztec pattern in orange and red tones with green, black and white added in. It looks a bit like a rug, but I'd be able to find it on the hooks by the door. No risk of it blending into a black hole.

'Excellent,' I say. When I get to the till I ask, 'Can I wear it now, please?' I walk through the shop feeling very prepared for winter indeed, and the feeling lasts the drive and all the way home. When Zara unlocks the front door I squeeze her free hand.

'Thank you. Thank you for preparing me for winter.'

Sophia
Jönköping

I HAVE BEEN sleeping better since our sheep-spotting outing. I filled my camera roll with forty-eight images of sheep. We first found a field just outside town with white, fluffy sheep but realised we couldn't get close enough, so we made another attempt at a city farm where two sheep lived with a goat and a donkey and I could spend a considerable amount of time petting them all and taking the pictures I needed. It worked, and I'm a genius.

I know I have to visit my parents, and I *want* to visit my parents but it's like booking a hair appointment—it's lovely once it's done and you feel all new and glossy and refreshed, and don't have to think about it for another three months. But calling to book it gets put off for weeks. I decide to get it done.

ME: How about I come over tomorrow evening?
MUM: Can't wait.

Mum starts listing the food courses she'll be making, and I know I'll be having a bowl of cereal before we leave, as there's nothing on the menu I can eat.

I WAS SURPRISED when Blade asked if he could come with me and even more surprised when I heard a voice that sounded a lot like mine saying 'yes'.

'Are you a fan of strained silences interrupted by the occasional "Pass the salt" or "You're a disappointment we'll never recover from, even if we reach the ripe age of one hundred"?'

'It can't be that bad.'

I just shrug. It *is* that bad.

'Remember that there'll be three courses, and the fork on the left is for the first dish, then you work your way in.'

'Soph, I've been to a dinner party before.'

'And you need to take your shoes off because Mum cannot stand the idea of dirt in the house.'

'It's going to be fine.'

NOW ON OUR way with no time to come up with a last-minute excuse, I wonder what I was thinking. Out of the corner of my eye, I see the intersection that signals my parents' street.

'Next right,' I instruct Blade, not taking my eyes off him.

'There' I say and point. 'The house on the left. With the dark green front door.'

We park on the empty, lifeless street outside my childhood home and an automatic light flickers on along the walkway through the front garden when we step onto it.

I give Blade one more glance. He looks . . . good. Some part of me feels proud that someone like him would come with me. Even if it's not technically a date, he is here *with* me. He has finally dropped the beanie, and his soft-looking curls are delivering perfect, flowy movement and volume. They're begging me to run my fingers through them. As a stim, of course. A sensory stim, because hair like that would feel *very* good on my fingers. No other reason.

I wipe my feet four times, then step back another time and wipe them again. *No mud. No dirt. No germs.* Blade wipes them once. And then I ring the bell.

My mother opens the door, as is the standard. My father will have been shooed off the sofa twenty minutes ago and chased off for a shower and a change of clothes. I can see the familiar scene in front of me. *Twenty minutes! TV off! Seriously, Harald? Yes, yes, it is only your lastborn child but a dinner table is a dinner table. Ten minutes! Where is the remote? There—off.*

We take our shoes off by the door and place sock-clad feet on the shiny, newly washed wooden floor.

My mum is an herb, perhaps the ever so popular *Ocimum basilicum*—basil. It has plenty of complex flavours and spends a lot of time in the kitchen. The herb can also make a ball of dough or even some cheese look fancy. She wears a wrap dress and her short blonde hair looks like she's just had her roots done.

'Hello, darling.'

The table is already laid out, and I count four places meaning none of my brothers are here. I imagine the fast excuses they would have delivered when asked to join for a midweek dinner with Sophia. There is a carafe of water and a bread basket in the middle. The whole house smells of deep cedarwood candle this time. I wish Mum would stick to one scent and not keep changing them.

Mum reappears and presses a glass of Prosecco in my hand then turns to Blade.

'Sophia's co-worker. We've heard so much about you.' I cringe. Actually, so much for *so much*. If I remember correctly I have mentioned Blade in two fleeting group chat contributions and one phone call. And it hits me. I didn't tell them he's my co-worker. Is it that unlikely that I'd turn up with an actual *date*? A man who might be interested in me romantically? Not even my own mother thinks it's possible for me to find love, so what hope is there? I mean, fine, I've brought a man home. Or even a boy when I was younger. But still. I feel the heat climb my cheeks and look at the floor.

'Thank you for having me. I'm Blade.' He produces a bottle of something red from a plastic carrier bag, which I hadn't noticed before. 'And actually, I came here *with* Sophia. I'm here with Sophia.' He sounds almost as awkward as I do but I know what he's trying to say. *Thank you. Oh God. Thank you!* I need to chip in. Mum looks at us both.

'Yes, we came here together, Blade and I.' I wave my hand between us. 'He drove us here in his, well, in Sixt's vehicle.' I see Blade's eyes light up with amusement, which, unfortunately, I take as an encouragement to continue my monologue. 'I still have my car, and my driver's licence is not in need of renewal until next year, but the car is a very big car and it makes me nervous, so in the end it was a great thing that Blade drove us here.'

'I see,' Mum says. 'Sophia, you look very nice tonight. Did you put makeup on?'

I simply nod.

I PUSH THE food around my plate mindlessly. Somehow food always tastes less appealing when I need to use multiple utensils and a napkin properly and more delicious when it's eaten in private with hands or just the one fork.

'I keep saying that Sophia needs some time off. She's always working,' my dad says in his strong Swedish accent.

'I like work. It's relaxing and enjoyable. Job descriptions are clear and easy to carry out.'

'We're going on a cruise to the Med in July, just organised the upgrade to a balcony suite. You should take a holiday sometime, Sophia,' Mum says.

'I don't enjoy travelling,' I say. They know this. Travelling is not a break, to me. It's an extra workload of packing and unpacking and writing lists of what you might otherwise forget. It's getting used to a new place and not sleeping well the first night. Then when you're just about used to it, it's time to leave. I'm about to interject that my uncle didn't like travelling either, and then I remember that apparently that's not true. He did travel, at least once. The reassurance I've always felt that he was *like me*—that there is *someone* that I'm like—is somehow rocked by the discovery that he lived abroad. Maybe I'm not like anyone, after all.

'The weather will be perfect in July. Hot but a change from here.' Blade says, continuing the holiday talk. I can't help but smile.

'Have you been there?'

'Well, no, this is my first holiday in quite a while,' he says and my parents don't quite know what to say. A whole dinner in English is too much for them to handle, and they go back to offering sauce and wine.

I sit quietly, because whilst we're on the topic of work and holidays, I could also say that I've been working every hour possible for the past five years to prove I can run the business. That if I lose my business I won't know who I am any longer. I am happy to exist as the Sophia who owns a flower shop, but if I'm just *Sophia,* I'm simply one of the other 100,752 women in Sweden with that first name. For the second time this evening it's as if Blade has read my mind. Or, rather, my feelings.

'But speaking of work, Sophia seems really good at what she's doing. The business seems to be thriving. This whole trip has been really successful so far, and Vincent seems to be really pleased with her work. But I imagine it's not easy for her, not knowing the future of the shop.'

My mum carefully finishes chewing before replying.

'My brother was very proud of his shop and wanted to make sure that it would be properly taken care of and run successfully, which is quite understandable. Especially given Sophia's . . . *challenges*.'

I shrink. I attempt to eat a potato because otherwise I will simply confirm to the whole table that I do have *challenges*. But no, look at me, at least I'm not challenged by eating this potato here, even if it did touch the sauce. I swallow it with great difficulty, the traces of sauce tickling and burning my throat as it descends.

'Well, she's excelling. She's been running a business for four years now, and not just making it work but making it work successfully, from what I can see. I couldn't run a business for a year if you asked me to. I can't imagine wanting to end the beautiful thing your daughter has created.'

Dad coughs. Then looks at Mum.

'Could you pass me the salt, please?'

WHILE WE WAIT for dessert I walk around the room pressing my index finger into the flower pots along the windowsills, checking the moistness.

'Sophia.' I jump. 'We do water our plants.' How can I explain again that I don't doubt it, I *have* to press my fingers into the soft soil? Mum goes on. 'We've discussed this and you know how I detest this type of controlling, ritual behaviour. What would your old therapist Karin say?'

Karin. If asked who I wouldn't want to meet in a dark alleyway my answer would have to be Karin, closely followed by the Portaloo bully.

'I do it to Lina's plants also. She doesn't mind.'

My dad and Blade appear behind us, trying to break up the tension by showing family pictures on the mantelpiece.

'That's Sophia there, crying over Santa.' He laughs.

'I was scared of Santa too. Didn't really have a father figure so a man barging into the house with gifts was a bit of a terrifying concept to me,' Blade says.

'Every single Christmas, Sophia would ask if Santa was coming. Not because she wanted presents but so she could hide well ahead of time!'

I think Blade can see the agony on my face, and I imagine he must be wondering how this photo has made it onto the mantelpiece in this home where there ought to be moments of joy instead. He clears his throat.

'My mum used to tell me not to worry, that he was a human just like her. Mum used to say it unsettled her at first, how I was scared of something other children loved, wondering if I'd be brave enough for the world. But then she figured all I needed was to find out the truth and I'd be okay.'

Two sets of eyes stare at him, not sure how to respond.

'So what do you *do*, Blade?' Dad says.

'I'm a full-time carer. To my mum.' I wish he would have said journalist. Now there'll be questions at best and harassment at worst.

'I read about the carers' strike here in Sweden. Paid less than cleaners, aren't they, carers?'

'It doesn't make you rich, no. Carers could do with more support.' Blade doesn't seem to mind the questions. He has that deep confidence that lets all comments bounce off.

'We all have a choice, don't we? I didn't receive any help,

left with no grades and yet within ten years I'd made my first million. Hard work and determination is all it takes.' My mum nods and smiles, but I can't help to think that its half-hearted, lacking the usual flair and flavour. Quite like a basil leaf that's slightly dark and wilted and less fragrant. The ones you need to put in some cold water to refresh.

'That's great to hear.' I thank Blade in my mind for not adding what I know he thinks: *Not everyone has those opportunities. Not everyone has the ability, and not everyone has that privilege.* He lets it slide. Mainly because his eyes are fixed on a family picture. One of the few we have with my uncle. It was taken on Midsummer. I'm wearing a crown of *Alchimella, Nigella,* evening primroses and spray roses. *If you add roses to your crown, you'll find love,* my uncle said. Blade moves closer and studies our faces. Closely.

'That's my uncle,' I say. 'And those are my brothers. Hampus, Pontus and Mattias.'

We're alone in the formal reception room, my parents having retreated to the kitchen, waiting for my mum to serve us coffee and place a box of chocolates on the table so that she can remark when I take three instead of just one. *I guess you do have a few odd years until your thirties when your metabolism slows down and sugar becomes your greatest enemy! Ha!*

I turn to Blade and say quietly,

'I wish you would have met all my brothers. They're loud and ruthless but can also be wonderful. Especially Mattias. When I feel down he sends me pictures of animals he's met at the clinic.' My brothers' presence has a way of taking the focus off me, which is welcome in some situations where I prefer to remain small.

'If you need to . . . well . . . just take hold of my hand, you can squeeze it.'

I should point out that his hand is not an instant-release

anti-anxiety medication but when my Mum comes round the corner saying in a high-pitched voice, 'Who would like a chocolate?' I think that the hand may well do the trick, so I simply nod at him.

And when we leave, after he's asked me if I'm ready to go, and all I've managed in reply is a silent nod, and the door closes behind us, and I hear Mum and Dad's voices immediately starting to discuss us, I do reach out in the dark and find the hand.

LATER THAT NIGHT Blade opens a beer and hands it to me.

'How did you know I needed that?' I ask.

'There are some things a glass of milk just can't take the edge off.'

I reach for it. He adds, 'It's alcohol-free.'

'Thanks. Actually I'm starving. Do you still have that snack bag?' I didn't eat much. It's hard to eat when I need to balance a napkin on my lap.

Blade comes back with goodies and I immediately begin stuffing my face with salty crisps. I think how easy it is for me to eat in front of Blade.

'You're different, around your parents,' he says. 'You stop all the little things that you normally do. Like twirling your hair or rubbing your index finger over your thumb nail. You even have a different posture, like, like—'

'Like an Arabian horse.'

'Not what I was looking for but, yes, maybe. They're elegant right?'

'I always felt like a strongly built pony.'

He laughs.

'I can see that it's complicated,' he says, and I shift on my log, finding a better position.

'It's very simple, actually. They just want me to act normal, when I clearly can't. There. Simple issue. With no solution.'

People think problems are hard to solve, but there are ways to shuffle around, dig into it, find your way around it.

'My family is just my mum and me, and neither of us is very normal. But we just are.'

My family and I never just are. We sit and ask polite questions about each other's jobs. We talk, in that everyone is constantly saying please and thank you. We never had pets growing up: dogs shed too much and cats go to the bathroom *inside*. We got a fish who died after a year. I wanted to bury him, but in the end he got flushed down the toilet and I cried. *It's only a fish, Sophia,* Dad said. So then I thought perhaps it was better if I didn't ask for another pet.

'Your body loosened up, though, and the usual things you do, you started doing them once we arrived back here, in the woods.'

How is it that he knows all my quirks? And then I think about how I must be comfortable enough to do them in front of someone I've known for about two minutes but I'm not comfortable doing them in my family home. Then I think that maybe I better finish my unmasking book. I mean, *of course* I mask. It's survival instinct. People have been accused of being witches for less than my behaviours.

I shift my body weight on the rock I'm currently using as a seat.

'I had a sort of therapy called ABA, applied behaviour analysis, when I was younger. It's based on changing *unwanted* behaviours. I'm only learning now that maybe it was toxic. What if the behaviours didn't need to change? Or couldn't because they're part of who you are? How about accommodating differences instead of extinguishing them?' Every time I hear the word *therapy* I go cold. I would never set my foot in a therapist's office again. They're forever associated with Karin and her dark bob. 'Do you want to hear something I read?' I squeeze my fist so hard it starts pulsating like a heart. 'With ABA, half of Autistic children become indistinguishable from their neurotypical peers. That's the goal. Making sure we don't stand out.'

'How does it work?' Blade asks.

'I had to learn all sort of things. Mainly to appear normal. Stimming—like when I flap my hand against my thigh, that appears pointless to most people, so my hands were held in place. But to us it's not pointless. It calms us down. If I can't do it, I feel as if I'm about to drown in anxiety. And eye contact? It had to last for five seconds or I wouldn't get my reward. I was trained like you would a dog.'

'That seems pretty artificial. The last time I had more than five seconds of eye contact was when I proposed.' I sit up. Straight. I reckon I just spontaneously did four seconds of intense eye contact. Possibly more.

'You proposed to someone?'

'A year ago.'

'What did she say?'

'*No.*'

'No?' I can't imagine anyone saying no to Blade. In fact, I don't think I've managed it once in the short time I've known him. I wanted to say no when he stopped at the side of the road—but couldn't. I want to say no every time he wears that silly beanie which doesn't cover his ears—and I can't.

'It was definitely a *no*. A *maybe* if I'd upgrade the ring and try again in a year. I crossed path with her a few times since. Now there's no eye contact. We both look at the ground if we run into each other.'

'But . . . why?' I'm supposedly bad at understanding people's motivations, and this is the first time I agree. Because, *why?*

'She said she wouldn't just be marrying me, it would be like marrying me *and* my mum. Basically I came as a two-for-one package, and the main product wasn't enough to entice her to buy it. Can't blame her. A carer isn't exactly the most attractive profession you can list on a dating app. Caring, yes—carer, no.'

'Do you miss her?'

'Not any longer. Not her. Does it frustrate me that there doesn't seem to be a woman my age who could enjoy staying in with an old lady every day of the week? Who doesn't need me to always be more, do more and have more to be worthy of them.? Yeah, I guess. I don't think I've ever been enough to anyone, not even Mum.'

'How can you do more? You are here because of your mum, because this is important to her. You carry, shop and prepare for *me* every waking minute. I don't see how you could possibly do more.'

'I like doing those things for you.'

'I think you're the first person who does.'

There's a comfortable pause. I'm trying to think of what to say next when Blade continues.

'There is nothing wrong with you, Sophia. I don't know if anyone's ever said that to you. Nothing wrong at all. You were left in a freezing car because those meant to look after you didn't get it. Didn't get *you*. Maybe they thought they were helping you, but it seems to me that everyone who tried to help you and protect you did more damage than good. But it was never your fault. None of it.'

Tears start rolling down my face at his words. I always knew my heart was broken, but didn't realise someone else might be able to see it too.

I think about all the so-called 'problems' I have. The emotions that seem to come at me with such force I can't contain them inside my body, that I have to flap my hand for them to begin to subside. I think about all the things my parents wanted to be different about me. All the things they didn't like, that didn't fit into their image of what I should be like.

I think of sitting next to Karin. I would have liked to stay on my feet, walk around the room the way I can in the shop when I talk to a customer, because the movement helps me focus. One time, I was bending forward, looking intently in her eyes, and began telling her of the origins of cherry blossom trees. My uncle had sent me a postcard with one on the front, and I kept it in my coat pocket. Karin turned her whole body away from me. Dramatically, as if she'd seen something indecent. I was trying to connect, but she didn't want to talk about flowers. So I stopped. Then I reached out my hand and sat with it mid-air, like I'd been taught, like she wanted me to do. She finally took it into a firm, quenching grip. *Good morning, Sophia. Good girl. That's how we greet each other.* By the time it happened, my hand had begun shaking.

My tears have stopped. Like an automatic irrigation system that's completed its next cycle.

I speak quietly. 'What do you think people should do when they're in my position?' I always knew that Autistic women are three times as likely to experience domestic abuse. I just never thought it would come from my own family. Or if that is even the correct word for it. But I decide that having a word, even the wrong one, is better than having nothing. This is the first time anyone has called my experience *something*, and it's like it suddenly exists as a solid shape rather than blurred around the edges. I will hold on to these words for it until I figure out what to really call it.

'I think they have a choice. You can do whatever you feel you need to do to heal.'

'But I love my family.'

'You can love your family and still be angry with them. You

can love them and still wish they had treated you better. Loving someone doesn't mean they don't have to take responsibility for what they did. But you need to do what *you* want.'

'I am angry, when I think about it.'

'So you tell them that and let them step up. What you need is important. If you give them another chance to be what you need them to be they, should consider themselves the luckiest people in the world.'

I nod.

'Thank you.'

Blade turns away from me, tilts his head upwards to drain the last of the beer.

'Let's pack up. We're moving locations tomorrow, remember.'

Zara
London

ZARA HAS NO time to think about what she looks like or prepare anything much because Edith is following her around the house. She has started doing that increasingly, like an attention-seeking pet. She moves to the sink—Edith follows. She goes across the room to the fridge—Edith is behind her. She even stalks Zara to the bathroom. Zara takes her time now, wondering if she'll still be outside when she emerges. She opens the door and yep, she's there. She starts talking immediately.

'I think I might have been a bad mother.'

'Oh.'

Zara realises this is a sitting-down conversation and so she closes the bathroom door and ushers Edith into the living room and gestures to her to sit down.

'You are a wonderful mother,' she says.

'Blade is scared of me.'

'He's scared *for* you. That's very different.'

'Is it? The fear is the same. Of, for, they're irrelevant here. I've made my child full of fear. I've always asked too much of him.'

'Lots of people our age are scared. It's a generational thing.'

'Some days all I remember are the bad days. When I raised my voice at him. Or missed a school play. When I let him watch TV for a full day so I could have some peace. That's all there is in my brain.'

'Everyone has those bad days.'

'But they have the good moments too. Mine start to disappear, to fragment and blur around the edges, then move out of reach. I'm left with my mistakes and flaws.'

Zara tries to imagine for a moment being only her flaws, being the time she lost her shit and yelled at her sister or when she didn't quite tell a friend the truth and never owned up because she got away with it.

'I came out of the shower and all the good memories had gone. It's empty,' Edith clarifies.

Zara glances at the time, realising lost memories will take more than the fifteen minutes she has. *Screw it.* You stick up for your girlfriends—and Edith needs her.

'So we make new memories. Right now.' Edith's brows pull together, confused.

Zara gets her phone and feels a pang of guilt but then picks herself up. She messages Eliza, her beautiful date who is kind enough to bring cupcakes to her friend and who she thinks—hopes—will understand.

> Can I make a last minute change to our date venue? Elm's Terrace. There's wine and me and Edith. Turns out I can't leave her after all. Emergency memory-making needed. Sorry x

AS SOON AS Eliza is inside the little terraced house Zara is able to relax and abolish the nerves that had inconveniently built up. She doesn't check herself in the mirror frantically or wonder if her laugh sounds rather loud and off-putting. She has given her date the task of choosing a game from the shelf in the far corner of the living room, whilst she prepares a plate of snacks, and Eliza goes for a simple pack of Uno.

'I used to think it was all about a man, a man called Uno, that perhaps it was the inventor's name,' Eliza admits. 'Now I know it means *one* in Italian.'

They attempt a round, soon realising there is no way around Edith showing her cards, and instead spread them out on the table in front of her, letting her pick with them on full display. It's a bit like playing with a child, Zara thinks and ponders how wisdom and naivety can live in the same body to such degree. Humans are just a mix of emotions and thoughts and it's a wonder anyone is all right at all, thinking about it.

'I am in awe of you for looking after Edith, even if it's just temporary,' Eliza says as Zara fills Edith's wine into a colourful cup, to just the right level for it to not spill when it's drunk.

They let her win, Edith. Then they put the game away and before they have to think of something to talk about, Edith has picked a topic.

'One day I didn't leave bed at all. Today you'd just call it a duvet day and argue that kids need it, but in my day there was no iPad and no excuse for a mum who couldn't face the world.'

'We do need duvet days, Edith,' Eliza offers.

'Let's find some pictures of good days.' Zara gets up from the sofa and Eliza's eyes follow her. The photo album is thick and brown, and the leather has peeled off in patches. Zara opens a page at random. Edith and Blade on a beach.

'Remember this?'

'I look like a good mum there.'

'You are a good mum.'

'I don't know if I can trust pictures. There's this one photo I don't know what to make of.'

'Which one?' Eliza asks.

'I'm not sure where it's gone. I'll show you if I find it,' Edith says.

Zara has moved on, flicking the pages, looking for the most joyous moments.

'Someone's birthday party,' she says, showing them what looks like a dinner party in this house. Oversized nineties shirts and plastic earrings.

'Do you go to many parties?' Zara asks gently.

'You mean like this one? I've been known to host the odd tea party, yes.' Eliza smiles at her.

Oh Zara is in *luck*. A woman who thinks a party means tea and that everyone deserves good memories.

IT'S ONLY TEN o'clock but Zara knows Edith by now. She's calmed enough to not have that anxious empty stare, grounded by pictures and images she recognises. She wouldn't follow Zara around any longer, but she's still not in charge of her memories and only sleep can restore them.

'I'll take Edith up to bed,' she tells Eliza.

Eliza starts assembling her belongings into a pile and drains the contents of her glass in order to bring it to the kitchen. Zara quickly stops her.

'Will you not stay for a while? Finish the bottle of wine?'

The wine glass swiftly returns to the table, and Eliza's hands let go of the phone and sweater she was about to put in her bag.

'Of course. Would love to.'

'Right, I'll only be a minute or two. Make sure she's all

tucked up and happy. Then I'll be right down again. I feel like there are still some memories to be made tonight,' Zara says.

UPSTAIRS, AFTER WATCHING Edith brush her teeth and get changed and before going downstairs to the living room where a very sweet, very spell-binding estate agent waits for her, Zara hovers, hoping Edith will collect her memories whilst she sleeps. Every last one.

'Edith,' she whispers into the dark. 'Remember—it's just your memories that are gone. Blade still has them all. The good memories. And I'm sure you made enough of those.'

Blade
Tenhult

WE'RE BOTH RELIEVED not to have dinner plans the next evening and to be able to retreat to our camp site. Sophia so that she can reset from her visit to her parents and me so I can come to terms with what I now know and have been waiting to dig into: Sophia's uncle's name was Sven. He went to London in 1996. My mum had his address. I know what this might mean.

I step out of the camper to call my mum quickly. Carefully thinking over what I want to say, need to ask, without getting anyone's hopes up.

We're doing twice daily calls now, on recommendation from the neurologist, to keep me a constant in her life even when I'm not physically there. Consistency will be key in helping her stay in the present, going forward. Especially if—when—she moves into a care facility. I am sitting on one of the two large logs that Sophia has dragged over, and we're having a gourmet meal of hotdogs with bread and potato salad later. I have the phone held out in front of me as video calls are better for her. Zara holds the phone up for Mum and I see only her chin and nostrils.

'Would you like water or milk with dinner?' Sophia asks as she walks past. Mum misses nothing.

'Was that a female voice?'

'Yes. I've been sharing the ride with a friend, kind of.'

'Please do tell. I'd very much like to know the *kind of* friend it is.'

I sigh. I don't even know what this is myself.

'How about I write and explain it in a message? We're about to eat.'

'But how's it going, Blade? Have you found him yet? Do you know what happened to Sven?'

I pause, thinking through my choice of words carefully. 'I don't know if I've found your Sven yet, Mum. I'm working on it still, have at least one more possible option to track down. And then . . . then I'll let you know. What I've found.'

I can tell she's frustrated with my progress, or what seems like a lack thereof, but she doesn't know just how close I *might* be. If Sven number five isn't our guy, that increases the odds that maybe—just maybe—Sophia's uncle could be. Sure, it sounds like he only travelled to London, no idea if he ever lived there. For all I know it was a short business trip and he saw little more than the airport. But I'm dangerously close to feeling a sense of hope. That I could actually find Sven, that I could make my mum happy, that she might go willingly to a care home where she'll be looked after and treated well and I won't have to spend all of my time worrying, constantly, about what could happen to her. But hope is no guarantee.

When we end the call I ignore Mum's request for more information, on both my search and the female voice she heard. Sophia interrupts my train of thought.

'So your mum, you said she goes to this bus stop everyday and just sits?'

'She's not exactly just sitting,' I reply. 'She's waiting for someone. Unfortunately it's someone who will mostly likely never come.'

'Maybe she's a *Paeonia*. They live long lives and resent transplanting so are best left alone,' Sophia suggests.

'That sounds about right.'

'I'd love to have a Paeonia in my life. They're wonderful flowers.'

'Are they hard to look after? I keep wishing I'd had a sibling—someone to share it all with.'

'I hardly ever see mine. And the only thing we share is trauma.'

'Still. Siblings are the only ones who know your roots, that completely understand where you are coming from. You can't share the full memory of your childhood with anyone other than a sibling.'

Not having any siblings mean it's all on you: you end up being solely responsible for a parent's loneliness or happiness. You're the difference between their declining or thriving. We all know having a baby means being responsible for a tiny human life, but no one tells us that when the circle repeats itself with an ageing parent we get something much more complex. Instead of a newborn blank page, we have a fully formed human being with an illness, a temper, a history and a lover called Sven.

'I guess all families are complicated, and we just have to do our best to simplify them,' Sophia says. She uses a thin stick to push earth and moss around on the ground. I wonder if I've ever seen her hands still.

'But I'd like to think most people at least start a family out of love,' I say. As someone who has yet to start a family, and who never got to see his mother find that kind of love, this thought is even more calming to me.

'You're a romantic, Blade!' She may be right. I probably am.

I realise then that I've placed my hand at the back of Sophia's log. I'm not touching her, but it's there, in a protective gesture which I wonder if she notices and can feel. She continues to move the stick along the ground.

'I think I would like your mum and your life. It sounds quiet, and nice,' she says.

But she doesn't know the reality of it. That she would actually fit into it is too good to believe.

'It's very different from your posh life,' I say, removing my arm from behind her back.

'Posh? In what universe do I have a posh life? Have you even been to Svedala? It's not exactly the Italian Riviera, and the last time I checked Blom's Blooms didn't have a royal seal of approval.'

'You run your own business. You don't even look at the prices when you shop, just chuck stuff in the basket. Your parents have a cold press juicer and an Italian coffee machine. You have cashmere throws and wear Prada T-shirts. We come from different backgrounds, that's all. I'm not judging you.'

'Except you are. Listen, these T-shirts my mum orders for me online because they don't scratch me. You know the little tag at the back of the neck? Feels like a bloody noose around my neck. And I can't even cut it off because then there is still a small annoying bit that practically cuts my skin, or so my brain tells me. These shirts enable me to think and work without being distracted, and yes, I'm privileged that I have parents who can afford them. But just because they do, that doesn't erase the years of ABA therapy they put me through. Doesn't change the fact that they've always wanted and still want me to be different. My parents may own nice things, I may own some nice things, but that doesn't necessarily make it all easy.'

'I know. I'm sorry.'

She's too worked up to even hear my sorry.

'And most of those nice things I never asked for and never needed. But I had to be grateful, and I was reprimanded when I didn't like them. 'Oh, this expensive doll Daddy bought and you haven't even taken it out of the pack.' No one asked me what I wanted. Which would have been Legos and chapter books.'

'Sophia, I'm not saying you had it easy. I know that you didn't. I'm just saying we have different lives, different lifestyles.'

'Well, of course we do, everybody does. But we all have to learn to live with them. We have to learn how to make ourselves happy, how to accept what people give you even if it's not what you wanted. You open the doll and stroke her hair and sit strategically for a while where your parents can see you. You learn to make the best of the life you have.'

I can see that she's close to tears again.

'And then . . .' She attempts to speak through what is now very loud, very snotty cries. 'Then you . . .'

I reach my hands out in a question, and she nods. I pull her close and hold her. She sobs but then it turns into a different, calm cry.

'Then what happens Sophia? You were saying?'

'Then you grow up and find you don't know how to be, how to have a life you actually want, if you're not doing what other people want you to do.'

Sophia
Tenhult

YESTERDAY WAS SIXTEEN hours ago but I can still feel his arms around me. I might have cried for a minute longer than needed just for them to stay there. I've been toying with what to say all day—in between dealing with a stall holder who claims to be allergic to flowers and is insisting I move any arrangements out of his vicinity—and have come up blank.

I decide to take the bus back after work rather than wait for Blade, and when I arrive I sit outside in silence. It feels empty without the van but our recently constructed outside living area is enough. I prop myself up against a large log with my sweater as back padding and settle in with my laptop. I go over the delivery note of what needs to be sent up from Svedala in the next delivery, and then my thoughts drift to the dinner with my parents and the picture of Santa and how Blade had said something like it was the most natural thing in the world. I suddenly get this urge to say something too. To explain to Mum and Dad that I'm not the only one who feels like their body is an anxious mess and who wakes up having had nightmares of an old ABA-therapist and their reinforcements. There is a whole online community who feels the same way, and perhaps if Mum and Dad won't listen to me,

Sophia, who doesn't score high on IQ tests and who doesn't have refined culinary or literary tastes, then perhaps they'd listen to what @Autistic_ProfNed posts when he isn't lecturing at Harvard. I find the quotes that speak for me the most and paste them into an email.

SUBJECT: Professor Ned's thoughts on ABA

Then I feel like I deserve a voice too even if I have no title or any of the things my parents render important, and perhaps in the shadow of Ned I can have one—perhaps he is the preface that I need.

I compose a second email, this time only containing Sophia's thoughts on ABA.

TO: Mum
SUBJECT: Why I keep my distance

Mum, there are things I have to say, things I want you to know. The reason I moved away is because I was never allowed to be who I wanted to. I moved so I could survive. Only Mattias let me be who I am. You got my brothers to pinch me when I stimmed. I know you did what Karin asked, and maybe it's all down to one bad therapist, but it still happened. Wasn't there some instinct that said that this was wrong? I moved away and muted the bloody group chat because being around you exhausts me. Being around people I love exhausts me. Do you understand how that feels? Even now when your name pops up as a notification on screen I feel like I hear your voice shouting at me.

I never liked the things you all like. Travelling, new places all the time, new restaurants with new food and breakfast buffets with every different pastry you could want but no porridge or Rice Krispies. I just wished and waited for the day I would grow up. When I'd be able to start a life where I'd be happy. When I could be who I was.

Sophia Ven
Blom's Blooms
Stora byvägen 28
347 44 Svedala
www.blomsblooms.com

I'm surprised when I get an almost immediate reply. I don't even have time to close the laptop before it pings. The Basilicum must be alone in the kitchen today.

FROM: Mum
SUBJECT: Re: Why I keep my distance
My girl, I'm sorry you feel like this. I wish you would talk to me. Emails are for work, paperless invitations and mailing lists. Will you talk to me?

I think about different methods of communications, non-verbal people, and how they're all valid and we all have a choice. That *I* have a choice.

FROM: Sophia
SUBJECT: Re: Why I keep my distance
I too am sorry I feel like this. I can't talk because I don't find the words easily. This is how I find the words, so please just read them.

Best,
S

THE NEXT MORNING I wake up early, before the opportunity clock.

'What are your plans today?' I ask after my morning swim. The water feels even warmer than in Eksjö and I stayed there until I couldn't possibly stay any longer. I can't believe we lucked out and found another spot with a lake. *A hundred lakes with you,* Blade had said. But we're running out of time.

I have the morning off since the market is finished in this town, and I'm determined to do something with it.

'Research. Do you need help with anything?' He gives me the impression that he'd drop said research, drop anything, should I need help.

'I have some errands to run, some things I'd like to see in town. Perhaps you want to join me?'

'Sure, I'll come.'

I ENTER THE address in the sat-nav and Blade drives.

'So we're going on a fun day out?' Blade asks.

'Yes, pretty much.'

When we arrive he looks at me doubtfully.

'We're going to a garden centre? On your one day off?' Blade says.

'You are hanging out with a florist. This is my idea of fun. Window shopping.'

'Should have known it wouldn't be laser tag or the movies, shouldn't I?'

We walk down the aisles, and after I pick up what I need we browse plants. I mumble to myself as I walk.

'Have you memorised the names?' Blade asks.

'Almost all of them, yes. I'd read the botanical encyclopaedia when I was a child. Kind of became a little party trick. My parents would ask me to name a flower in Latin, and I delivered every time. They were very proud of me in those moments.' I made the most of my entertainer role, revelling in the pride of my parents when I made their friends laugh or exclaim *Amazing!*

'What about this one?' He touches the leaves of a majestic green plant.

'*Hydrangea Mmacrophylla*,' I say instantly.

He stops at another.

'This?'

'*Rhododendron camtschaticum*. This is an interesting one. It started out as one plant but was reclassified in the 1990s, because it was deemed to belong to a distinct genus.' I look at Blade, never missing a botanical teaching moment for eager ears. 'It happens sometimes. DNA research may find it belongs to a different family than initially found, or Latin language rules may change. So a flower can become something else. This one over here had its name changed from *Rhododendron camtschaticum* to *Therorhodion camtschaticum*.'

'It had its name changed in the 1990s?'

'Yes. Like I said, it's not uncommon, although it's a struggle for plant-lovers to keep up with. *Botanical Monthly* do include it in their news section but not everyone is a subscriber.'

I can see Blade thinking, like a cartoon character he does that thing where he puts his hand to his chin and stares into space.

'You may just have helped me an enormous amount, Sophia,' he says finally. 'Do you mind if we head back home?'

Blade
Jönköping

FLOWERS CAN START *out as one type of plant and then be reclassified. Name change in the nineties.*
    I sit with these thoughts all afternoon. The animal sounds don't bother me any longer. Sure, I still wouldn't want a bat crashing into me, but I've definitely hardened these past weeks. I'm also less anxious.
    Am I jumping to conclusions? What grounds do I even have? A gut feeling from a comment about flowers. *Seriously.* But I can't help wondering, could Mum's Sven have changed his name? Is that why I'm finding nothing on this last guy I've been trying to track down? Who keeps records of name changes in Sweden? Google Translate and a search on Swedish search engines tells me where I need to apply to view records. *Am I seriously contemplating applying for records of every name change involving the name Sven?* All this rather than look closer at Sophia's uncle. Because it's clear now. I have only two options left: it's either Sophia's uncle or one of the Svens changed his name.
    This is it. I've cracked it. *I must have.* Sven must have changed his name. Which means he's still out there somewhere.

I NEED TO speak to Sophia, properly, discuss everything there is to know about her uncle and at the same time share my mum's story. I'm putting it off. If I've really found Sven, it means my trip has come to an end, and I only have days left to talk to her about what I have no choice but to label *feeling*s. In the end I can't blurt it out however hard I try, but I manage to get the message across that the evening will involve her, me and a location that isn't the camp site.

'I was wondering if you'd like to go somewhere tonight?'

'Clarification, please.'

'Similar to the way I went to the garden centre with you, I'm hoping you'll join me. In town.'

I JUMP AROUND the camper-van and open the door for her. Her long legs descend. I've started opening the door for her because it takes her a while just to gather her things and get out of the vehicle. I'm waiting for her with the door open like a valet car-park employee. Can't believe Sophia has agreed to go out with me. Sort of.

'It's just a short walk from here.'

'You don't have to,' she says, and I give her a curious look.

'Have to what?'

'Take me out.'

'I know I don't have to. Tell me if this doesn't beat the garden centre. Or the sheep spotting,' I say.

'I did come out of there with a new pelargonium, didn't I?' she says.

'I'm not sure pelargoniums are the right tell for whether or not a date is successful.' Then I kick myself. Mentally. Obviously. Mentally kick myself because since when is this a date? Since when was last time a date? Luckily she doesn't seem to notice.

'Here we are.' I stop in front of an American-style up-market diner which I found after extensive googling.

'You're taking me for breakfast?' she asks, delight on her face.

'All-day breakfast. I called to confirm they can do a porridge, and it's no problem as long as the order is put in before kitchen closes at ten.'

Instead we order omelettes and pancakes with Nutella and powdered sugar. She eats like I've never seen her eat before.

'Go ahead. It's got your name on it,' I nudge at the last pancake.

'No it doesn't.'

I drizzle the letter S across it in melted chocolate.

'Now it does,' I say.

She eats it.

'So. I can eat with you around. I can sleep with you around. I'm starting to think maybe you have my name on you as well.'

This may not be a date. But if it were, it would be the best date of my life.

'What are you thinking about?' Her sweet voice cuts through the heavy silence. I don't know if I can be honest now. Or maybe just not yet.

'Just questioning every choice I've ever made.'

'Same.'

I glance at her.

'Really?'

'Currently questioning why I put this strapless dress on when the straps feel like iron wires on my skin.'

'Why did you put it on?'

'I wanted to look nice.'

From her forehead to her chest, Sophia's skin goes pink. It always makes me think of strawberry milk it she does this. She looks down at the dress. It's dark green, tight around the waist then flares out into a skater skirt ending just above her knees.

I literally was speechless when she came from the back cabin to the cockpit, climbing over the basket of dirty laundry with a few swift moves.

'It looks amazing on you,' I admit. I clear my throat.

Get your shit together, Blade. You still have questions for her.

'Shall we go?' I wish I could stay here forever, watching her, but close to ten is apparently when the waitstaff start to hover around your table and the till machine in a small town like this.

'You ask for the bill, and I'll go ahead and calculate the split.' She is already bringing up the phone calculator.

'Sophia, I'm paying for this.'

'No, no. Disposable-income split is fair, Lina and I do it all the time—although we make similar amounts, so it's easy maths—and it's only acceptable to let slip when signalling romantic interest, when you ask someone out with the intention of romance, meaning in a date situation—' She stops and stares at me. I can literally see the realisation forming in her brain: *Oh.*

Sophia
Jönköping

THERE MUST BE something with the lighting, because Blade looks *very attractive* from where I'm standing, which is at the top of the stairs about to follow him outside. His arms are definitely bigger and more defined, and he's clean-shaven and wearing, dare I say it, a very flattering navy blue cardigan over a polo shirt. I don't even mind the silly beanie that rests on top of his head. I'm too busy being mesmerised by the shadows the streetlights cast on his face. His hair is tinted almost blue in the dark.

'What?' he asks as I stumble out of the establishment and onto the pavement as if it's a late night bar and not an all-day-breakfast joint.

'What what?'

'You're staring.'

'Oh. Right.' I should avert my gaze, but I like looking at him. I *very* much like looking at him.

He walks back towards me, and we stop right underneath a streetlight.

'Just . . . look at us. How far we've come. I mean both literally and figuratively. I'm not counting down the days we have left of this torturous trip any longer because well, it's stopped being torturous somewhere along the road. And tonight? It finally feels like we're friends, like we almost *like* each other,' I say.

His hand brushes against mine, and I can't talk when that happens. I have to stop and breathe. And think.

'Sophia, I *do* like you. Very much.'

Oh? *Oh.*

I continue to stare at Blade—and realise just how much I like him. This once annoying, frustrating, lost man who crashed a funeral has turned into so much more this past week. I can see him as the thoughtful, caring, kind person, his mum must know him to be. And his best friend. And now me.

I take a step forward, closing the gap between us. My skin is hot and sticky, and I know his must be too, but I don't back up.

Blade veers slightly away, and I'm expecting him to break this silence, or to move away from me, but then I see he's only shifting his footing. I look around me for a second, to the empty street and the silent clouds moving above us then back to Blade. His attention has remained fixed on my face. I shiver with a cocktail of fear and want, feeling my lips tingle. The moment stretches out and then he's leaning in, diverting slightly to the left so I know he's not going to kiss me. I keep still, keeping us in this strange limbo, feeling his lips so close to mine. I'm being a coward.

'Sophia.' I can feel his breath on my neck, and I lean towards it because it's so warm and comforting.

I pull back slightly because I have to. 'I need to tell you something,' I start. Why is this so hard suddenly? I've said this same sentence to boys many times before, yet suddenly I wish I didn't have to, that I could say it then laugh it off as a bad joke the minute I'd done it. I don't want to be the Sophia that can't kiss, I want to be the Sophia that could kiss a man like Blade.

'Tell me what's going on inside your head. You can trust me.' He lifts his hand and cups my face in his palm.

I want to trust him. I want to talk to him without it feeling like jumping off a cliff. It petrifies me. I lean my face into his hand. That's all I allow myself. Then I say it.

'I don't kiss.' My chest tugs as if I've ripped off a Band-Aid. There, all in the open and on display for him to see.

'Okay. Can you explain? Explain so I understand.' He didn't laugh or tell me I'm strange or, worse, just lean in and prove how very wrong I am, and that he, a man, knows my body and what it wants better than I, its owner, does. He always explains things so I *get* them, and now he's asking me to clarify the same way, without making assumptions.

'Mouths have bacteria. And they scare me. Mouths. I know that sounds crazy, and I know that I am in fact, most likely, to some degree, crazy. But I can't seem to get past it. The germs.' Memories of wiping my feet at the doormat, using hand gel in the car after a shopping centre visit. *Don't touch the side railings, Sophia.* But I had to touch the side railings, didn't Mum understand? Because if I didn't my arms would flap. And my reward would be taken away. *Germs.* My only option was to become so scared of germs that that fear trumped my urge to touch the railings. I scared myself out of meeting my body's needs. Even if I know why I'm so deep in it now, I may never be able to change it. And now I'm scared that this man won't want me. But could he? *Could he?*

'What do I do, then? If I can't kiss you.' The last bit comes out as a croak rather than speech and I look at his mouth. It's funny how I like looking at it so much when I don't actually want it . . . Have I done this with other mouths? Presumably I've seen lot of nice-looking mouths before and yet I can't remember eyeing them up.

'Well.' I attempt to come up with some sort of plan. Ideas. Turns out I have plenty. But my cautious brain is reprimanding me. *Danger, danger, detain her!* I guess I *could* run my fingers over his collarbones, which have just a slight hint of a tan. I could breathe warm air onto his neck and nuzzle my nose against his jawline. Then I could press up against him and feel my breath fade away. There are many options that don't involve saliva, and I can't stop my mind from exploring them.

'That's okay, I understand.'

He understands?

'Here's my idea, then. There are other places I could kiss you, Sophia.' *Other places.*

'We could try that.'

He leans in and brushes his lips over my shoulder. Very softly. Impossibly lightly.

'Close your eyes, Sophia,' he requests. My eyelids fall immediately shut. Eyes closed, I feel him close to me like a warm blanket. I'm anticipating his next move like I've never anticipated anything. I could stop this torture and *thing* which will obviously end badly just by opening my eyes, or by reaching out my hand and pushing him away.

I do neither.

His lips finally brush the skin right beneath my ear. And then there's another pass of his lips over the same patch of skin.

'You can tell me if you need a break or if you'd like me to stop.'

Talk? I'm supposed to be able to *talk?* I manage a shake of my head. His fingers trickle down my throat and I feel myself parting my lips ever so slightly then closing them, pressing my lips together. No. *No lips.*

'Blade,' I whisper. 'Not my lips.' His fingers halt, lifting off my skin right above my collarbone. I feel the loss of his touch immediately.

'Not the lips,' he whispers back. 'You can trust me.'

'Okay.' I urge the shock out of my expression.

Blade kissed me. On my shoulder. And my neck.

In fact, he's still doing it.

'Blade,' I hiss. I think I should try to be feminine. I hear my mum's voice in my head: *Especially with your stature, Sophia.*

It's good. This is what people do. They kiss each other. On multiple body parts. Like shoulders.

'Let's go.'

'Do you feel fit to drive?' He is, of course, but I'm not fit to be a passenger. To sit next to him and have my hands on my lap, looking out of the window as if this didn't just happen.

'We could stay here, but there's no lake and our morning view will be of—' he stops for a minute and turns to look '—a balloon shop and a bakery.'

'Bakeries are good. They make breakfast.'

'They do.'

We somehow make the steps between the pavement and the RV cabin. I switch on the lights and then I'm back in his arms again as if nothing happened.

'Close your eyes,' he instructs again.

I do.

But my mind can't quiet. My eyelids must have fluttered with doubt.

'No. Don't open them. Not yet.'

I don't.

'You could have this all the time, Sophia. Think about it.'

'It's not possible.'

'Is this not enough?' Blade presses into me now, with his whole body, hips against mine. As If trying to make a point.

Enough? This would be more than I've ever had, more than I could ever have imagined for myself. Even just being touched once the way he touched me would be enough. My fear is that it's not enough for *him*.

There's another kiss on my temple. When his lips reach my eyelids they are featherlight and I feel like I'm about to cry.

Then it all stops. Because I'm actually weeping. Still with eyes closed I stand there, in a camper-van, my arms pulled tight around me, and I weep.

'Open your eyes. Please.'

I do then. I see houses and a sky that's dark grey through the windows and Blade's eyes looking back at me. My tears don't make him uncomfortable. Men hate tears. They tell you it's silly and that it's a manipulative technique. Then they raise their voices and shout because they can't stand them and will stop at nothing to quiet the noise that is female sadness. But not Blade. He rocks back and forth then scoops all of me up into his lap, and I can't remember the last time I've been held like this, probably sometime in childhood before I shot up on the weight-and-height curve and my outstretched arms were met by my parents with a *You'll break my back, Sophia. Use your two good legs.*

'Let's get you to bed,' he says and I let him walk me there. He swiftly gets the bed down and folds the duvet to the side. I sit down on the side of it, too tired to move. I'd like to blame it on two rare alcoholic beverages, but it could very possibly be the way this man seems to tug at my emotions like no one else. I would be terrified if it weren't for the fact that everything has felt lighter, more manageable and less my fault since we started this journey. That's not something a cocktail can do.

'I can't take my shoes off,' I say. He bends down and undoes my sandals, fiddling with the small leather straps and metal clasp.

'Here. Get in.'

'I can't,' I mumble.

He looks at me confused.

'I have to take this off. I need to sleep naked.' He looks at me then down to the now strapless green dress when he realises what I'm asking him.

'Sophia, I'll undress you. Then tuck you into bed—which is all I'm going to be doing tonight—but how do you think I'll get a wink of sleep?' He laughs softly, a sweet sound.

'I promise I will turn off the opportunity clock tomorrow morning. One night only.'

He pulls back and looks down at me on the bed. He slowly reaches for the top of my dress and pulls it down so gently the sensation is like being stroked. By satin. I shiver. When the fabric reaches my hips, he looks me in the eyes for the first time.

'Stand up.' I do what I'm told, and the dress slips off my hips and onto the floor in a messy pile. My underwear is simple cotton briefs and a bandeau top.

'Now get into bed.'

I lie down on my side and pull the duvet all the way up to my chin, just how I like it, even in summer.

'Good night, Sophia,' he says before walking off. I hear the clink of a water glass being put down on the shelf next to my bed. In case I wake up thirsty.

An Almost-Retired Storage Facility Manager
Malmö

THE RENT-A-SAFE MANAGER will miss this routine when he retires. What new routines will he have when he no longer opens the facility up with the keypad at eight every morning? When he doesn't make his coffee in the small staff room at nine, inspecting the shared fridge and bin carefully to identify any offences: un-labelled personal food items, expired food, glass in the food-waste bin. And when he won't take his Tupperware out of said fridge at precisely twelve fifteen and place it on the glass plate of the white microwave, which has been there almost as long as he has.

His wife seems to have a lot of routines. None of which he is part of. Cleaning the kitchen on Mondays, the bathroom on Tuesdays, stroking her face at night with those round cotton discs that don't fluff like the loose stuff, two chapters read before turning out the lights each night. He wants to sleep right away, when his head touches the pillow, but he bears it for her, the light. Waits quietly until she places a floral bookmark in her novel and rolls to her side and flicks the light switch to make it all dark and peaceful. He's never told her that he waits for her. Maybe she doesn't know? But this is the thing with words: they fall into routines of their own, and his were never to say, 'I love you', 'Thank you' and 'I'll wait to sleep until you're ready because you're my person in this world.'

He shakes his head and turns now to a routine he does know. Something he can handle. The English number he will keep calling until he hands in his key and picks up his last check.

He listens as it dials, then to the generic voicemail greeting he's spoken to a couple of times. Read his number out and hoped they'd call back.

No one ever did.

He stands up and takes his mug in his hand, heading to the back kitchen for a coffee refill. One more week with his routine.

Sophia
Jönköping

THE NEXT MORNING I wake up alone and it takes my mind a minute to piece together where I am and what happened last night. Blade kissed me. Not my mouth—but in a way I actually enjoyed, without laughing at me or making me feel insecure or strange. He likes *me*.

This is all moving too fast. I'm starting to believe that maybe there is a planet where I can breathe and exist and love, but then I think that astronauts receive years of training before they throw themselves out there, and I have only briefly known this man.

I am sipping my cold milk when Blade comes in, a paper bag with baked goods in his hand. I move my mouth into a smile. He sits down next to me on the fold-out-sofa bed I haven't put back yet. He hands me something fluffy and sugary and still warm.

'Good morning,' he says softly.

'Good morning,' I reply with a hoarse voice. I worry my panic and want and confusion all show plainly on my face. But all I see is a fondness in his gaze, as if I'm the only person he wants to see.

'I'm sorry if I made you feel uncomfortable last night, if the tears were because of me. Let me know if there's anything you need me to do. Anything at all.'

'I don't know what to do with what I'm feeling,' I admit in a burst of words.

'If it's any consolation, neither do I.' He leans in, then hesitates for a moment, but finally kisses the top of my head.

I think that maybe I've started to change. I no longer identify as a grass flower but something else. I brush the hair off my face and look up at him. There's something he has to understand.

'I'm currently a peace lily, *Spathiphyllum*. They're lush and green and lively-looking. But God forbid if you forget to water them. Unlike many other plants that just sit there without making noise and then suddenly die on you, the peace lily wilts like it has lost its soul, all within a single day. You give it some love and it perks right up. Like nothing ever happened. Then once in a while when it's feeling super grateful it grants you a single gorgeous flower.'

He laughs.

I press on. 'What I mean is this: I'm not an easy woman. I may look it. I'm all quiet and compromising. But when you really get to know me, I'm not like that, not really. I have needs that I don't even know how to meet myself.'

'Not understanding what you need doesn't disqualify you from having people try to give you what you need.'

'I mean, yes, maybe? But I can only go so far away from what I need. I want to compromise, to meet in the middle more, but I can't.' The not kissing. Touching the topsoil of houseplants when I'm in someone's home. Moving while I talk. The fact I wipe surfaces with two different types of antibacterial spray because they both are said to kill 99 per cent of bacteria, so if I use two, one of them will surely kill the

1 per cent the second one doesn't and vice versa. These things are difficult for some people to understand, let alone live with.

'I've spent my life compromising. Isn't that what life and love is? It doesn't have to be a fifty-fifty thing all the time, does it? Right now my mum and I have a zero-one hundred balance. It's like the disposable-income split, exactly like that. Give me ten per cent, Sophia, and I'll give you 90.'

'What if I don't know what I can give? Or even what I need in return?' Because it's the truth. I've been raised to be like everyone else, to hide everything that's me. I grew up and continued the masking. I've tried to be every sort of person there is, and not one of them has worked. Not even my own family can figure me out. And now I'm trying to figure out what part of invented, made-up me this man likes, because if I don't know that, then how can I continue to be what he wants?

'Here's what I think we should do, just for now. You go to work, I will go and do my stuff. We both come home this evening. Then we repeat again tomorrow. Because remember what you told me about being ready? We are never ready for the day.'

I nod. That makes sense.

I lean into him and let myself be held—I've never had anyone to lean into before.

Zara
London

'REMEMBER THIS WHEN it's my birthday in two months.' Zara *loves* birthdays. Loves feeling the presence of her friends, loves handwritten wishes on cards, loves hearing her mother recall the story of her birth and loves receiving the message from her parents at exactly 11.32 p.m. (they stay up to send her it)—it is the time she entered the world.

'You will have a birthday week. Seven days of dedicated celebration. There will be seven cakes,' Blade promises, laughing at her choice of compensation.

'And balloons?'

'A lot of balloons.'

'Good. How are we so different? You won't even allow me to sing Happy Birthday to you.'

'I have no idea. But thank you, Zara.'

Honestly—the things Zara does for her best friend. She sighs and refills her mug from the filter coffee pot, hoping it's still somewhat lukewarm, and settles down to tackle the Swedish name-change records Blade sent over. There are a lot of Svens who have opted for a different name, it turns out. Facebook is a gift, and Zara ticks men off fairly easily, only having to send a couple of messages to confirm. Edith has gone over to the neighbour's, something that is happening more and more often. Pushba told her the children like having someone to talk to when she's busy cooking or cleaning.

Zara is four hours in when she finds him. Everything matches, everything Edith has said. She presses Dial on Blade's name.

'Hey. I think I found our guy.'

Edith
London

AT HOME, I'M watching an episode of something with actors I seem to recognise but can't place, when Blade calls me on my iPad. For a minute I feel a familiar tug at my emotions. I think it's the same one I felt years ago when I started working and dropped him off, six months old, at nursery. The feeling of wanting him to be with me but also knowing that he needs to be somewhere else.

'Mum. Listen, I have some photos of who I think is your Sven. I want to show you. Is Zara there?'

'Yes.' She is sat next to me, just close enough that I can feel the side of her body.

'Okay, great. I've sent her the pictures. Where do I start? He moved back to Sweden after three years in London, changed his name for whatever reason—he's now called Fredrik—then married and had a child the following year. A boy. Then two grandchildren. He worked for an accountancy firm until he retired two years ago.'

'Here.' Zara passes me her phone with the pictures. Blade has sent all the ones he's found. From teenage years and graduation to family shots and old age.

I sit quietly and solemnly for what must seem like an age to the young people.

'It's okay, take your time,' Zara says. I can see the look on Blade's face, it says *I can go home. Finally.*

'This is all great, Blade,' I say. 'I particularly like the family picture. It looks like they were a lovely little unit and I just adore the child's red dungarees.'

'Okay. This is good, right?'

'There is just one problem.'

'I knew it. Whatever it is, we can fix it. I was going to suggest we bring you two together via FaceTime, if he's up for it, of course. What do you say?'

I take the phone from Zara and put it down on the table, looking straight at my son through the screen.

'That sounds very lovely, and looking at this handsome man here I wouldn't quite mind a FaceTime date, if I may say so. This man in the pictures you sent is not the man I'm waiting for. He's not *Sven*.'

BLADE THINKS I'VE lost my mind. Which we all know I have—that's not what we're debating here. But I have not yet lost *all* of it. Not yet. Blade went off and sulked. Swore in his head, I'm sure. He'll pick himself up and continue. Something floats in my mind, just out of sight. I know it's there but can't quite see it. I'm waiting for it to move into view the way moving clouds do, but it doesn't. I think it's a picture. Not one that Blade found but one that I found.

Next to me Zara is still scrolling on my iPad. I lean into the shape of her body. It's nice sitting next to another human.

'Look. I'm googling olfactory hallucinations. Apparently they're a thing.' She's been avoiding getting involved in the

Sven business. Apparently today we are avoiding Sven by focusing on the dead-rat smell that only I can smell.

'I see.' But I don't see at all.

'Sometimes you may smell things that aren't there. Other people do too. Look here.' She opens a message board where someone named @john1951 has written that he can smell rotting cabbage and burning bonfires in his apartment.

'It's not just you. If the doctors had informed you about this it may have reduced the anxiety. I'm sorry. How does it make you feel now?'

'There is no dead rat,' I say.

'There's no dead rat,' she confirms.

'It says here that you can put your timer on thirty minutes when you start to smell whatever you're smelling, go do something else, and if it still smells when you come back it's real. If not it's a hallucination.'

When you start to lose your balance and need a cane to help you walk, you feel a little bit unsafe all the time, not massively but a little bit. When another part of you stops being reliable it is hard to keep believing in yourself. I swallow and fold up my reading glasses. I read somewhere that children can't understand pretend until they're school age. So even if you tell them there are no ghosts they'll still be afraid of them. If you are specific and tell them there are no ghosts in their room because you're there and ghosts really dislike humans with your specific hair colour and blood type, that will work. Perhaps I can tell myself that there is no dead rat because rats detest the sound of Zara's tapping on the keyboard, and I'll find some relief.

'I wish I would hallucinate freshly baked buns or clothes on a washing-line,' I say. 'Instead, I get an animal cadaver.'

Thinking again of the photo Blade showed me, I say to her,

'I know Blade's upset. I know he wanted that to be Sven. But that's not him. I know it's not, or at least I think I do. Tell me, do you think I have lost my mind?'

'No. I think you know the face of someone you love, Edith. No matter how lost you get.'

Blade
Jönköping

IT'S NOT HIM. I tried to convince myself that Mum was wrong but she won't be moved. The name change record had come through when I had just left Sophia and the best morning of my life. Goosebumps were replaced with other goose bumps, and I thought that was it. I'd found him.

'Are you sure?' I ask Zara an hour later.

'Positive. There are times she knows exactly what she's talking about, and this is one of them.'

'The name change made sense. Everything made sense. He lived in London during the time frame, he was the right age.'

'So what's the plan now? I assume you're not heading home yet?'

'No,' I say, part answering the question with Sophia in mind. 'I . . . I think I found him. He's the only option left. I just need to be certain and have enough information for Mum when I break the news to her that he's passed away.'

'I'm sorry he's not alive. But she will be able to handle it. She's stronger than you think.'

But she wasn't always strong, was she? When the day was over and she was too tired to cook dinner and would sit in her room crying and everyone left, I was still there, watching her unhappiness envelop her. My life's mission became keeping Mum happy, being her reason to move forward and choose joy. Zara should know this.

Maybe moving in with Mum was an attempt to keep being her reason? To once more give her enough to keep moving forward? To finally lose the anxiety I've carried? If I can make her safe and happy enough, then I'll have done my job. That was more important than anything else. More important than living. But time is running out for us because I won't have the luxury of talking things out with her before long. To find answers to all the questions I still have for her.

Except Mum might have given me a chance to do just that. She sent me here, to Sweden.

'I'm going to talk to Sophia. This is my last hope.'

Sophia
Linköping

I'M HAPPY. FLOURISHING. I'm moisturised and hydrated and focused. And I haven't even remembered to take my multi-vit chewies for a week. I've had the best week of my adult life.

I've started writing emails to my mum. I am yet to receive a reply. The emails make me feel freer, but also like the distance between us is getting bigger with each message sent and each message ignored. I'm turning into someone else and I'm desperately waiting for her to be acknowledged. I do this before going to bed, sending it off into a void, knowing there won't be a reply until the next morning because Mum goes to bed at a sensible hour. I always feel lighter afterwards, as if whatever I've written down isn't my problem any longer, that I've sent it off for good. I scroll through my Sent folder and read what I've written.

TO: Mum
SUBJECT: Achievements

Hello Mum,

Vincent has been showing up to look at my work. He was my uncle's friend, if you remember? Having him there made me think about when anyone showed up for me last. Watched anything I do. I was terrible at school plays, ballet performances and recitals. I remember the first one, I looked for you in the audience and saw you in a red sundress. I remember thinking you were the prettiest mum in the room. Then I went on stage and I messed up. Not tripping on my laces, or forgetting the steps, or singing out of tune. But worse. A Sophia mess-up. You see, the music was too loud and it was so crowded on stage, and I wanted to be off it and in your arms. My hands went over my ears covering them, blocking it all out. Until someone led me away.

We tried again. And again. I tried all those things that we have pictures of that now sit in photo albums and on Facebook, that are emotional milestones for parents. Then I stopped getting parts, and I dropped out of activities. Until there was nothing to show up to and no public accomplishments to watch.

But that doesn't mean I haven't done things, that I'm not doing things. Vincent can see it. Maybe one day you can see something good I do too, even if it's not what you expected from me?

Sophia Ven
Blom's Blooms
Stora byvägen 28
347 44 Svedala
www.blomsblooms.com

TO: Mum
SUBJECT: ABA

Hello,

I wonder if you read about ABA before you found my therapist? I have now, and it says it can treat 70 per cent of people with Autism. I'm trying to imagine what I was like, how you could look at me and feel I needed to be treated. Therapy was the worst thing that's happened to me. It ruined my ability to say no, taught me that I didn't have bodily autonomy and primed me for being taken advantage of. It made me scared of face-to-face situations because I grew scared of the consequences.

Sophia Ven
Blom's Blooms
Stora byvägen 28
347 44 Svedala
www.blomsblooms.com

TO: Mum
SUBJECT: School

Hi Mum,

I hope you read my last message. And the one before that. I was thinking about school today. Because I had to have lunch at a food court, and it reminded me of the cafeteria. There were smells and strange consistencies and a variety of dishes brought together resulting in an odour that stuck to my nostrils like glue. I never knew were to sit, back in school. I would stand in the cafeteria with my tray, and there were always seats available but I realised I couldn't pick one. It wasn't just picking a seat, it was a strategy. There were seats I wasn't allowed in, that were reserved for best friends and where I'd be turned away as I approached. Then there were seats that had a free space next to them or, worse, several free spaces. That would mean the bullies could take them, could get close to me. And chew loudly in my ear and watch as I'd start to shiver. They might pour a packet of salt on my food. And finally watch me get up and leave without having eaten a thing.

Do you know what I did in the food court today, Mum? I left after one bite.

I wonder if I would have been a different person if I hadn't been forced to go to a mainstream school. I could have been a person who liked to learn, who wasn't always hungry, and who felt calm and safe. I read about a boy on Twitter, he gets to skip playtime and replace it with quiet time in the library, he gets to skip PE and have shorter days. I kept thinking about him, because I'm so happy for him.

I always thought I failed, but maybe it was school that failed me?

Goodnight.

Sophia Ven
Blom's Blooms

Stora byvägen 28
347 44 Svedala
www.blomsblooms.com

WE ARE DOWN to the last days of the trip, and the joy I feel at being able to say, 'I did it!' is covering for the other feelings I have about the trip with Blade coming to an end. He is helping me today, having told me the search and interviews have concluded, he's done with his research. When we arrive late afternoon, the marketplace is already full of people, covering the ground, blending together into a one-coloured carpet-like blur like moss phlox, *Phlox subulata*.

'Where do you want the crates?' Blade asks and I nod towards an area at the edge of the common.

'We're really just waiting for it to finish so we can pack up. Getting it all ready.'

This was my favourite installation. I did something entirely different and used geraniums, sunflowers and others to create something that borders on art. I've made six different installations across the common each with a different theme. *Dream, Grow, Now, Play, Breathe* and *Think*. They're large, upright and brimming with colour and character. There is no motif, I haven't shaped them as a teddy bear or a large sun, just how I imagine each feeling in my mind and the word made out from shades of flowers.

Blade comes up behind me with a churro in his mouth. I'm amazed at the speed at which he located and bought them.

'Did you plan to spend the whole day eating?'

'Plan to spend the whole day in awe of you.'

He reaches out to touch me, and I recoil.

'Food courts are number three on the list of public places

with the most germs. After public restroom sinks and escalator handrails,' I explain.

'Got it. Sorry.'

I produce a wipe from my pocket and hand it to him. The sharp smell relaxes me and I inhale deeply, as a familiar voice comes up behind me.

'I could tell you were nearby from the smell, sister.' I turn around and am face-to-face with Pontus, brother number two. 'Where there's antibac spray fumes, there's Sophia.' He laughs. Blade's face remains still.

'You're here,' I say.

'I am, yeah.'

'Nice to meet you.' Blade says and they shake hands a minute too long, as if neither wants to be the first to let go.

Hampus comes up behind them, with Mattias next to him.

'Hi, sister,' they say in unison.

'Hi, brothers one, two and three.'

'This is pretty damn spectacular,' Hampus says. 'I don't know much about art, but this feels like, well . . . art?'

'Who did you work with?' Pontus asks. Taking a step back and joining the others so that my brothers are lined up next to one another, a trio of blond, bulky men who both look like me and don't.

'Just me,' I say. It's usually the answer to everything in my life. 'I work with no one.'

'Incredible,' Mattias says, smiling at me, then turning to our brothers. 'Why don't I take you for a proper tour and we let Sophia work?'

THEY COME BACK half an hour later, with bags full of purchases and words of praise.

'I had this idea of you with an apron behind a counter selling tulips,' Pontus says, and Hampus nods in agreement. 'Thought you might have a stand here selling flowers, so I wasn't even keen to drive over when Vincent called.'

'Vincent called you?'

'He said we needed to see this.'

'He did promise us free vouchers for the beer tent as well,' Hampus adds.

Knew it. My flowers alone wouldn't have been enough to pull them in. But they came. Showed up. And I think that's a first.

'Well done you,' Mattias says.

I look at the ground which is now brown rather than green, littered with beer caps and popcorn.

'Thank you,' I say.

Vincent wanted them to see this because I've done a good job. Because he's proud of me. He is the closest link I have to my uncle, and I can't help but think he'd be proud too.

Sophia
Linköping

WHEN WE ARRIVE at the field where yesterday's bustling scene has been replaced by still and scattered litter on trampled grass, Blade helps me unload my crates and boxes to pack up, then he hovers.

'See you at four. I'm not going anywhere today. No more places to visit.'

'Later than that. I'm meeting Vincent.'

He has asked me for a meeting to talk over the project and say thank you before I leave, but I'm guessing it's more my uncle and old times he wants to discuss. I don't do reminiscing. My memories of him are mine, they're childhood and warmth and a very big hole in my life ever since. Listening to another person talk of my favourite person in the world is like watching a movie: I may smile and feel touched but it's not me or my life.

'So I'll wait for you at six, then?'

'Perfect.'

'I HOPE YOU eat pizza?' Vincent says. He has stubble today, and I think that would be a helpful detail for my sleep routine should the sheep fade from my memory.

'I do.'

It's not busy at five o'clock and we choose a table by the window, where prams are pushed past and college students flock in groups with Fjällräven backpacks.

'How are you finding it, this project? I take it that it was a bit out of your comfort zone.' I have a water, and he has a Coke, full sugar. I take a sip and am glad he added that last clarifying bit, or I might have started into an explanation of the satnav and drive to the project.

'It's been good. Thank you for the opportunity. I do look forward to being at home with my plants, doorbell and regulars, though.'

'I never could get your uncle as far as this town. He also liked it best close to home.'

'Really? I thought he had the shop busy with projects and sales? A thriving and booming business,' *How else would he expect me to save up more than a million?*

'Not at all. He made just enough and was happy to make just enough. Sometimes he'd have lodgers when trade was down, recession of 2006 and the early nineties recession.'

I remember this now. Faintly. An Afghan woman in the spare room, so I'd slept on a blow-up mattress in the living room when I visited.

'It's a bit of a different situation for me. I'm not sure you're aware, but I need to buy my brothers out.' Every time I say it I feel embarrassed, as if I've failed already.

'Well, you've had quite a few years to learn to stand on your two feet and show that bunch what you are capable of, am I right? Doing that well. I can have a chat with your brothers, if you like. They were very impressed with your work, Sophia.'

I think of the message Mattias sent me last night. I know

he's proud of me, but I still don't think I'm ready to confront them.'

'It's better not to. But thank you.'

The food arrives. Pizzas with garlic sauce and white cabbage salad on the side. More Swedish than meatballs and Zlatan.

I crease my forehead as I think for the first time: perhaps I got it wrong. Perhaps the five-year period was not there to allow me to make enough money to pay my family off, but to allow them to change their minds about me. For them to see that I am capable and deserving of the inheritance.

'My uncle must have had quite a few lodgers, but I think I only met one of them.' I say, shuffling the pizza around on the plate, not able to finish it all whilst also talking and having the added distraction of pedestrians walking past on the other side of the glass. 'I used to receive letters for one of them.'

I stored them for some time but must have thrown them away eventually. They never looked important and it's rude to open a stranger's post. I search in my memory for the names of the lodgers now. The Afghan woman was definitely Damsa.

'I think he was lonely,' Vincent tells me. 'If it was up to him he'd have had you living with him full time.'

I let myself imagine that childhood. Going to a different school, quiet dinners for two every night and practical clothes that suited gardening.

'I think I might have loved that,' I allow myself to say then close the chapter as one that wasn't meant to be.

'Trust me, it was enough for him just having you for holidays and odd weekends. It was the getting back from England and taking on the business that needed a settling-in period. Easing back into solitude. He solved that with people staying.

He wasn't one to go out and socialise, but having someone around helped ease the loneliness. He could read a book and they could cook, and at the end of the night they hadn't both been entirely alone, there'd been the turning of the pages and the smells of the food to remind them of each other's existence. Was more like himself when I saw him a couple years after he got back. Your birth probably had something to do with it as well.' All I can hear is the name of a certain country.

'England? My uncle?'

'He lived there for some time. Before you were born.'

'But he hated planes. I didn't even know he owned a passport. The only holiday of sorts he took was when he drove to Germany to buy cheap wood crates for plantation. He told me he was an oak, a *Quercus robur*, because his roots were so strong and he planned to grow a hundred years old. In Sweden.' The statement brings a wave of sadness—he didn't grow like an oak. The image of a chopped-down tree, its rings visible on the stump, comes to me. If you trace the rings with your finger and count them you find out how many years the tree grew for. I imagine an oak tree stump now, fifty-two rings. He died way too early.

'Well, he definitely spent time in England.'

BLADE IS WAITING outside when we come out of the restaurant. He's still to take off his beanie, not even for a second, even during this heatwave. As we arrive at the car and I sit down, I realise that he remembers things. Like that I want my seat warmer on. Constantly. Things that he shouldn't remember. No one else does. When I was a child no one reminded me to take a snack because *Big girls pack their own school bag, Sophia* so I'd arrive at the dinner table famished and with a feeling of my stomach being turned inside out from emptiness. But Blade just casually drops little hints. Or actual snacks. In my lap.

'What's this?'

'It's a cereal bar. I thought it was a decent one because it seemed the biggest brand in there.'

'Why is it in my lap though?'

'Thought you may want to eat it. I take it you didn't finish your food so there's room for it.'

Well, no, I hadn't. Too many thoughts in my head. Too many things to look at outside the window. Too many Vincents opposite me.

I open it and turn towards the window when I eat, aware of each crunching sound my jaw makes.

I message Lina.

> ME: Blade hands out snacks at the right time. Continuously. Feel strange. Might have to hand flap for release.
>
> LINA: Wow. He seems to have evoked quite an emotional response in you. You only hand flap stim when I put on Bambi.
>
> ME: I DON'T LIKE ANIMALS DYING ON ME.
>
> LINA: Exactly. Blade reaction is right up there with an orphaned-deer kid reaction. Just saying . . .

I close the conversation and notice twenty-three new messages in my family chat. There's an instant stress ball at the base of my stomach, but I open the thread. I can ignore up to twenty messages, but any more than that I need to at least chime in with a one-liner.

> ME: All good. Working hard and keeping busy. Vincent is happy enough. Thank you for the pictures and updates everyone.

Then five minutes later I open it up again.

ME: Did my uncle go to England before I was born?

MUM: He lived there for a year, yes, then started the shop. Not sure what happened to him there as he never travelled anywhere after that trip!

Blade
Linköping

HAVE DEFINITELY BEEN a carer for too long. Now that the person I care for is in a different country, I replace her with other people. Other people like Sophia. She's none of my business. An adult with her actual life together. Business owner, own apartment, cashmere sweaters. All at twenty-five. But can I stop caring for her? Nope. I note when she eats and I try to be one step ahead. I count how many glasses of water she drinks a day. Fuck—am I creepy? Just not used to being free.

'Did you know that my uncle's profit was only marginally bigger than mine?'

Sophia says from my right. 'When times were hard he had lodgers. First his old university friend and then a refugee through a council programme. I'd forgotten about it. Or assumed it was a favour and that he didn't get paid. He also went to England, to London, I learnt. All this time I had no idea.'

I freeze.

'London?'

'Yes, London. City in the United Kingdom with ten million inhabitants and landmarks such as Big Ben and the London Eye.'

'Did he ever talk to you about . . . his trip? Someone he met during the trip? A woman . . . ?'

She looks at me as if I've asked a highly inappropriate question, like what colour underwear she's wearing today.

'No. He said I was the only girl for him.'

'When was this trip?'

'It must have been before he started the shop. He never left it for more than a week. And I know when he bought the lease It's in my documents. The end of 1996.'

I'VE CALLED MUM and I can see the minute she answers that it's not a good day. The opposite from yesterday. There's something about how the eyes focus on something in the background rather than me and how her arms hang heavier down her sides.

'Hi, Mum,' I say, hoping to reach her. I miss her. Not just the good days but, I'm surprised as I realise it, all the days. All the versions of what Mum is now I miss, and not just the memory of her. I hadn't realised, but the thought shifts something inside of me, something heavy that's stood in the way of our connection ever since she changed.

'That looks like a forest.'

'Yes, Mum, I'm outside this little village called Tenhult at the moment.'

'Those look like pine trees.'

'I'd say so.' A *Pinaceae*. I hear Sophia's voice echo the Latin name for it and can't help but smile.

'You shouldn't be out this late, Blade. Remember I only have one son. It's not safe out there.'

'I'm okay. I'm an adult now, remember? I'm here looking for Sven. Travelling around Sweden in the hope of finding him. Remember?'

She is agitated now. Eyes moving erratically and even from here I can sense a panic build up. *I wish I knew what she was going through when this happens.* 'Is Zara there?' I ask.

'Right here!' She appears from where she's been hovering, taking the iPad off my Mum and holding it with one hand whilst the free one squeezes Mum's hand. Touch grounds and connects her to the moment.

'Sweden plans end badly.' Mum's voice is high-pitched. Different.

'I'm okay Mum. Sweden is nice. This is probably my favourite place so far.' I keep talking in the hope that the sound of my familiar voice will relax her. 'I have a friend, the one who the packages belong to, with me. Yesterday we picked a litre of wild blueberries and there's a lake where we swim every evening.'

Mum moves closer, then farther away. She is really not here now and I look at Zara.

'Make sure she's safe, please,' I plead. 'Keep reassuring her.' I wish I was there. Giving instructions but not being the one to implement them makes me feel helpless.

'You won't find Sven—' She is cut off abruptly, and her next sentences only make it halfway to me. There's a slur in her voice which I haven't heard before. I make out only a couple of words.

'I'll calm her down and put the TV on for her. I'll call you later,' Zara says, and a split-second later my screen is empty, facing the dark woods.

What did she say? I message Zara. The reply comes ten minutes later and sends a shiver down my spine.

> **ZARA**: She says you won't find Sven any other place than Hornton Street, at the bus stop. Like she's always told you.

Then again, five minutes later.

Your Mum has a new screensaver. I only noticed it now. OMG.

Zara's second message arrives and I zoom in on the picture, which is of Mum's phone. My head is spinning with thoughts as I'm standing up, my back to the camper-van where Sophia will be brushing her teeth and preparing to read a chapter in her book. Waiting for me.

She *has* a picture of him. There's a drawn circle around his face, Mum's shaky hand not quite managing to make the lines meet at the ends.

It's a picture of a newspaper clipping. The scene is busy: there are women in cycling shorts with high ponytails secured with scrunchies. Men with suits cut too large, legs too wide for it to be today. Sven looks off-camera. He is tall, his head above the others and he's wearing a dark grey T-shirt. The hair is light and very similar to the hair of someone I know well. I know this face,: I've seen it before.

In a framed photo in Sophia's parents' living room. And in the photos she messaged me to show to my mum.

I found him.

I now know something about Sophia's uncle that she doesn't. As for Mum, I have a task ahead of me that I'm not looking forward to. To tell her that she won't be seeing Sven, that there is no chance of ever finding out why he didn't turn up to meet her. That she won't ever find the resolution and peace she craves. I have to go home and be there for her, and Sophia will stay here.

What a fucking mess.

A part of me is angry, angry at a man I never met. He should have looked for her. Not spent his days drawing and telling stories. He could have changed everything. And why did he leave my mum? There is so much I don't understand. Who doesn't show up, doesn't get in touch but spends his life drawing pictures and idolising a woman? It's infuriating and doesn't fit with the picture of him that Sophia paints.

I've dropped Sophia off in town and have gone to a small coffee shop to think and put together what I have, which I will need to present to Mum in the gentlest way possible. I carry my tray with a black coffee to a table by the window and sit down.

Then Zara calls, and the ground shifts beneath my feet.

I have to go.

Edith
London

THE FIRST THING I think is that I'm not vertical but horizontal and that it's wrong. Like half of a crossword, I should go the other way. It's dark outside, so it must be early morning or late evening. There is the pain, but it's only subtle at first. I look around. The ceiling is spotty with grey, and I think that it's an angle we have neglected and also that I see it once a year so perhaps I can continue ignoring it, kind of like addressing my aunt's insensitive jokes at Christmas or buying napkins with Easter motifs. The pain nudges me. Like the soft nose of an imaginary dog, it probes me and pushes me to get up. Left hip, cheek, brain, thigh. I should call out. When you find yourself at the bottom of the staircase unable to get up, calling out is what you do. I know Zara must be in the other room, and even if I can't see her face in front of me right now I know which name to call: like a phone number, she has become a sequence of symbols I know will bring her here, although there is no face to it. I am about to open my mouth when I decide against it and close it again. Because I *feel* him, and I know I want to stay and see this through. Hallucination or not. If this is the only way to see him I will take it.

'You came.' I'm not sure if I say this in my head or out loud. Either way he can hear it.

'Of course I did. You know I did.'

'I thought we didn't meet?'

'We didn't.'

'But we were meant to meet. I was meant to end up with you.'

'I know. You always end up somewhere, even if it's not the place you had in mind.'

'And you. Where did you end up?'

'Edith. You know where I ended up.'

'I know?'

'Back where I started. The way I was before I met you. I didn't like it but I grew to understand, eventually.'

'Are you playing mind games with me?'

'I am one big mind game, remember?' He smirks and moves closer. I know that if I close my eyes, if I even blink, it will be over. I hold my eyelids open until they're sore. *Don't go. If you never came, you at least shouldn't leave me now.*

He stands over me. His face facing mine.

'I think Blade is almost ready to come home, don't you? He's found something you could never have imagined. That will change his life. You can make things right with him. And then you can let him go.'

I blink at my son's name, and a tear trickles down to my ear. Vertical. I need to get vertical, that's all I know. Because I have a son and a whole lot of people who need me vertical, well and safe. Then I piece together the emergency call in my head and call it out. Because now the pain is there, cutting through my beautiful hallucinations. I'd very much like to stay, but I also know that I can't, and as soon as I think those thoughts I see him start to slip away. I find the words finally and call out.

ZARA!

Part Three

So I'm not moving, I'm not moving.
—THE SCRIPT

Edith
London

I CAN STILL see his face when I close my eyes. Which I do a lot. Finally this disease did something nice for me. The lights are much too bright, and it turns out Zara is disappointingly nervous in an emergency situation. I half wished they had told her there was no room in the ambulance and could she jog behind it, please? The way she squeezes my hand then lets go as if I'm more fragile than I was yesterday and she shouldn't be touching me gives me an urge to push her and her concern away.

I try to remember what undies I put on today then want to laugh out loud because there's a habit that obviously never dies for you. Do mothers still say that to daughters today? *Always wear your best knickers because you never know if you're going to have an accident and go to hospital.* As if a girl has to look decent even when hurt.

Then I realise that I won't be able to go to the bus stop today, and the physical stab that follows that thought, always, without fail, is a little bit weaker than usual. Because I may see Sven again in my visions, I may even be able to learn to call him to me whenever I want. Like a particularly beautiful dream you can call on. *What will you dream tonight?* I'd ask

Blade at bedtime. *About a fire engine and lots of red gummy bears. What about you, Mummy? And I'd say, I'll dream about you and me. Maybe we'll go on holiday somewhere warm, pick shells on the beach and smuggle them back in our suitcases.*

Well, now I will plan to dream of Sven.

I'm still groggy and soft-limbed from medication when Zara walks back in, coffee in hand.

'Hi, Edith. I'm sorry I wasn't there when you woke up. Or when it happened.'

'You came.' Coming is what matters. Or wanting to come.

'I talked with the doctor and with Blade. You broke your femur, which means you'll have difficulty getting around for a while. It's going to be a tough recovery, they said, but you will recover.'

'I've broken a lot of things in my life. Nails, promises, hearts. It all turned out okay.'

She goes to sit next to me on a chair that's already pulled in place. She must have been sitting there whilst I slept.

'I'm glad you're so positive.'

'Could you be so kind as to pass me my phone?'

'Here. I've charged it.' She hands it to me, and I see no missed calls from Blade and no missed called from the random Swedish number attempting to dig up the past without my permission, delivering truths I don't want to hear.

'I think it's started now,' I say to Zara finally. 'The breaking down slowly, slowly. I didn't feel it before, when I was younger. I think when it's either your body or your mind you don't notice all that much? You compensate. Like when you lose your sight and your hearing becomes sharper as a result. But when a bone is broken and I also smell dead rat and think that coffee is kept in the freezer, then it's quite obvious, isn't it?'

'I wouldn't call you broken.'

'Tell me. How has it gone with Eliza? She brought me a doughnut yesterday from a big box that she had in the office.'

'She's lovely.'

'That's what I say about the GP or a particularly handsomely risen Yorkshire pudding. Not about a young woman you're dating.'

Zara laughs.

'Okay. She's fucking hot, and I think I really, *really* like her. Better?'

'Much.'

Sophia
Linköping

WHEN I GET back late afternoon, having walked the short distance from the bus stop, Blade isn't there so I undress and walk down to the lake for a swim. It's warmer now, and I don't even hesitate as I walk in. I dip my whole head under, tricking a swarm of mosquitos that fly above the surface searching for me in vain. I walk back barefoot with my body dripping water onto the forest path. I think that Blade's sweater would be nice right about now, the black one with the soft lining that he cut the tag off for me. Except when I get inside there is no sweater. There is no Blade. In fact, everything of Blade's is gone. I feel myself start to tremble. He should be here waiting for me along with all his things that he's moved into the camper-van from the tent.

Where did you go? I message him.

BLADE: Mum is hurt. I had to leave. I'm sorry. Speak soon.

I'm too much in shock to reply. *He's left me*, that's all I can think. After all that, he didn't even say goodbye. He just left. Speak soon can mean either I'll call you within the next hour, or what my history of almost-kissing men has taught that it's more likely to mean—never.

Here's the sad but true thing. A lot of people are like roses—*Rosaceae*. Beautiful, sweet-smelling and popular. But underneath the perfect display they are prickly, ready to hurt you. If times get hard, and the environment isn't exactly what they wanted, they revert to their true state of being, boring and unscented. This is exactly what has happened with Blade—and I should have seen it coming. Life is this endless confusion. Why I can't read people properly. Because this shouldn't have happened. He shouldn't have left. He said I could trust him, that I *should* trust him. But why would I trust someone who can walk away, just like that?

I want to shout. *I never change my routine for anyone, but then you became my routine despite all odds, and now you changed it!* I'm melt-downing so much I just sit and rock on the floor, and deep down I know it's my own fault for falling so hard. It's like I've waited all these years and finally released all the feelings I'd bottled up, unleashing them on this one man. I calm down slowly, and my senses start to catch up. I imagine Blade's arms around me, squeezing tight and pushing all the anxiety away. That helps. Because though I'm crying over him, he's the one I want to take the pain away.

Blade
Copenhagen

I DON'T KNOW how Mattias got my number, but here we are, I'm standing in the open space of the Oresund train heading back to the airport listening as he berates me. I don't even care that there's a couple within earshot who can probably hear it all.

'Fuck you, man.'

'I don't know what you think I've done, but I didn't mean to hurt your sister.'

'Well, from here, it looks like you stalked her, conned her into joining you on your research trip that no one understands, took advantage of her and then abandoned her in a camper-van hours from her home.'

'Do you think I planned this? To find out that Sophia was a part of this and to then fall for her? Then to leave her? Look, I am sorry, and I'll explain everything to her. But my mum got hurt and I'm all she has—literally, there's no one else. I don't have a choice.'

I hold my phone away from my ear, in anticipation of what I know will be more imminent shouting.

'Bullshit. Everyone has a choice. And you should have thought yours through more carefully before involving my sister. She's different. **Vulnerable.** Not like other girls. You don't just leave like that.'

His words trigger something inside me.

'You haven't seen what she's capable of. She's not like other girls, you're right. She's so much more.'

'What do you know about it? You don't even know her. You met her, what, eight days ago?'

'I'm not too sure *you* know her. Where was this big-brother, protective act when she was a kid? When she actually needed it? When your parents and her therapists made her life a living hell, where were you then?'

I press the phone to my ear now, because he's gone quiet suddenly. I can hardly pick up what he's saying.

'You don't understand.'

'Sure I do. You weren't in her corner.'

He's suddenly very quiet.

'We didn't think we could question anything. They were our parents, and there were professionals taking care of Sophia. Helping her. Yeah, it felt fucking wrong, but who was I to say something when I was just a kid too? So I would give her my sweets. I asked her how she was doing even if she never answered, and I let her play with my friends even if they didn't usually allow girls.'

'Okay, I get that. You were a kid too. We all do what we can, and we all screw up. Me included.'

'Boy, did you screw up. You just left her like that, all alone? She said she thought you understood her, you always slowed down and explained things so that she could understand. You should have known you couldn't just walk away like that, with no explanation.'

I stay still for a moment, then I let his words sink in, processing what they mean.

'I had to leave, there wasn't time, but when I come back I will go straight to her. I'll explain everything, answer any questions she has. Let me fix this, yeah? Because even if I don't deserve her, I can tell you that I want to be in her corner. I want to sort this out.'

There is a long silence, and I think he's hung up on me when finally he speaks.

'That's you and me both. But I'm not sure what she wants.'

Sophia
Linköping

IT'S BEEN TWO days since Blade left, and I'm about to finish my project. Me and my blooms have officially done it. I'm a long way from having the money I need, but I least I know I can do it. I can increase my revenue if I need to.

I've also survived for four days on only that one *Speak soon* message from Blade. I catch a glimpse of myself in the mirror by the door on my way out and wonder how the chaos inside me isn't more visible. If my outside matched my inside I'd be a nice, modernist sculpture: head sideways, nose instead of eyes and eyes on my chin. Instead I'm still me: blond hair, tired blue eyes and the beginnings of a stress pimple on my forehead.

MY BROTHER CALLED to ask what time I was leaving, and I didn't know why he asked until I spot his pickup truck in the distance. I hear it before I see it and stand there motionless, waiting, as he drives all the way up to me and parks.

'Hej.'
'Hej.'
'You okay?'

I remember that he used to ask me that. After therapy. After a roadkill incident. After the bullies had gotten hold of my hat and dipped it in the toilet. When he climbed into the car after hockey practice and sat close to me, so close his warmth spread to me. And I'd say yes or no, and that would be it. No further questions when I did no further explaining. He'd hesitantly turn around and go off and join our brothers, until the next time.

Today I decide to try something new.

'Not really,' I say. He takes a step closer, kicking at a pinecone.

'I'm sorry. That you're not okay now. And you know, for all the times you weren't okay then.'

'Not your fault.' I follow the pinecone with my gaze. It stops rolling but rocks back and forth on the path as if it's anxious.

'Maybe not, but I was still sorry it happened to you. I *am* still sorry, Sophia. So genuinely sorry.'

I nod. It's one of those sentences that covers more than just one moment, that transcends time and changes something in you.

'What's that noise?' I can hear faint quivering from the truck. 'Did you bring work? If you did, can I pet it?'

'I don't tend to drive around with patients.' Mattias says with a slight smile. 'I don't have an ambulance licence.'

I walk over to his truck and peek into a window where I think the noise is coming from.

'Wait a minute.' My brother dives into the backseat and emerges with a pet travel cage.

'He's yours. I bought him. I've checked him over, and he's fit and well, no hidden illness, hips screened and cleared and no family history of arthritis. He looks set for a long and happy life. I've microchipped him already so he won't lose his owner.'

'His owner?' I manage. A very cute, very distracting black

nose is peeking out at me, pressing against the thin bars of the cage.

'You. You're his owner.'

I should scald my brother, tell him all the reasons why I can't have a dog and why he definitely shouldn't give me one, but as he opens the cage's door and I see the face—oh what a face!—which has a white stripe running from between the large curious eyes to the black nose, I can do no such thing. All I can say is

'Thank you. Thank you for giving me my own pet.'

'You deserve to have a pet, Sophia. When you were a little girl and now.'

Mattias hands me a bag which I'm too busy to look into but assume is dog food and other necessities, and he squeezes my shoulder. I look closer at the *(my!)* puppy and he sticks his head out when I unclasp the sides of the door and carefully open it all the way. I notice that next to the white stripe is a small orange drop, not quite even enough to be a snowdrop, but rather it looks like a wonky-shaped cornflake.

'Cornflakes,' I say and take him into my palms where he fits perfectly. Maybe being big-boned and having large hands isn't so bad after all, if they can hold a whole puppy with a white-and-orange nose called Cornflakes.

'Call me if you have any questions. I promise you—it feels good, almost healing, to take care of animals.'

I think about something then, something that could be a timeless moment for Mattias and how I wish that for him like I had mine.

'How are you?' I ask, the puppy already in my arms, wriggling and crying softly.

'I'm okay.'

'I'm glad you are. And I'm sorry if I've forgotten to ask you that over the years.'

'Thank you.'

He hops into the truck. Before closing the door, he calls back to me.

'Sorry if I went too hard on your boyfriend. I meant what I said about him being an idiot for leaving you. But I think he actually likes you, and whatever reason he had to leave, I think it must have been a good one.'

Eliza

London

ELIZA HAS GONE over to Edith's house to repack her hospital bag. Eliza is used to being in people's houses, entering their lives, moving things around then putting it back to how it was so they won't notice a thing, when the viewing is over. A bit like a ghost she, thinks, playing interior dress-up when no one sees then disappearing again.

There is a racket coming from the front door, and Eliza goes to check, wary and with headlines of seniors' properties targeted for break-ins on her mind. What she sees on the other side of the door doesn't look like a robber.

'Oh, sorry. I thought Edith was home.' The woman is small and covered in children. One strapped to the front of her and one hanging off her arm.

Eliza keeps her hands to herself, seeing that the woman wouldn't have one free to take hers anyway, but smiles widely.

'I'm afraid Edith has had an accident. I'm Eliza. I'm here to pack a bag for her and bring it down to the hospital.'

'Hospital? Is she all right?' The genuine fear that flies across the woman's face as she breaks a hand free and wipes a sweaty strand of loose hair off her face tells Eliza that this is one of Edith's friends.

'A broken leg. But she is recovering well. Can I get you a glass of water?'

'Yes, please. Don't worry—I can help myself. I'm Pushba, by the way.'

The little boy has let go of his mum's hand now and strolls off towards the garden, knowing his way around the house perfectly.

'Jake brought a ball.' Pushba nods towards her son. 'We'll be making Get Well Soon cards for Edith when we get home.'

Eliza watches on as Pushba fills a glass with tap-water and drinks.

'You know, I never had a fucking village,' Pushba says.

'Excuse me?'

'Yeah, she doesn't know swear words yet.' Pushpa laughs and nods to her baby. 'You know, first they sell us the dream of the perfect family. Then when your husband leaves, you think 'Oh well, at least there's wine and girlfriends,' but all your girlfriends have either moved to semi-rural towns up north or still have their husbands. So there you are with no one checking in on you apart from the delivery drivers. You're covered in baby vomit, fantasise about more than four hours sleep straight and are left with only the wine as your coping strategy.'

Eliza nods. She can't really relate to her story, but she can at least sympathise.

'So one day I thought "Screw it, I need baking goods and there must be a village somewhere willing to give me some fucking flour." I knocked on three doors, and then I found Edith.'

'We all found Edith,' Eliza remarks.

Pushba drains her water glass and places it in the sink then smiles at Eliza.

'I'm sorry. I'm just chatting away.'

'No worries at all.' Eliza likes the woman. 'I was just about to head upstairs and pack a bag for Edith.'

'I'll come and help.'

Pushba leaves the garden door open so Jake can find them, and the two women go upstairs.

'It looks like they were about to change out the summer wardrobe,' Pushba comments, and Eliza looks at the boxes with wool garments and moth balls balancing at the top. It's a bit early to bring out the jackets, but then Edith must have had a reason, rational or not.

She runs her fingers over the fabric, before picking the box up and moving it to the side. She doesn't know why she does it, a life-long habit of feeling pockets before putting things in the washing machine. She is of course not near a washing machine, but in a bedroom; nonetheless, her hand finds its way into a pocket. Then another. Her hand digs around and keeps pulling something out of pockets, placing the finds on the floor. She knows Zara has been looking for this.

Why the coats? Was it because she was meant to meet him in winter?

Pushba comes up behind her.

'Letters,' she says, with interest in her voice.

'Yes,' Eliza replies. 'It does look like letters.'

Blade
London

I'M PACING NEXT to the luggage carousel until my one suitcase eventually turns up. Zara meets me at Arrivals, and I silently take one of the two Costa cups she's holding.

'Okay. You're too quiet,' she says as I fling my smaller bag onto my shoulder. I stay quiet until we reach the car park.

'Where is your method of transport?' I ask.

'It's a car.'

'*Car* would be too great a compliment.'

Her Fiat from about last century has only a left blinker: don't ask me how she gets out of having it fixed. And of being fined. As I sit down I'm also reminded that the seat warmer can't be switched off, a wonderful feature in July. At least if you're Sophia.

Sophia.

'She's okay, you know. Your mum.'

I feel guilty for having thought of Sophia, Zara having misread the pain on my face. The guilt comes out as anger when I speak.

'You were meant to keep her safe.'

'It was an accident. Accidents happen. The only thing that could have prevented it would have been living in a house that doesn't have stairs. She's not a child, she's not frail, she's not even a danger to herself, really. You smother her.'

'I watch out for her! What am I supposed to do, let her wander off and just hope she makes it home eventually? I guess I wouldn't have to wonder much. She'd just be sitting at that bloody bus stop all day.'

'She lights up when she's at Hornton Street, like she's got this purpose again. She can be unaware and frustrated at home, struggling to find the right items and words, and then we get on the bus together and her focus shifts. She's clear and determined and knows exactly where she needs to be. How could you not support that?'

'Her doctor told me to keep her away.'

'Well, her doctor doesn't know her like you do, like I do.'

Zara flicks the indicator switch with an aggression she usually reserves for half empty ketchup bottles. I can't help thinking she imagines flicking my nose.

'She's still a human being, a woman. She's not dead yet, you know,' she says.

I'm furious now. I know. I bloody *know* all this as she's *my* mum and I've been taking care of her for three fucking years whilst Zara has only had a glimpse. I swallow my anger and continue to listen.

'It's real to her. And that means it's real to me, and it should be to you. That's why I tell her he *may* be real. I respect that that's her reality, you know? Who am I to say my reality is more important than hers? If she wants to wait for him, then I can let her.'

I feel that familiar defeat, the sense of *Fine, you're right, but I don't like it.*

'Why? Why wait for this man? It doesn't make any sense. And don't say love, please. He never turned up, he left her for all intents and purposes, and she's just been pining for decades, unwilling to let go. She just sits and sits at that damn bus stop.'

'If you didn't always know where you were, would you not go to the one place you know means something to you? Where you are yourself? What moment would you go back to if everything was slowly slipping away from you?'

To Sophia. There is no hesitation, no thought process involved. The name is simply there. I want to un-think it, unsend, but it's been thought. *There.* If I couldn't remember how to make tea or where I lived, at least I know I'd never forget the way I felt when I was with her. And I'd want to be back in a forest clearing in a warm July with her.

'Even if she's unwell and even if she's your mother. And so what if she can't do what she used to? She can still have purpose somewhere. Right now, this is her purpose, and if you take it away, then what's left? What does it matter what it is that makes us get up and live every single day? As long as something does, we're good.'

I'VE NEVER REALLY been to hospital before, only for day appointments and a half-day stay for an MRI Mum had to get done when her memory began fading. I relate to it more as a TV set for medical dramas than an actual place where people are sick and other people work, and I'm half expecting a hot couple to appear from the on-call room adjusting their scrubs. The nurses get me some sheets and a pillow for the chair, which apparently turns into something resembling a bed, and I walk to the patient room.

As I walk back to Mum's room, I read a sign informing relatives that visiting hours are between two and five and that flowers aren't allowed in the general surgery wing. *Flowers.* I wonder what flower Sophia is now. Something trampled on and left behind and—

No, this is for the best. Things have changed in the past day.

Every hope I had of Mum being safe somewhere and me being able to embark on some sort of life which may include Sophia has dwindled and shrivelled. It didn't work for someone like my ex, who already lived in the same city. How could it work with Sophia?

Mum is still sleeping. I untwist the IV line coming from her left arm.

'I'm here,' Zara says behind me. 'Do you want me to stay, or shall I see if there's anything edible in the hospital Costa?'

'I'm fine,' I tell her. 'I'll wait here until there's a round, and they can update me.'

'Should be at five but there are always emergencies, so you never know. I missed the one this morning, but Eliza was here to get the update.'

'Eliza?'

'Edith's friend. Well, my friend too now, actually. Your mum introduced us. She's an estate agent on Hornton Street.'

I shrug. A friend? Mum has made friends? There is so much Mum does that I know nothing of, that she is capable of. If only I'd stopped to see. I pick up a 'Get Well Soon' card off the side table. *From Pushba, Jake and Ella. We're making cakes for when you get home*, it reads. A child's drawing shows a stick person looking sad in a hospital bed and in the next image happily eating a brownie. Underneath it is a PS: *I came over last night to borrow some tape. You weren't there, but Zara gave it to me. It's for my school project lighthouse. I'm using two garden pots and paint! Jake.*

'This is also a friend?'

'Your nextdoor neighbours. They borrow flour and eggs now and again. And, as it turns out, tape.'

A memory of a quiet, friendly family I've never stopped to talk to comes to mind.

Zara grabs my arm suddenly.

'Eliza just texted me. She was packing Edith's hospital bag, and guess what? She found more letters.'

A HEALTHCARE ASSISTANT comes in and checks Mum's vitals. I'm awkward under her gaze and presence, having been absent initially, my guilt not yet dispelled, but Zara chats on.

'She'll be on anticoagulants for some time now. Physio sessions. The good thing is that Edith was so active and fit.'

We have her walks to and from the bus stop to thank for that.

Statistics I read during my trip here wheel through my head as she talks. Life expectancy after a bone break: one-year mortality rate is 21 per cent. Odds of survival worsen with increasing age, of course, but thankfully women are less vulnerable. And Zara seems to talk about the future, as if there's no imminent danger to Mum's life. The numbers mean at best my mum has only a one in five risk of dying this year. Numbly I think, *Who would I be if I didn't exist to keep Mum alive*? I don't want to find out. All the dreams of freedom have gone. Freedom means nothing when you're alone.

'How long will she be here?' I shoot a grateful smile to the girl who's just finished up and is wheeling the blood pressure monitor back into place in the far corner of the room before leaving us be.

'A week?' Zara answers. 'At least that's what they said yesterday.'

I nod.

'Hey, let me go check Costa. Hospital rooms have the same rules as Christmas Day and road trips—there's no limit on snacking and food consumption. Anything goes. I'm not missing the opportunity.'

Mum stirs. I watch her open her eyes. The front of her arms have freckly age spots, and spider veins break the skin on her legs. I pull the blanket up in case she's cold. I've seen all these marks before but today they make me sad, seeing them against the backdrop of the crisp hospital linen: she looks older.

'Hey. I'm back,' I say when she notices me.

'Why? I didn't ask you to come back.' She is very alert all of a sudden.

'Mum, you broke your leg. Of course I came back.'

'From what I remember, you have no medical qualifications, and so your presence in the event of a bone break is wholly unnecessary and based on sentiment. Sentiment I do not have time for. I've been trying to tell you.'

'Now is not the time, Mum.'

She keeps up appearances, but I can see her face relaxing. She slaps my shoulder gently, as if there's a speck of dust or a bee perched on it.

'I guess it's not bad that you came. I have some more letters for you. Zara is looking for them. I think they're important because I've been keeping them safe. Inside books.'

'I know, she just told me about them. I'll read them. Try to rest.'

'I have been resting for too long.'

'Fine, don't rest. Maybe try some tap dancing.'

I must say, she drifts off incredibly fast for someone who doesn't need rest. There's buzzing from under her pillow, and I slide my hand in gently, pulling out her phone. For a minute I think of Sophia and guilt washes over me, then I come to my senses: it's just a Swedish area code, nothing more. I step away from Mum's bed and press the green button to accept the call.

An Almost-Retired Storage Facility Manager
Malmö

THE MANAGER OF Rent-a-Safe is excited about his handover. For a whole morning he gets to tell a young person how things are done! Being well aware this may be his last organised and dedicated opportunity to do so makes it sweeter. From now on, he may have to make do with telling strangers they're using the bus card upside down or that the shelves should be stacked differently in Ica. But this? This is to be treasured. The manager arrived half an hour early (not to work, no, but to have a coffee and be able to make it look like the young person was late. By 8.50 he has had two coffees and does not want a third one. Unless there is an opportunity to ask the young person to make him one. Then he would have a third coffee.).

The man arriving at the doors of the small back office at a minute to nine is not quite as young as he'd hoped, but it will have to do. In the desert every cactus is a flower, as his single colleague says when he's hitting the fifty-plus nightclub on a Saturday night.

The young person stands expectantly after the manager has said hello. Always good to keep them waiting. Always want everything right away these new generations. App this, app that. But there's no app to help him now.

'What is this?' the young one asks. Oh, yes. There's an empty desk with a single key. It would blend in if there were even just one other item next to it, but alone it stands out, demands attention.

'It's a numbered key to a safe. You should have encountered plenty of them if your CV isn't fraudulent.'

'Yes. Well . . . What am I supposed to do with it?'

The manager sighs. Soon this key will not be his responsibility, his desk will be clean. But for another seven and a half hours it *is* his responsibility.

'The contents of the safe need to be collected, but we can't get through to the owners. The initial payment only covered the first five years of storage. They have been in default for a year now.'

The manager finds he almost knows the phone number by heart now. It ends with five-nine. The age his father lived to. Memory is a funny thing. He dials it—one last time, he tells himself.

No one wants this safe. The manager knows what people want. He's watched enough reactions when people discover long-forgotten treasures hidden away in storage. Feels like the man on that *Antiques Roadshow* programme he does, watching all the faces smile and say, 'That's not what I expected,' when really they're contemplating if it was worth the petrol spent to drive here. Yes, the manager knows what people want; good at reading people, he is.

He tips his mug to the side and scrunches his face up, realising it's empty. Hoping the young one may nod and mouth 'Shall I get you another one?' He doesn't. He's busy studying the file and Excel sheets the manager gave him.

The manager is just about to hang up, like he always does,

when he stalls. There's a rustle at the other end of the line. He clears his throat. The man (Young! Why is everyone these days sounding so darn young when he himself is sounding so darn old?) on the other end speaks.

'Hi, this is Edith's phone.'

The manager's English is not great. Not very often that Englishmen rent safes in Sweden, which would give him a chance to practice. It's not even English that he speaks now but Swenglish.

'This is the Rent-a-Safe person. Well, erm, manager. I direct the Rent-a-Safe office.' He stops and hums to himself. That's how it should be—he *should* be directing things. Yet it seems no one wants his directions any longer. Not when he's driving, because now there's satnav, and not when at the workplace because now there's *taking initiative* and *working with minimal supervision*. He recommences his vocal delivery. 'I have a safe that belongs to this number. We are about to dispose of its contents since it's unclaimed and payment overdue. Unless you'd like to sort it out.'

'A safe? In Sweden?'

The manager very much wishes the young person wasn't here for this once-in-a-decade phone call he has to conduct in Swenglish, but there you have it. He senses that this will not be the teaching opportunity he had hoped and that at four o'clock he will rub his hands together and say, 'Shall we call that a day?'

'Do you have a name? Whose name is the safe in?' the young man asks. There is bleeping in the background, sounds like a kid's toy low on battery. *Oh.* Hospital sounds, he realises.

'Yes.' The manager doesn't have to look at his paper. He's known the name for almost a decade now. His wife suggested he search for the name on the Facebook, but he has *some* principles doesn't he? One doesn't exploit one's clients.

'It belongs to a Sven Haneman.'

There's a long pause. 'Thank you,' the young man says finally. But he's not sure whether the thank you is for him or someone else. It's a sort of—he hates to say it—*general* thank you, without clear aim or target. Then the young man's voice can be heard again.

'How did you get this number?'

'The safe was rented by Sven Haneman but the name to contact about it was given as Edith.' He pronounces the first name 'Ed-it.' 'So will you be sorting it out, then? Or should we throw it all away?'

There is silence, then a rustling and a croak.

'Thank you. Yes, I do believe I'll be coming to sort it out.'

'Excellent news, excellent. Well, good day, then,' the manager says and hangs up to write his last note as the Rent-A-Safe manager—about the collection of the safe's contents and payment within a fortnight. Then, he can begin his retirement. With an empty desk.

Even without the satisfaction of having lectured a young person on his final day, the manager leaves the facility, happy to be headed home. His wife is cooking beef Wallenbergare.

Blade
London

I DON'T THINK I can read the letters Zara found while sitting next to Mum, so I go and sit outside the hospital. They are dated, and I have to read it twice to make sense of it: *2016*. Years after Mum and Sven's missed love story.

Sven,
 I am so sorry that I didn't find you before it was too late. Life feels so endlessly long doesn't it? Like one long slog. Drain the pasta, wipe your shoes off, don't forget to pack lunchboxes.
 We talked about dying once. As we walked through Brompton Cemetery and read the inscriptions on the tombstones. Couples' names written next to one another and sometimes whole families: five, six, seven names in a vertical row. It never made me sad, reading their names, it made me feel like more life than death existed. That there were so many people that had lived. That life was somehow more powerful than death. Giving off the impression that it could win.
 'I don't know where I'd want to go once I'm gone,' I said.
 'Ashes are less trouble, less environmentally taxing. I'd like to not be a bother.'
 Which made perfect sense. You never wanted to be a bother.

'But where? Ashes can go anywhere.' I thought about ashes then.

'I guess everyone likes a field. Some people don't like the ocean. Too windy, too salty, too crowded, can't swim. But do you ever hear someone say, "I don't like an open green space"? No. I wouldn't think so.'

Then you laughed, and we sat down and ate our sandwiches.

I wonder if you are one with a Swedish rapeseed field now, glowing yellow and bright.

I hope that you are. That you didn't feel you were a bother; even at the end, you would have hated that. That you found a field you liked and could be at peace in. I hope for that and so much more for you, my Sven.

I fold it up again, as if I've read something secret. Mum looked for Sven in 2016 and found him. I can't believe I never found them—the answer was always within the walls of our house. She's written an endless stream of letters but never sent them. Folded neatly into blank envelopes, no stamps. All this time she's known that he was dead. That it was too late.

Sophia
Svedala

MY HEART BEATS an extra beat, and I break a sweat when I see his name pop up on the screen. Then I see that it's only the rental details for the camper-van. *It's obviously paid, you just return to any Sixt location, hope you're doing okay,* he writes underneath. I read it fifteen times as if there ought to be some hidden meaning in there. Then I read it backwards but still can't find anything more.

'I hope you had a good trip,' the man at the desk says as I hand the keys over and he prints the invoice.

'It was good until Markaryd, thank you,' I reply, and I don't even care about the look I get. This man, with brown hair and blue eyes is a blanket flower *(Gaillardia aristata)*. He is a common feature on our streets and I'll forget him when he's out of sight.

'There you go—your invoice.'

'Great,' I say.

ONCE I FINISH the bus journey from the car rental office and finally get off at Svedala station I hesitate. It's empty apart from a stream of teenagers exiting the youth club and a couple of cars in the supermarket car park. I have three options now: my house, Lina's house or the shop. I'm not sure I want to talk about what happened. Kept inside me, I can pretend it's not doing any harm, that it isn't as big as it feels.

I go and settle Cornflakes in my flat, and he goes straight to sleep, not realising I need him for company. The journey has exhausted him, and I sit on the floor and stroke him gently before I get up and slip my feet into my trainers and head out to the store, picking up the same bottle of wine I bought last time I was here. Turns out I can't stand the loneliness after all. I take the Welcome Home notes I left myself and toss them in the paper bin.

IT'S JUST BEFORE seven o'clock when I knock on Lina's door. The first thing that's different is that it takes her almost five minutes to make it to the door. When she does open it, she looks surprised and flustered.

'I have wine,' I say. 'It goes well with vegetables and Sophia.'

'You're back!' She hugs me and when my face is leaned against her shoulder, I notice the second unusual thing, and that's a pair of men's shoes next to the doormat.

'You have company,' I say, my voice deflated despite me willing it to sound excited.

'I met someone.' She looks so pleased that I hug her a second time. 'Please may I introduce you to Tim.'

'Hello, Americano,' I say and stretch my hand out to the tall, handsome coffee customer my best friend has had her eye on for months. 'Nice to meet you.'

He laughs, and the grumpy attitude that we would joke about seems to belong to another person entirely.

'Usually it's just Tim, but I accept in a small town like this I'd stand out enough to earn that nickname.'

'How did this happen?'

'Remember that he started to buy two drinks? And we thought he'd lost his mind as we saw him go to his car and there was no one in the passenger seat?'

I nod. We had plenty of theories. Including that he just wanted to show off his disposable income and that he found life choices so hard he bought two different types of drinks. All of them turned out to be wrong.

'Well, the other drink was for *me*,' Lina says, unusually flushed and pink-faced. 'He just couldn't bring himself to give it to me.'

'She was always so busy and stern-looking. Every day I'd tell myself I'd offer it and ask if she'd sit with me and every day I bailed,' Tim chips in.

'That's the cutest thing I ever heard,' I agree.

'Right?' Lina says and clings to his arm.

'Do you want a drink?' Tim says. I think how quickly he already seems to feel at home here, and my stomach sinks at the memory of how I shared a space with someone too, just a couple of days ago.

I give them the bottle of wine I brought.

'I'll leave you to it. I'm so happy for you guys. Actually, this wine also goes well with lamb and new love, I've been told.'

Lina promises to call me tomorrow and that we'll have wine night this week now that I'm home. I walk back to mine, the now wine-less shopping trolley rolling behind me like a dark shadow bouncing and struggling over the rough pavement, with a strange mix of happy and sad that I can't categorise. But then suddenly I can, because this is a feeling I know well: happy for them, sad for myself.

And I thought it had finally changed.

Blade
London

FIVE DAYS AFTER her accident Mum gets to go home. She's made an incredible recovery. Unprecedented, the medical team told me. A physio will be coming twice weekly and a nurse every day to begin with but she's fit enough to be home. Eliza got a cleaner to come in while we were in hospital and Mum has spent the first hour rearranging items and moving them back to their original place. I hold onto the letters and sit with the words they contain, waiting for a moment to speak to her. Zara left a lasagne in the oven and a bowl of rocket in the fridge, but once we got back she headed home. Now it's just Mum and me again.

This time I know I've got it right. The story. Mum's story.

My anger is gone. Can you even be angry at someone for forgetting? For sending you to look for someone they deep down knew died years ago? When you know how much she never wanted to forget?

I sit down next to her on the sofa.

'I need to talk to you, Mum. I met someone in Sweden. Someone I really like.'

'A girl?'

'A girl. She's called Sophia.'

'That's a lovely name.'

'It's a long story, and I think I better start at the very beginning. With Sven.'

'He didn't turn up.'

'Zara gave me this. She said you photocopied it from the library.' I hold out the A4-size picture of a gathering outside the town hall. The one she used as her screensaver. I point to a face in the crowd.

She doesn't reply. Instead she touches the hem of her long-sleeved T-shirt, a bit like Sophia would, and looks straight at me. The slow nod that follows feels like a drawn out, hard-fought-for confession. The thought of my mum and him both alone, on different sides of the North Sea tugs at my chest. But then I remember that they weren't all alone. One had me, and the other had Sophia.

'You weren't really waiting for him were you? Not that afternoon and not now. Because he did come, didn't he, Mum? We both saw him in that picture from the archives. He did turn up that afternoon in 1996. It was you that didn't turn up, right?'

Her eyes meet mine. I repeat what I just asked.

'*He* was waiting. But you never turned up, did you?'

Sophia
Sweden

THE NEXT DAY I wake up to a crying puppy.

'This is your home,' I tell Cornflakes. 'And I'm your company. It's just me. It will always be me.'

I settle him on my lap and stay in bed with him. The shop can wait. In all these years it's never opened up a minute after eight o'clock, but what has that done for me? What has all my work given me?

At ten there's a knock at my door.

Lina has a floury apron and a hairnet scrunched up in her hand. Cornflakes barks and nips at her trouser hems until she crouches down and acknowledges him with large enthusiastic strokes.

'The shop is closed,' she states.

'I'm having some time off.'

'Two customers have been in asking for you.'

'People miss me?'

'You're an institution, one of the monuments in this town. Yes, people will miss you if you don't show up to work. I suggest you don't go missing again.' She eyes me from top to toe. 'Go pick a grey sweater and a pair of jeans. Socks and sneakers.'

'Okay,' I reply, happy to have been told what to do and for the element of choice to have been eliminated.

She's still there when I reappear five minutes later dressed and with my hair pulled back into a ponytail.

'Good. Let's get you some breakfast.'

I SIP MY hot chocolate sitting on the chair outside her shop so I can see any incoming customers to my own. I've sifted through the online orders and have a couple of deliveries to make this afternoon, but apart from that it's a quiet first day back.

'My dad has asked to meet me. He's attending a conference in Malmö and suggested he'd drive over to see me,' I say. 'He should be here around six.'

'Has he ever been here?'

'A long time ago. He's always very busy.'

She snorts.

MY DAD IS outside at six sharp with a box of chocolates in his hands.

'You don't drink wine, and I couldn't bring you flowers.'

I take the box from him. There are milk chocolates, white chocolates and only a few dark ones. I wonder if he remembers that I don't eat dark chocolate and whether he looked at the ingredient list before choosing this one, or if it's by chance.

'Right. This is lovely,' he says as he sits down on my two-seat sofa after a tour of the shop downstairs.

'Thank you.' I don't know what to say. Having my dad in my house feels rather like a stranger having asked to come in to use the bathroom and I'm standing around waiting for him to leave so I can resume normal business.

'Mum said you've been emailing,' he says finally. 'She waits for them every evening.'

She does? I thought she'd be in bed, seeing them in the morning. I hadn't realised she'd wait up. That it was something she wanted to read.

'We have. I have things to say, things that I needed her to know. I . . . I didn't have a great time in therapy.'

'I used to complain about the cost. Five hundred bloody kroners an hour and another one hundred in petrol both ways.' Dad remarks. *Did you think of the cost to me?* I let the silence settle around us again.

'The car,' I hear myself saying, fortified by Cornflakes's body lying heavy on my lap. 'I hated being left in the car outside the ice rink.' I look at my puppy so I'm not sure if Dad looks at me or not. He replies with some delay.

'I let you stay in the car because I wanted to keep you safe. Those boys in hockey class were bullying you, and if they saw you carrying on—'

'*Stimming.* It's called *stimming.*'

'Right.' He takes a moment. '*I* know that. But if *they* saw it, things would have gotten worse.'

'You could have talked to their parents.'

'We thought they might turn on you even more if we brought it up. Made a big thing of it. We thought it would run its course.'

Well, it did, I think. *A ten-year course.*

'So you locked me up. Away.' I struggle to talk. As if it's my turn to introduce myself in a new group, palms sweating, but I know that I'm right. Before, I didn't: everything felt wrong, but I assumed it was me.

'We did it because we loved you. We thought it was the right thing to do,' Dad says.

Then he is quiet.

'Let me go and top up these drinks,' I say because that's something people say in quiet pockets of air. In the kitchen I message Lina to please come over and that she can bring Tim if he's around. I need someone to talk about the weather, current politics or the national hockey teams.

The minute they arrive the atmosphere changes. *Mutual relief.*

'You friends are very nice, Sophia,' my dad tells me as they leave an hour later.

'I should have visited before,' Dad says. 'You really have been running quite the business here—it's successful, it's working. And I like what you've done with the inside.' His hand sweeps in a half-circle motion, toward the shop.

'Thank you, Dad.'

He doesn't hug me when he leaves. He ruffles Cornflakes's furry tummy for a long time at the doorstep then pats my shoulder. I feel like we are closer—but we still have some way to go.

'Righto, then. Bye.'

Edith
London

MY NEUROLOGIST TOLD me that a new study found there to be twenty-seven human emotions. He told me this as he warned that I may be experiencing a shortening in range, perhaps only really feeling happiness, anger, sadness and contentment. Or, he said, I could be finding myself within a mix of them and not always a rational one. *How wrong was he,* I think now. How very wrong. Look at me skilfully singling out just the one pesky emotion. *Regret.*

'I'll read the last one you sent, yeah?' Blade says, and I want to cover my eyes like a child, but then I think that this is what I want, isn't it? I want it to happen now because in a few years I may stop talking about mössas and Hornton Street and start talking about a naïve woman who didn't come to meet Sven when she should have, who chose the wrong man and ended up alone for a lifetime. So I shush it and keep my hands in my lap.

S,

I know you would do anything for me—for us. I know it will hurt you, and so I cannot face telling you in person. Or with lengthy words. I'm sorry. I can't take Blade with me. I'm not allowed to bring him out of the country without his father's permission. He is promising to come back and be involved, that this has been a wake-up call. He'd come back into both of our lives, then. And I feel I have to give him a chance, to give Blade a chance at a life with both his parents.

I'm sorry.

Blade stops, folds the letter up and waits for me.

'I got as far as that small alleyway next to the church. Then I stopped. I wasn't going to meet him but I desperately wanted to move closer so that I could get a look at him. But if he saw me hovering he might have thought I could be persuaded. I couldn't allow myself to be persuaded. Because I couldn't leave you behind. But I also couldn't bring you.'

I interlace my fingers as though in prayer, as if the mere mention of a church requires it. *God,* do I hate habits with a passion.

'He had come back into the picture, your father. Promising exactly what I'd wanted—love, co-parenting and financial support. But to get it I had to stay. To give us a chance. Even if I'd said no I couldn't have gone, because he wouldn't sign the passport form. I couldn't take you out of the country. He said it was because he loved you too much, because he was going to be a father to you.'

'He didn't keep the promise. He didn't stay around.' The pain on Blade's face, still visible after twenty-nine years, reminds me of exactly why I made the choice to stay. To try. He wanted a father.

'He didn't.' In fact, he disappeared faster than a British heatwave.

'You chose the wrong man.'

'That I did.'

'Why didn't you try to find him? When Dad left? When I was older? You could have had a second chance.'

'We are allowed second chances, but we can only take them if our first choices don't ruin us.' What would I have said? It was too late.

Blade perches forward on the chair, as if he's about to stand up and sprint off, then moves both hands to his face.

'My God, Mum. You've lived with the regret all this time. It's drained you. I saw it sometimes, growing up. It was . . . hard for me to watch.'

'Yes,' I say. The guilt when I think of Sven, of him never marrying, of dying before we found a way to reconnect. Then the guilt for letting my choices affect my son. For being a broken parent.

We'll just wait for time to pass and with every day we'll forget each other more until we're just each other's bleak memories, like running barefoot on summer grass, or hearing on the radio that the Berlin Wall had fallen. Our love story will be memories and marks of time and nothing more. I'd think. *That's what we're doing. Waiting for time to do its thing.*

Turns out I was left to age and forget alone.

In the end I'm the only one waiting. Because Sven died suddenly seven years ago. Before I could find it in me to look for him. Then I started to get cloudy, everything blurring together, but within the haze he was always clear, and I knew I had to find him. That he was what was unresolved in my life. Some days that's all I had. But it was enough.

Sophia
Svedala

AT NIGHT I reread all the messages I have from Blade, but it's like watching your favourite Disney movies as an adult. The magic has disappeared, and you see the cracks, the plot holes and the special effects that are too obvious.

I can't hold off any longer, so I message him.

> I got a dog. I'm still crying a lot, but at least I'm not alone. Started taking a daily vitamin because my main source of nutrition is cereal and milk. I've seen my dad and I didn't feel like everything about me, from the way my hair falls to the sound of my voice, was wrong this time. I think that's progress. I think we can work it out. Me and my dad, I mean. And maybe even me and my mum. She reads my emails.

THE NEXT DAY at five o'clock he video calls. I've looked at my phone so much the past week that I'm amazed the screen, or one of my retinas, hasn't cracked. Apart from work emails and group chats there's been nothing. His voice is tired and hopeful and just as I remember it.

'Soph.' The abbreviation of my name makes me feel little, but not in a bad way. Everyone needs to feel little sometimes. Even very tall women.

'Speaking.'

'That's good. It helps when you call someone.'

'Well—*Hej.*'

'Hey as well.'

'Got your message. I'm glad you responded to me. But I'm sorry things haven't been going well for you.' He pauses briefly before continuing. 'I think that's mostly my fault. I couldn't have stayed, I needed to get home to my mum, but I also shouldn't have left in that way.'

'I needed an explanation. I needed more from you.'

'Your explanation starts now. I need to start from the beginning though. My mum got ill three years ago. It was slow at first, but the disease has been progressing rapidly. She started digging up her past, her memories, while she still could, before she forgot it all. She wanted me to know who she was and what she'd given up. She was looking for someone in particular, a friend, someone that she loved and was in love with. She knew she had to meet him, but kept forgetting that she couldn't. But she would return to the bus stop every day, always waiting for someone who would never come.

'Because she couldn't just say that to me, a mix of denial and her memory fading, I agreed to go to Sweden and look for her lost love, so that maybe she could stop waiting. I had only five leads, five possible names that corresponded to what she could remember.

'The first one lead me to that funeral, where I met you. The former schoolteacher, who had the right name, right age, right town but wasn't mum's Sven. The second lead was your uncle. But at the beginning, when you said he'd never been to London, didn't even own a passport you thought, I dismissed the idea that he was the right one. Svens three, four and five all didn't pan out. I'd given up any hope of finding him until you said you'd learned something new. That he had travelled, specifically to London, and lived there. The more you shared about your uncle, the more it became clear he could be the one.'

'Someone loved my uncle. Wanted to be a family with him. And I never knew.'

'It's strange when you find out your parent, or uncle, wasn't who you thought.'

'It's funny, because I do know who she is. I've known your mum all along.'

Blade looks at me, not quite understanding.

'I told you Sven never went to London. That he never had a relationship. I always found some comfort in the fact he was like me. I could live and be happy even if I were alone, because he was happy even though he was alone.'

'You are like him, he was like you.'

I nod.

'But he did find someone. Just like Vincent told me, he went to London. He spoke about her, what she would do if she lived with him. How she would play with me and teach me a new language and run the shop with him.

'He never said her name. She wasn't real. Or at least I thought she wasn't. He would talk about her like he was telling me a story, creating a fairy tale for me, for us to live inside when the world was too much for me. Remember the drawing you asked about in my shop? The one of a happy family? And the one in the camper-van?'

'Yes.'

'She was Miss Marigold. Your mum.'

Blade pauses, but I can see something building in his face.

'Yes, my mum was your Miss Marigold. The love they had was so special he told you stories about it. Because he was happy. And I am now too, not just because I found Sven for my mum, but because I found you.

'You coming on this trip was the best thing that's happened to me in years. I felt freer, more seen, more alive when I was with you. I felt more like myself, and that there might be more to life than just caring for Mum full time. But then I had to leave.'

This is a lot of information. I tense and then say, 'You know how I like directness. Explanations and reasons. Why did you leave with just a message?'

'I had to go right away. Mum had a fall and was in hospital. I panicked. I didn't think you could handle it, me splitting my attention and focus with my mum. But it was selfish. I'm so sorry, Sophia.'

In my family we only say sorry for stepping on each other's feet or spilling a glass of milk. I blink at the unusual use of the word.

He continues.

'I learned so much on this trip. Your uncle and my mum loved each other. He did turn up that day. You were right, he was a good man. And my mum made a wrong choice, much like I did, much like we all do sometimes. But like her I want to make it better, to apologise and to hope that you can forgive me. Because the most important thing I learned on this trip was how much I love you.'

Then he tells me there is a safe that belonged to my uncle waiting to be opened an hour's drive from where I am. A safe with something he wanted Blade's mum to have. My anger has faded over the course of the phone call, as I have started to understand. *If Blade hadn't come to find Sven we would never* have met. *If my uncle didn't love his mother, we never would have met. If I hadn't gone on this trip with Blade, I wouldn't have tried to save my shop, I wouldn't have learned to stand up for myself, I wouldn't have learned to fight.* And most importantly, Blade left not because he doesn't want me but because he's also scared. And he's back now.

Blade
London

I GET OFF the phone as I walk through Kensington Gardens on my way to drop off a box of chocolates to Hamptons. Mum tells me the estate agent who helped her is called Eliza and wears sad footwear. I think that description will be sufficient. The peonies, and the roses and irises are still blooming in flowerbeds behind the black railings but all I can think of is a grass flower.

I write to her, the call not being nearly enough. *What flower are you now?*

I FIND ELIZA right away and she seems to recognise me.

'Edith's son, hi!' She is pretty and energetic, and I can imagine her in a promotional video for a new-build eagerly demonstrating the hot-water tap.

'I've got something for you. A thank you, for being there for her and being so kind,' I say.

'It's no problem at all. She's become a friend.'

'I still have a hard time thinking of my mum as having friends.'

'Oh, she has a lot. A whole village, I'd say. She's become a bit of a legend around here.'

My mum. The woman who can't be moved. Which brings me to the other reason I came to see Eliza.

'I'll have to keep that in mind when we look for care homes. She's agreed to move, but only on the condition that you sell her house and that the sale process involves many teas, coffees and chats. She has accepted she'll lose Hornton Street and the bus stop, but she hasn't accepted that she'll lose you and everything else this place gave her.'

Eliza smiles.

'I'd be happy to. And we'll stay friends. Tell her we can try for an open house-style viewing if she would like a bit of a crowd and refreshments.'

I nod. It sounds perfect.

'Did you know she set up a neighbourhood food bank while you were away? Milk, flour, eggs and, bizarrely, tape. She has regulars. An open viewing will be just what she needs.'

As I leave the estate agency, my phone pings with Sophia's name.

I'm currently a touch-me-not (Mimosa pudica).

I google, and it turns out it's a real ball-shaped purple plant.

The compound leaves fold inward and droop when touched or shaken, but usually reopens a few minutes later, the description says.

A sensitive plant. I can work with that.

Sophia
London

TWO DAYS AFTER my call with Blade, I receive an email with a ticket attached to it. It's from an Eliza, but the message says that it's sent on behalf of Edith. *Edith.* I'm going to meet Edith, Blade's mum, the woman my uncle loved so much he'd do anything for her. The woman he loved so much he'd even leave her be, to let her do what was best for her son. I can't pack flowers, but I can pack things that calm me. From what Blade has told me, his mum has similar difficulties to me because of her disease. I know all about being sensitive to light and touch.

I know that Edith will be waiting for me at her address, and I also know that Blade won't be there when I arrive. Blade and I are messaging again, slowly building up trust. Figuring out what things might look like if I decide I can handle his life.

As if she knows I need the encouragement, my mum has sent me an email, which I read outside Arrivals, waiting in line for a taxi. I open it and smile to myself. All my emails have gone unanswered until now, but as it turns out, not for nothing. She's listened, which is all I ever wished for. To have a voice.

FROM: Mum
SUBJECT: Me communicating. Finally.

Dear Sophia,

I'm sorry this has taken me a while to write. All I ever wanted was to give you everything. Your father and I worked so hard for our house, for the clothes you wore, to give you kids everything we didn't have. I wanted you to look like the other girls in school. I never did. One time my classmate's mum brought a black bin bag with clothes and dumped it next to your grandma's car. 'Here you go,' she said. 'Your girl is a bit smaller than mine, and some of this may fit her.' I didn't have the heart to tell my mother I could not under any circumstances wear the most popular girl in schools' hand-me-downs. It would be social suicide. Because the relief on my mother's face was bigger than my shame. Her girl wouldn't freeze and she wouldn't have to choose between grocery store money or buying me clothes.

You see, Sophia, we were poor. I told you to do things like eat your food, think of all the starving the children in Africa, but in my head I thought 'Think of me.' We weren't poor in the sense you may think of it but gosh, yes, we were poor. I did my homework in the dark because I didn't want to waste electricity. Squinted my eyes to the point of my mother thinking I needed glasses.

So when I started making money, I wanted to make enough of it. I would stay late at work. I found a babysitter for you all. I enjoyed my job but even more so I enjoyed buying things for you, Sophia. I enjoyed the girls looking at you when you arrived to school, glancing at your new glittery trainers. When you wanted to cut off the labels and rip off the sequins on a skirt, I thought, There goes all my effort. And I couldn't understand why you would want to. Does she not know what I'd have given for those clothes when I was her age?

I thought the only way forward was to give you more. There were so many things we did wrong, because we didn't understand you. But that was our fault. We didn't try hard enough to.

I never meant to hurt you, not then and not now. Knowing that I did hurt you pains me more than I can ever tell you.

Your Mum

PS I thought you loved the babysitter?

FROM: Sophia
SUBJECT: Re: Me communicating. Finally.
I loved her because she put on Cinderella as many times as I wanted whilst she did her nails, and she let me scrape my food into the kitchen bin. I never ate when she was there. It was fine, but I would have loved my mum there instead.

Sophia

PS Why did you never hug me when you got back home? I saw families doing it on TV, so I ran to the door when you were back, but you never scooped me up.

FROM: Mum
SUBJECT: Re: Me communicating. Finally.
But you never liked hugs. You would stiffen and stand still as a statue.

Mum

FROM: Sophia
SUBJECT: Re: Me communicating. Finally.
Research shows trees respond to hugs. Plant cells can perceive pressure waves. Trees are still and unmoving. Meaning, I still needed to be hugged. I might still.

FROM: Mum
SUBJECT: Re: Me communicating. Finally.
You're in London now, but I might go and hug a tree for you, since you say they can respond.

I smile as I type my reply.

FROM: Sophia
SUBJECT: Re: Me communicating. Finally.
That sounds good. Try to find a Weeping Willow, they're the best ones to hug. They need the emotional support;)

My mum is going to go hug a tree, just for me.

FORTY-FIVE MINUTES LATER, a taxi drops me in front of a white house with a red door and a wild and unruly front garden.

I can tell immediately upon meeting her that Edith is a rubber plant, a *Ficus elastica*. You might mistake her for something romantic like a lilac, or gorgeous like a rose, but that would be to underestimate her. She has large waxy leaves and can adapt to any situation. I know instantly that I can get along well with a *Ficus elastica*.

'My girl,' she says and pulls me down towards her. 'Finally I meet you. Would you like me to show you the way to Hornton Street?'

I manage Edith's wheelchair onto the ramp of the red bus and park it in the dedicated space. When we get off the bus, she asks me to stop. It's busy, and the pavement is dirty. Everyone walks faster than what I'm used to.

'I will wait here. You go ahead. Straight ahead and on your right, a large rust-coloured brick building. You can't miss it.'

'I can't leave you here,' I object.

'I have a lot of friends here. Half the neighbourhood. I'll spot one of them soon enough. Go.'

Blade
London

I'M HERE TO meet Eliza again, bringing the power of attorney form that Mum signed, and Mum's message an hour ago makes little sense. I know she's up to something.

> You're meeting someone. Be at the bus stop at three o'clock.

I make my way to the bus stop and sit, watching as people pass by, on their way to work and school and home, I imagine. To live life.

The knot that's formed in my stomach keeps growing as the appointed time approaches. Did Mum feel this every time she stood here? I look down at my shoes, the leaves, the squares of the pavement. Then I look up and see her. Her arms sway, and she walks fast, too fast. Her eyebrows draw together and then—there it is, the smile. She's here and she is smiling: that has to mean something. The town hall is to my left, and the library to my right, and there we are in the middle at the bus stop which must have seen thousands of meetings just like this one.

I walk towards her, and she nods as if to say *Yes, it's okay*, and then I sweep her into my arms.

'Sophia. You're here.'

I pull her close to me.

'I'm sorry,' I mumble into the top of her head.

'And I'm sorry for not making it clearer that I was *in*,' she says.

'Sophia, I should have never left the way I did. I should have talked to you, explained, given you a chance to react and figured out a way to handle this. Together.'

'And now? Are you sure that we can figure it out?' she asks. 'I can't cook, I won't move anywhere because I have my business, and I still don't like kissing.'

I laugh.

'Soph, I'm going to suggest something.'

'What?'

'That maybe we give kissing a try.'

I can see her mind spinning.

'Look, I think that's what you want too. And it's just something to try. Soph?'

I trace her jaw and the soft lines of her face with my fingers and feel her lean into my touch.

'Yes. We should . . . try.'

'Sophia, I know you. How your lips twitch and how you need to breathe deep breaths whenever something makes you emotional. But if I got this wrong and you don't want to, then that's okay too.'

'Okay let's try. Let's get it over with,' she says.

'Wow, you're such a romantic.'

'Sorry. I mean . . .'

What does she mean?

I take a small step closer. 'I'll talk you through it so you know what to expect, okay?'

'Okay.'

'First, I'm going to brush my lips against yours.'

I let my lips brush against hers, and the widest, sweetest tingle goes down my spine. And she stays, doesn't move her face away.

'What do you think?' I ask as we pull away from each other.

'This is what I think, Blade. Mouths contain eighty million bacteria but I guess it's like with E-numbers or the aspartame in a Diet Coke. The minute you taste it, you forget it's bad for you because it tastes so sweet.'

I smile as I pull her into a big hug.

'That is the most Sophia of all answers.'

A COUPLE OF hours later I'm sitting with Mum, Sophia and Zara. There are Hobnobs, Digestives (today's small choice for Mum) and teas, and we let her take her time. I asked Mum if she wanted to be the one to open the safe in Sweden, that it could be arranged with a video call if nothing else, but it's a firm and very conclusive no.

'I couldn't even pick up the call. Let Sophia do it. It was her uncle.'

Sophia will go and collect it as soon as she arrives back in Sweden.

'Did he ever talk about a lost love? About a girlfriend?' I ask Sophia now.

'Not a girlfriend, no. He said I was his one and only love, and that for some of us there are only a few people in this world who can love us truly.' She looks at me now. Looks at me and doesn't look away.

'That's the truth,' Mum adds.

'He said it was like tending to certain flowers. They won't

grow for anyone. 'I once tried to control a marigold, a *Tagetes*, Sophia,' he said, 'but I couldn't, and so I had to accept defeat and not try to plant it again.'

'You're as stubborn as a marigold, Edith,' my mum suddenly says, and we all look at her.

'Miss Marigold. He drew you, Edith. We both did. I have the drawings with me. I'll talk you through the life he imagined for our stick family. I know so much about Miss Marigold. Her favourite season was autumn, she loved to dance and meet new people, and she could make anyone feel like they'd known her for ages.'

We all sit quietly for a while.

'And why wasn't he in any pictures? Graduation? The shop website?'

Sophia answers this without hesitation.

'He hated pictures. Big crowds. Small talk about the weather. Those connections that don't feel like connections at all. Do you think you'll find *me* in many photos? That's really not strange. I'd be as surprised to see him in a group photo as I was hearing he'd gone to London and had a *life*. All this time I thought he was a loner. And that that was what was in store for me too, if my efforts to change failed.'

'I have a feeling you'll find the odd picture once we pack up the house. But I can't for my life tell you where I would have hidden them,' Mum offers.

Sophia continues. 'I think Edith brought out his love of people. When she didn't turn up he went back into isolation. They both did.'

'I made the wrong choice. Obviously I could not be trusted to make choices, so I didn't. I focused on Blade and that was that. Trying to survive the heartbreak,' Mum says.

Everyone falls silent.

'What are you thinking about, Soph?'

'I'm thinking that if this didn't happen, we wouldn't have met. Perhaps I would have been isolated too.'

'One more question, Mum. Why didn't you answer the phone?' I ask, ready to wrap this up and move on.

'I think it's simple.'

'Go on.'

'I didn't want anyone telling me what I already knew. That it was too late. And it was all my fault.'

IT'S SOPHIA'S IDEA. At first, I tell her it's impossible. Then Mum overhears us and gets involved. Once that happens there's no return.

'I've always wanted to move to Sweden. I planned it all those years ago and wouldn't it be fabulous if it happened?'

'I'm not sure moving would be wise. It can increase symptoms and speed up onset and progression,' I argue.

'There is a time to listen to prognosis and the world of science and then there's a time to take a leap and listen to your heart,' Mum insists. Can't argue much with that.

Sophia is fully on board. It warms me seeing how she'd rather fight to have my mum move with us than take the easy way out and leave her in a care home we'd visit once a month. She never suggested that I move to Sweden—she suggested we both do.

'I'm very sure she's not a vegetable plant, but even if she is and didn't like having her roots disturbed, I have experience with moving even the trickiest plants. Transplantation is never fully impossible under the right conditions,' she insists.

'In this particular instance I'd like to argue that my mum is not a flower, nor is she a bulb,' Blade says, smiling.

'We will all turn to soil and grass and plants in the end,' Mum chips in helpfully.

'I'm never going to win with you two, am I? Ever.'

'Quite possibly, no,' Mum says at exactly the same time that Sophia says, 'No.'

'Miss Marigold belongs in that shop. Well, at least in the town,' she adds.

Two very determined women. That's what I'm up against from now on. And I don't mind. Not one bit. Of course, Sophia has thoroughly researched the topic of moving with dementia and provides all the arguments.

'The small town will be easier for her. I've read about people with dementia making the move in the early stages to escape the sensory load that is the city. The noise, the smells, congested pavements, getting lost when roads and architecture keep changing. In Svedala, she would have the freedom to still walk out the door alone. Be in nature.'

I give in.

'So. Sweden it is.'

I just got a whole lot busier. Apply for papers, get Eliza onto fast-tracking the sale of the house, find a decent care home in Sweden, transfer the pension. But anything should be possible. My mum is finally going to start a new life abroad aged sixty-five and I'm coming with her.

WE ARE PACKING. It's a big task, and we figured it's better to start right away. Mum is sat in the armchair and I'm following instructions. Somehow as she gets more clouded, more tired, her alert days, the days when she is herself, become brighter. She is efficiently guiding me around the living room's drawers and shelves. What used to be a cluttered house, her home for twenty years, will soon be bare and minimalistic with only the large furniture pieces left. Today Pushba is helping, her youngest child on the floor with wooden spoons and kitchen pots to keep busy. It's loud, but Mum likes noise. Apparently a toddler banging on a metallic pot drives away other sensory experiences, such as the smell of rat.

'We'll miss you.'

'I won't sell to anyone unless they're the type of person who lends their neighbour a pint of milk,' Mum says.

I shake my head at her.

'I can't believe that for years you wouldn't move, and now you've just agreed to move to Sweden. You were the woman who can't be moved.'

'I was always meant to be there. If I could have been with the man I loved, I would have spent my life there. I was meant to have my overseas adventure.'

'Look at this,' Pushba calls from the other room, where she is helping clear out Mum's wardrobe. In her hand is a glossy photo of two people on a park bench, tulips blooming behind them. Mum and Sven. Pushba smiles.

'I found it at the bottom of the box of winter coats.'

Sophia
Svedala

LINA PICKS ME up on the other side of the flight, and seeing her makes the physical illness I feel at being away from Blade subside. I stand still and straight with my bags in my hands as she hugs me.

'Cornflakes is with Tim,' she explains when I scan the car for him.

'Can you pass by an address in Malmö?' I ask. 'I need to collect something. For Edith and Blade.'

THE MANAGER IS young and keen.

'There's been quite a search for you,' he says, when I tell him what I'm there for. He shows me which safe is Edith's, then hovers next to me as I carefully put the key inside. The key is small and insignificant; it reminds me of a bicycle-lock key or the small silver ones you get on a rubber wrist band at public pools. There's a wooden box inside. Nothing else.

'Aren't you going to open it?' The man's disappointment is obvious.

I press it to my chest and breathe in the smell of earth, still there in the wood after years inside a square, metal space.

'Not just yet.'

I CALL BLADE as soon as I've got the contents.

'This is what was inside,' I say, showing him. It's an intricately carved wooden box, much like a jewellery case or where someone might put their sewing needles and thread.

'Did you open it already?' he asks.

'Not yet.' He watches me carefully as I unclasp the metal latch. The lid doesn't immediately spring open, and it takes me a second attempt and more force for it to comply.

'It's letters,' I say. 'Hundreds of letters organised according to year. There are Post-its separating them. It's my uncle's writing'

'I'll get Mum,' Blade says.

Edith is on crutches now, starting to bear weight on her legs. She shuffles over to the sofa and Blade holds up the screen so she can see me.

'It's letters. All letters,' I tell her when she's sitting down. 'He wrote to you.'

'Are they stamped?' she asks and I flick through a pile again to confirm.

'No,' I say. 'Not a single stamp.'

Edith closes her eyes as if she's on a rollercoaster or a high cliff she doesn't want to look down from.

'I'll read them all when I get there. One by one.'

'They span twenty years, Edith,' I say. 'From 1996 to 2016 when he died. All these years you were both writing to each other, but never sending the letters.'

I GET MY laptop up and ready and wait for it to be four o'clock. I log on five minutes early and then sit there, staring at the virtual waiting room with my heart beating fast, until one, two, three, four members of my family finally arrive. *I can do this.*

'Hi, Sophia,' they all say in different tones and pitches.

'Thanks for tuning in,' I say, as if I'm hosting a radio show.

'We're listening.'

I take a deep breath that stretches my insides to the point of being almost painful. *Ready.*

'I'd like to keep the shop,' I say. 'I don't have the money to buy you out up front but I'm happy to pay instalments. Or have you all be shareholders and you get a part of the profit. But the shop is my life. It's what kept me going when things in my childhood and its various components almost killed me. I can't lose it.'

There, I said it.

'I think a shareholder agreement sounds very wise,' Mattias says, the first one to speak.

'If that's what Sven wanted, then why didn't the will say so? He meant for you to use the shop as a gateway to life. Your first five years was sorted. Then you'd have to stand on your own two legs like everyone else,' Hampus says.

'Or maybe he thought the five years would be sufficient for me to learn to stand my ground and fight for what I want in life.'

Pontus's head is constantly bobbing off to the side.

'Sorry, how long do you think this will take? Djurgården is playing MFF.'

'As long as it takes to find a solution,' I offer.

'Listen, I don't need money upfront,' Pontus says. 'Not a problem if it comes as small payments from profit.'

'That's assuming Sophia can make a profit,' Hampus argues.

'And that's where I have almost five years' experience and trading history to show you,' I counter. 'You've also seen my work and are familiar with it.' I'm grateful for Vincent's decision to invite them to see it firsthand despite me telling him not to.

'I say let's get an agreement drafted and then take a final decision,' Mattias suggests.

'That sounds reasonable,' Hampus says.

Pontus has gone off-screen completely now, the sound that emits tells us that either his team just scored or he has witnessed a murder in his living room.

'He'd sign over his own mother to watch the game. Don't worry, he's in,' Mattias says.

'Great,' I say, avoiding the words 'thank you' because I want to have authority and women in general need to say 'thank you' less. 'I will handle this.'

When we hang up I'm surprised at how easy it was—one conversation that undid years of worrying. I think perhaps there will be other things in life I can approach head-on and solve, and that I'm capable. Sometimes conversation and communication are good things that I don't need to be afraid of.

The drafted shareholder agreement arrives back signed by all three brothers within a few days after I sent it off to Mattias. I skim it fast and then sit in stillness.

I have no payments to make at the end of next year. *It's mine.*

'How did you convince them to sign so quickly? I didn't even know that you wanted it to turn out this way,' I ask Mattias as soon as he answers my call.

'I didn't want you to have to wait another minute. You've been in limbo for way too long. You needed that closure fast,' my brother says. 'I can't just stay out of things all my life. I've been in a surprise-party planning group chat for four months, and so far I've contributed the word "Great." I need to get involved with life and what happens to people. So—here the right thing is easy. Much easier than whether we buy helium balloons which are bad for the environment or go for confetti that has to be hoovered off the floor for hours.'

I pull the corners of my mouth into a smile.

'The problem was never yours. It was that you didn't have enough people standing up for you. I followed Mum and Dad, and for some reason they couldn't see what harmed you. They couldn't relate to you.'

That hurts. But he's right. I was so different, not the girl they'd dreamt of after three boys. I didn't like dresses and would wail when my mum tried to do my hair. Karin told them she had solutions. That I was treatable. If you don't understand something perhaps you'd believe anyone who says they do? They couldn't relate to me, so they couldn't stop what was happening to me.

Mattias continues.

'Honestly, it didn't take much. You've stayed away, and they haven't seen you in action. They've imagined you holed up in your uncle's old flat selling some flowers now and again. When they saw you handling a big project and what you created in their town, it was an eye-opener. What would they ever be able to do with the business themselves? I think being shareholders is the perfect solution. They'll all see firsthand how very capable you are. They'll profit from something *you* are doing. Trust me, their relationship with you will change.'

THE SHOP IS mine. *Forever.* I don't have to sell, and I don't have to scramble around and find hundreds of thousands of kroners. No more contracts in market towns that make me feel overwhelmed and anxious. Just me and the flowers in this small space I love so much. If this past month has taught me something, it is that yes, I *can* do it if I have to, but I don't *want* to. I want my home, Cornflakes, Lina and the same pasta salad every lunchtime. On top of those joys, I get to email my brothers a quarterly profit statement and witness their reaction to the fact that Sophia, the one who no one believed in, is doing well.

Then I write to my parents. My parents who now follow Autistic accounts on Twitter and like their posts. *I love you*, I write. Because I have a lot of love in my life, and I'm not stingy. I am happy enough to give love even when it's not fully earned yet. And I think that maybe love is worth something, maybe even a lot. We don't get each other but I'm no longer an annexe to the family home. I've moved out, broken free and found a plot of land to build myself on. I'm a cottage now. With wonky windows and a messy bedroom. Mum can come and visit as long as she's happy to see a cottage. She may never go shopping with me or say, 'My daughter is my best friend.' But there is love, and in the end a person you love and who loves you is sometimes enough. I can cut strings and end my relationship, or I can build on the little we have and give them a chance.

I love you, Mum, I write a second time. *Tell Dad I love him too.*

TO ADD TO my feelings of lightness that evening I get an email from my dad a few hours later, whose email address I didn't even know before. I mean, I must have known he had one, just like I know he has a shoe size, but it's never been relevant to me to know it before.

FROM: Harald (Dad)
SUBJECT: Interior design changes you may approve of

Hi Sophia,

Spoke to Mum. Just to let you know the framed picture of you and Santa which has been on the mantelpiece has been replaced with a group shot of you and your brothers in the Azores anno 2012. I hope you will come and see the changes soon.

Dad

I think that maybe I *could* go back there soon. That things won't magically change overnight but perhaps they will have in some small way. Perhaps next time I'll try to not take any sauce with my potatoes—to say, *No thank you, I'd like them plain, please*—and see what happens.

THAT EVENING I log onto my Twitter, and instead of lurking around and following hashtags I make my own post.

> @THEGRASSFLOWER: Unmasking is a terrifying prospect but I think it will be worth it in the end. #ABA-ptsd.

I think I might finally be finding myself. It wasn't about getting a boyfriend, about adding that one missing piece. It was about shaping and attending to all the small pieces in my life, making sure they fit as smoothly as possible. It's a process I have to continue all my life, but that's okay, I know how to do it now.

Blade
Svedala

'FLOWER STATUS?' I ask, coming up behind Sophia and pushing an empty coffee cup into the sink in front of her. She smiles.

'Lucky bamboo? *Dracaena sanderana*.'

I kiss the top of her head.

'See you later. I'm headed to Mum's.'

SOMETIMES THE BEST way to resolve trauma and past heartbreaks is to just start living, to do the opposite of what it wants us to do. Trauma wants us to stay scared, locked in our old ways and not move forward, and that's what we have to be brave enough to resist. This is exactly what Mum and I are finally doing—moving forward.

Mum has finally moved into her own apartment with a view over the garden. It's just down the corridor from the library and very far from the common sitting room, an important and non-negotiable requirement. Sophia has taken her on a tour of the local amenities, entering each location as a pin on her phone map as they go along, as I'm putting the final touches to her new home. The flat is perfect. Light, cosy and not at all what I had feared. This is not an institution but a home. From her apartment she walks out into a corridor where the front door is clearly seen, and once pushed open she'll find herself in a large, enclosed garden. Benches lined along paths and a vegetable path in the far corner. Mum is enjoying being the newest arrival and having neighbours stick their heads out of doors to spy on her or offer general advice. 'Don't go to Mindfulness. It's basically just gaslighting yourself into thinking you're doing great.' and 'The liquor store does next-day delivery if you tell them you live here. VIP treatment.'

I've unpacked the bags and hung the very colourful clothing up. Her wardrobe reminds me of a Picasso painting with its yellows and purples forming various patterns against the white shelves. I put the framed pictures up and deposit a stack of hardbacks on a bookshelf. I have added a room fragrance stick to the cabinet, high enough for it to not spill over should a clumsy arm lash out at it. At the bottom of the bag Mum packed herself, I find the bunch of flash cards. Some old and some recent, the neatness of the handwriting giving their age away. I take out the empty white flash cards I've brought with me: They're made out of cardboard so sturdier and no risk of paper cuts. When I'm done writing I put them in the mix with Mum's old ones. The move will be disorientating, we've been told. She may struggle at first. We'll be close by, though. Mum will be okay. I can love her and be just her son now, not her carer. We can build a relationship where we get to know each other again.

Where we take a walk or grab one of those ridiculous Swedish bakery goods that always seem to be filled with fluffy vanilla-flavoured double cream. A relationship where I'm not reminding her to take a pill or do her exercises, or feeling the desperation rise inside me as she won't do what she's told. My shoulders sink low with relief at the thought of this new life. I pull out the cards again and read the messages I wrote, hoping they're as neutral and pain-free as possible. Hoping my mum won't relive the pain every single time she reads it.

Sven did come that afternoon in 1998. He always loved you and never forgot you. He lived a good life. He died in 2016.

Then I add the most important part of it all. What I hope she remembers when old feelings stir and push at her sanity.

Everyone makes wrong choices. Everyone has regrets. You lived a good life too.

Sophia
Svedala

THE FIRST CUSTOMER of the day is looking for a bouquet for her aunt who's unwell.

'May I suggest some carnations? They don't just stand for love, captivation and distinction which one might think but also for medicinal purposes, such as for upset stomach and fever.'

'How lovely. These are very pretty, aren't they?' She looks at the flowers in the buckets I've shown her.

'Any colour preference?' I ask her. 'Although I'd stay clear of red. It was US President McKinley's lucky charm and he always wore one on his lapel.' The customer looks at me expectantly. I stop for breath and then add, 'He was, however, assassinated.'

'Oh. Should we go for a white mix, then?'

'Wonderful.' I start to work on them. All my focus spreads through my hands as I cut, bind and make something beautiful.

Sometimes when I go to sleep at night I don't close my eyes, I keep them open for a while. And I go through all my favourite parts of Blade like a map. When I start to tire, I close my eyes and continue. Here's why it sends me to sleep so well: it's endless. I never run out of places and at some point I always drift off with the warm fuzzy feeling inside me I've come to recognise as my new normal. When normal is like this, I don't need extraordinary. Who does?

I MEET EVERYONE at the old quarry after work. I'm carrying the biggest bouquet of flowers, and Cornflakes is on a lead next to me, lunging forward when he sees his human daddy. I let go, ignoring training techniques for today, and let him run towards Blade.

'This is the epic closure every love story should have,' Lina says.

It was Edith's idea, and she wouldn't let it go. 'The letters will come back and haunt me again,' she said. The more we thought about it, we could see that she had a point. The new Swedish neurologist agreed there's something to be said for closure, for the calmness it brings to a brain in uproar. 'It's not a bad idea making a ceremony of it. Perhaps even take some pictures,' she told us.

So here we are. I'm cradling Edith's and Sven's letters turned to ashes in my best porcelain vase. The ones they both wrote but never sent—now mixed together.

'So is this a common Swedish tradition?' Americano aka Tim asks. We all burst out laughing because, of course, we all probably seem barking mad to an outsider. Spreading letter ashes as if they're human remains. He should know that by now, seeing how much time we spend together. Even if I'd tried, I couldn't have pictured a better scenario than the one in which my best friend's boyfriend becomes my boyfriend's best friend.

I give Edith a hug and feel my chest expand from the joy of being together, the joy of being slightly unhinged, of there being no secret, of sharing grief with someone who understands.

I have kept one letter, with her permission. The words aren't for me, but they soothe me still, give me a sense of belonging I never had. I'm not the only one in my family. If I didn't know before, then the letter proves it.

> *I have a niece, Edith. She's not like my nephews. She needs me. I understand a little bit more of what was behind your decision now. What I mean is that I'll never be happy about your choice, but I understood your decision once Sophia was born. She's not my child, but she needs me, without me there'd be no one in her world like her. She has my brain, and I need to make sure she grows up knowing people will love her for it, even if it won't always feel like it.*
>
> *I hope you moved on. That you have a good life.*

Blade shakes the vase, and the fragmented ashes fly out, separating as soon as the wind touches them, flying off in a million directions within seconds, never to be reunited.

I reach for Blade's hand.

A Retired Storage Facility Manager
A good chanterelle spot

THE RETIRED RENT-A-SAFE manager and his wife have brought a Thermos flask and sandwiches. It's chanterelles season and he's looking forward to an afternoon of telling his wife where to find the best mushrooms and which direction to go.

He's always liked the forest. England has its Premier League and France has its baguettes, but do they have the fresh pine air and endless space that Sweden does? No, he didn't think so. He stops abruptly. There's a bloody racket! Who would bring a bloody racket to the forest when the retired manager knows that silence is what makes mushrooms reveal themselves? Shy things they are.

'Leave this to me,' the manager tells his wife, pressing the basket into her arms.

'Of course.' The manager's wife tends to always leave things to him; the bin, paying the bills, figuring out why she's sleeping in the guest room most nights.

He pushes through the shrubbery toward where the noise is coming from, appearing the other side of the trees covered in pine needles as if he's attempted to camouflage. He coughs. The air is bloody *polluted*. Ashes! In a forest! When the manager is about to collect his chanterelles! He is about to storm up and give the culprits a piece of his mind—there is a lot of it to give, since it's been resting and dormant since his retirement one month ago—when he stops in his tracks. What a funny-looking group. Not at all a group of teenagers frying sausages over an open fire risking the wildlife the retired manager holds dear. No—there's an older lady on crutches, surrounded by young people, and then there's a dog. It's on its lead, so no opportunity for him to complain there, he notes with disappointment. The ashes have cleared, but perhaps he got a fragment in his left eye because it's watering. Or perhaps it's the right one. It might be both eyes, come to think of it. The laughter of the group cuts through the silence, and the retired manager finds himself turning around, his feet sinking into soggy moss.

When he gets back to his wife he smiles at her. His face feels funny and distorted but when she smiles back at him he finds himself widening it nevertheless. He takes the basket from her, pointing also at the backpack carrying their picnic hanging off her shoulders.

'Here, let me carry that for you. Which direction shall we go?'

A Listening Tattoo Artist
London

THE TWO GIRLS walk in holding hands. The tattoo artist looks them over. He's good at guessing motifs. That's ten years in the business for you. He sometimes used to bet with Len, his older colleague, but then his girlfriend pointed out that it's unprofessional and he stopped. Have to listen to people, haven't you? He never did when he was young but at twenty-eight he's learnt. He has listened, and now he squeezes the water out of the sponge before leaving it by the sink, he puts the toilet seat down, and he doesn't whistle and call after women on the street. And so he does the guessing quietly in his head too, sometimes letting a vowel or word slip his lips. *Talking to himself*, they'll think. But lots of people talk to themselves and do all sorts of weird things, don't they? This is London.

The girls look too cool to ask for an eternity sign, a star, or—horror—some phrase in Chinese. Mind you, he hasn't had to do any of those since the jeans became higher-rise and girl bands went out of fashion. They could ask for simple initials or each other's names, he ponders: they certainly look loved up enough, the way they walk so close their hips bump into one another, as if they had magnets sewn into trouser seams. But he thinks they'll surprise him. If he and Len were still betting he'd *bet* they'd surprise him.

'We'd like matching marigolds,' the taller girl says, the one that already is sporting tattoos on her arms and collarbone along with pink shoulder length hair.

'Flowers, yeah?' the tattoo artist asks.

'Marigolds, specifically. We have some pictures.' She flicks through her camera roll and turns the screen towards him. Small, fluffy, asymmetrical, vibrant, delicate flowers.

He nods. This is good. There's obviously a story here and that's what he likes most—bringing stories to life forever. Etched on skin. Words don't come easily to him, and he never learnt to write, not like other people can, with full stops and commas and fancy words that make folk *feel* something. But he likes to think he can tell some sort of story through his work.

The shorter girl goes first, passing her bag to her girlfriend before lying down. 'So I can get it over with,' she says. This is her first tattoo, she confirms.

'Marigolds are resilient and stubborn and they've influenced us both. We're together because of one,' she says.

The tattoo artist gets to work on her thin, white, shaky wrist, creating black pixels that will stay with her for a lifetime.

Marigolds.

He likes when he learns something new at work.

Edith

Six Months Later
Svedala

IT'S TUESDAY, WHICH means Yoga. *Fabulous.* Much more so than yesterday's class which was conversational Arabic. The yoga instructor is getting married, and we are all excited to hear her gossip in between poses and deep breathing. Sophia dropped off a pair of shiny purple pants because my new friend Ruth keeps turning up in a leopard set, and I can't be seen as less, can I? Not in my first month. Oh, and someone died yesterday. Always sad. My other new friend Ruth and I were having a tea in my room and alas the nuisance and voices and general mayhem started. We took turns to peek out from the door and kind of stroll halfway down the corridor as if we'd forgotten something. *Oh, my scarf*, she mumbled. *My book!* I exclaimed. It was Ralph, as it turned out. At dinner we spoke about our memories of him (mine: he never returned the Jane Austen I borrowed from him for the Ladies' Book Circle. Ladies' Book Circle as in we read ladies' work, not that we're all ladies. I hope I get it back but can't be rude and ask).

The following day the chat starts again, because someone new will move in soon. This is the thing here. Things always happen, move forward. I am no longer in a rut between my house and Hornton Street, I am somewhere where things happen and where we can look out the window and see a removal van arriving with who may or may not be our new best friend. I said this last bit to Ruth, to keep her on her toes. Good to know that there are options. I quite enjoy being the youngest in the building too.

Sophia resembles Sven and sometimes when I look at her I forget that she is my daughter-in-law and think she is part of me. *We did it,* I think, as if Sven could hear me. *You said you'd take care of me, but I didn't let you because I thought I knew how to do life without you. Now I will take care of your niece as best I can.*

My Swedish is coming along nicely. I have learnt three swear words that I use when the Netflix won't work. I have a visit from a companion three days a week, and today we've come to Malmö. There is a strong gust of wind in the cemetery, and I wrap my coat tighter around me. I am quite looking forward to Swedish winter. The meals have gotten heartier, and we now get full-fat whipping cream with our pudding as if we're back in the 1800s and they're feeding us ahead of a hardships to come. I'm excited for snow. For a clearly defined black-and-white landscape that is easier for my brain to navigate than a world with colour.

'You may wait over here,' I say to Helen. She is a lovely little thing, but a woman needs privacy every now and again. I stretch out my hand and take the folding chair from her, a useful Amazon purchase which I use to sit down on in all types of places. Forest, beach and here. With him.

In my hand I have carnations, which are a symbol of love, Sophia says. Roses are a symbol of sorrow and grief, and God knows we have all had enough of that. While I can still remember people, I plan to love them.

As I lay the flowers down and look at his name I allow

myself to think of what could have been, the sunsets we could have watched, the times he could have carried my shoes flung over his shoulders or dangling from his hands when my feet got sore. I think of the times I could have cooked inedible meals and he would have grumbled but ordered takeaway saying, *You'll be the financial ruin of us, all those groceries gone to waste* as he tipped it into the bin. I think of getting tipsy and not feeling my lips anymore, just a soft tingle as I'd be pressing them harder against him, blood rushing there. I imagine him holding my hands to his lips and promising to love me always. Instead here I am. Promising to love the only girl he loved after me. To love Sophia.

Then I see him. Across the lawn, tall and straight and with the faintest of smiles. He has been dead for years but he is as real as the wind on my cheek or the ache in my right knee. I know that I can take out my phone and snap a picture of him, like I do with my other visual hallucinations. And some part of me knows that when I look down at the screen it will be empty. I also know that I can reach into my pocket and pull out the soft handkerchief with the perfume I've used for years and bury my nose into it, breathing in reality and forcing my senses to stay with me. Instead I stand there and just look at him. I smile back. I enjoy this gift that my brain is granting me a second time. I stand in the company of him, and I feel just calm, no fear, just blessed to have this moment. When I finally look up again, he's gone.

'Thank you for not being my Svennie,' I say after him. 'I had history all muddled up for a while. Ever so sorry about that. Ever so sorry about everything.'

Then I touch my hand to the cool stone and see if they come—the tears—but they don't, so I turn around.

And I think of all the quiet signs of passing time. Age spots. Wrinkles. Lukewarm coffee. Expirations dates. Melted ice. They happen so quietly you don't know if you are in the beginning, the middle or the end. Trying to guess is pointless.

Then I realise I have a feeling of peace inside. As if the rage, worry and faff that's filled me for so long has run out and my mind and I are only stillness.

I'm no longer waiting.

Acknowledgments

I am someone who says thank you a lot, perhaps excessively. The Swedish-British culture of politeness runs deep. Despite this, I am at a loss writing this.

Writing is not a lonely job; it's teamwork and so many people play a part in a book's journey. The fact that I've now written and published multiple books and get to call this my job still blows my mind.

Firstly, thank you to my editor, Meredith Clark, who makes lines better and leaves me the much-needed comments saying "not sure about this" and "what does this mean?" It's been a pleasure working with you and the wider MIRA team again.

Tanera and Laura, my agents at Greenstone Literary, there aren't words enough to describe what you do for my books (and me!). You are the first people to read my drafts, and I couldn't do this without you.

Mary at Darby Literary Rights Agency, thank you for loving my books and finding editors who love them too.

To the rights team at Darley Anderson Literary, Film and TV Agency, thank you for your hard work getting this novel into the hands of foreign publishers.

My writer friends: Emily Howes, you are forever who I come

to when this job gets the better of me. Your humour and shared suffering amidst deadlines and workloads get me through each and every day. Becky Alexander, my reliable, clever friend who always has time to read and cheer on. Perween Richards, thank you for reading my work and being my friend. Roisin O'Donnell, I'm lucky to have the support of someone who knows writing can change the lives of women; let's keep reminding each other of this and push on. My Curtis Brown Creative group, I am proud of you all and love that we still stay in touch four years on. This course was the start and I'm forever grateful.

Lizzie, you pick up the pieces and the admin balls I drop. Thank you.

To my accountant, John, thank you for support and advice.

Hugo, Therese, Freddie and everyone else in my life, thank you.

All the authors who read my ARC and say nice words or just offer your support online, it means the world. Also, a thank you to the sensitivity readers who provided feedback on this manuscript—your work is important.

To James, I'm thankful I met you. You'd be my campervan roommate of choice.

To my parents, thank you for the fact checking and proofreading. Because of you I won't have readers writing to me in a fury because I've gotten the distance between Svedala and Växjö wrong by a kilometre.

To my children, Alfred, Olivia and Ivy, you inspire me and challenge me daily—I love you.

Thank you to everyone who's been a part of this novel's creation or success. I wish I could give you all a blue *Hydrangea*, which Sophia tells me represents heartfelt sincerity and a feeling of gratitude.

Thank you.